The Best
AMERICAN
ESSAYS
2009

GUEST EDITORS OF
THE BEST AMERICAN ESSAYS

The Best AMERICAN ESSAYS® 2009

Edited and with an Introduction
by MARY OLIVER

Robert Atwan, Series Editor

MARINER BOOKS

HOUGHTON MIFFLIN HARCOURT

BOSTON • NEW YORK 2009

www.hmhbooks.com

ISSN 0888-3742
ISBN 978-0-618-98272-1

Printed in the United States of America

DOC 10 9 8 7 6 5 4 3 2 1

Contents

Foreword

THE ONCE COLOSSALLY famous author Washington Irving died 150 years ago this November. In many ways America's first professional writer, and one of the nation's first literary figures to achieve international fame, Irving is little read today aside from a handful of anthology staples. But for decades critics considered him our finest prose stylist, and his essays served as models for anyone learning the art of composition, as E. B. White's would a century later. In fact, one could draw a direct literary line from Irving's satirical New York essays and sketches to the arch manner of White's *New Yorker.*

Irving began his career at a time when the essay played a key role in the literary life of England and the emerging culture of the United States. In the eighteenth and nineteenth centuries many authors regarded the essay as a premier literary genre, the best means of showcasing their ideas, reflections, and — perhaps most important — their mastery of prose style. To be sure, the essay wasn't the epic poem, the supreme literary masterpiece to which few aspired, but the genre had a serious and discerning audience and kept many periodicals afloat. A list of the important essayists throughout those two centuries would amount to a roll call of many of the most significant figures in literary history. At the outset of his career, the young and ambitious Washington Irving clearly understood that he could secure a literary reputation on both sides of the Atlantic not by publishing novels but by writing essays.

First published serially here and in England, *The Sketch-Book of*

Geoffrey Crayon, Gent (1820) quickly made an indelible impression; Edgar Allan Poe noted that "the chief beauty" of Irving's work was "beauty of style."

Most of the "papers" or "numbers" (as Irving calls them, using the nomenclature of periodicals) collected in *The Sketch-Book* would normally be called essays. But the book is a mixed bag and includes — besides dream reveries, biography, criticism, and travel pieces — the classic tale "Rip Van Winkle," which critics have long considered a precursor of the American short story. Irving presents this tale, however, in an essayistic fashion, pretending that the book's fictitious persona, Geoffrey Crayon, had found the tale "among the papers of the late Diedrich Knickerbocker," an amateur historian Irving invented who conducted "historical researches" into the life of the early Dutch settlers. The tale is prefaced with a note attesting to the "scrupulous accuracy" of Knickerbocker and followed by another note from Knickerbocker himself, who claims that he maintains "full belief" in the story, and though it "may seem incredible to many," he is convinced after having met him that the shiftless Van Winkle's twenty-year-long mountain nap is "beyond the possibility of doubt."

Of course the whole performance is a multilayered fiction — everything has been made up by Irving. My point here is to show how comfortably early writers could cross genres within a single collection as well as blend imaginary elements into individual essays or essay-like sketches. Irving had picked up many cues from eighteenth-century British essayists, who freely introduced invented characters and situations into their periodical work, which also contained a residue of fact, wit, and keen observation. It was fully expected that readers would recognize these fictions for what they were, an honored literary means of shaping a moral or establishing an expository point. The essayists frequently invented epistolary exchanges from fabricated characters or imagined meetings and conversations. In fact, the uses of the "imagination" were one of the frequent topics of the early essay.

In one of his last essays, "The Writer in Winter" (see page 172), the late John Updike cites Nathaniel Hawthorne, "a writer who dwelt in the shadowland" where — in Hawthorne's words — "the Actual and the Imaginary may meet." Although not usually regarded as such, Hawthorne — who learned quite a few literary maneuvers from Irving — is a splendid essayist, and the comment Updike cites comes from what may properly be considered one of America's most famous autobiographical essays. Hawthorne calls it "The Custom-House," and it serves as the introduction to his novel *The Scarlet Letter.* The essay marvelously blends the actual and the imaginary: the author, appearing as himself and willing to disclose numerous factual details about his daily life, finds in a rubbish heap at the custom house where he is employed "a much worn and faded" embroidery in the shape of "the capital letter A."

So how and why did things change? When did the introduction of imaginary characters or situations or objects, no matter how trivial, become verboten? Why did compressing, say, two visits to one's dying father into a single trip for narrative purposes become a literary crime? When did someone writing an autobiographical essay need to supply an editor with sources and contact information so individuals mentioned could be called to verify accounts? How would such a popular writer as Damon Runyon ever publish his entertaining columns now with their colorful character "types," invented situations, and made-up dialogue? A columnist today who invents a shred of dialogue would soon be unemployed.

Around the time of the Great Depression in the 1930s magazines and newspapers began to devalue the traditional personal essay in favor of newsy and issue-oriented articles that featured interviews and reportage. This was perhaps to be expected, given the times and trends; less expected was the diminishment of the essay as a literary form in the world of letters and the academy itself. When the celebrated poet and influential critic John Crowe Ransom decided to publish an anthology of essays for college students he excluded many of the classic or belletristic essays that writing instructors had relied on for generations. In a famous and quite peculiar critical passage, Ransom writes that he considers poetry "democratic" and prose "totalitarian." By the 1950s, literature, under the supervision of the New Critics, consisted exclusively of three genres: poetry, fiction, drama. The essay had become — to echo the title of one of today's best literary journals featuring nonfiction — "the fourth genre."

When the essay was pressured to submit to the demands of professional journalism, its identity and status as a form of imaginative literature came to an end. In other words, the more literal the essay was expected to be, the less literary it became. E. B. White would come to feel by 1977 that the essayist worked in a marginalized genre and "must be content with his self-imposed role of second-class citizen." Considered suspect by professional journalists and devalued by literary critics, the essay managed to hang on largely through the creative efforts of such contemporary essayists as Joan Didion, Annie Dillard, Phillip Lopate, Edward Hoagland, Anne Fadiman, Joseph Epstein, Adam Gopnik, and a number of others who have been featured in this series and who write out of a dedication to the genre.

Has the literary status of the essay improved as we approach the second decade of a new century? On the one hand, I saw more published essays in 2008 than I ever have since launching this series in 1985. That surely is a healthy sign. On the other hand, it is still extremely difficult to find a mainstream publisher who will commit to a book-length collection of essays on diverse subjects. The essay as a work of literature is still more likely to be found in magazines than in books. A writer who submits a manuscript of separate autobiographical essays, each of which was independently published and stands alone, had better — if the proposal isn't rejected — be prepared to reassemble the contents and discover a "narrative arc" that will tightly hold the newly shaped "memoir" together.

The essayists who appear each year in this series come from a wide variety of literary practices, and many have their dominant genre or topics for which they are best known — poetry, fiction, journalism, humor, memoir, science, travel, sports, politics, criticism, nature, and so on. Dedicated essayists — the sort of writer who thinks, feels, and patiently explores ideas and emotions *essayistically* — are rare, even in this series.

It's always gratifying to hear from writers who have discovered through the series the pleasures of the essay as a literary form. It was especially gratifying this year to hear about such a discovery from an Irish essayist who happens to appear in these volumes for the first time, Chris Arthur. In response to a regular feature in Ireland's *Sunday Tribune,* "The Book That Changed My Life," Arthur recalled his first genuine exposure to the art of the essay. "Essays came into my life by accident," he wrote.

In 1989, when I was thirty-four, I was browsing in an Edinburgh book-shop and bought a copy of that year's *Best American Essays*, the annual collection that scours the USA's literary magazines, harvesting a yearly crop of excellence. I'd never heard of the series — then only in its fourth year . . . Like most people, I thought "essay" meant the written as-signments done at school. I had a vague awareness of it also being a lit-erary genre, something associated with the likes of Addison, Steele, and Lamb. Essentially, though, "essay" was something tedious. It had none of the appeal of what I considered real literature — novels, poetry, plays. *Best American Essays* changed all this. It made me realize the huge potential of this type of writing . . . *Best American Essays 1989* had a pro-found impact on my life. I read it avidly, then started to write essays of my own. It was as if discovering this clutch of brilliant examples acted to release a reservoir of words that had been building up for years. I'd tried my hand at poetry and fiction, but despite some modest successes it wasn't until the essay fell into my lap, courtesy of that *Best American Es-says* volume, that I found a genre in which I felt completely at home. I don't know how my writing would have developed without it.

Many fine essays are written for an occasion or an assignment. But others are more inspired than required. As Annie Dillard has suggested, essays are also born out of the same creative urgency as poems and stories, and as such represent what she calls an author's "real work." In this volume, readers will find many examples of real work, and I hope they come to understand what Chris Arthur ulti-mately realized — that essays are also *"real* literature."

The Best American Essays features a selection of the year's outstand-ing essays, essays of literary achievement that show an awareness of craft and forcefulness of thought. Hundreds of essays are gathered annually from a wide assortment of national and regional publica-tions. These essays are then screened, and approximately one hun-dred are turned over to a distinguished guest editor, who may add a few personal discoveries and who makes the final selections. The list of Notable Essays appearing in the back of the book is drawn from a final comprehensive list that includes not only all of the es-says submitted to the guest editor but also many that were not sub-mitted.

To qualify for the volume, the essay must be a work of respect-able literary quality, intended as a fully developed, independent es-say on a subject of general interest (not specialized scholarship), originally written in English (or translated by the author) for publication in an American periodical during the calendar year. Today's essay is a highly flexible and shifting form, however, so these criteria are not carved in stone.

Magazine editors who want to be sure their contributors will be considered each year should submit issues or subscriptions to: Robert Atwan, Series Editor, The Best American Essays, P.O. Box 220, Readville, MA 02137. Writers and editors are welcome to submit published essays from any American periodical for consideration; unpublished work does not qualify for the series and cannot be reviewed or evaluated. Please note: all submissions must be directly from the publication and not in manuscript or printout format. Editors of online magazines and literary bloggers should not assume that appropriate work will be seen; they are invited to submit printed copies of the essays (with full citations) to the address above.

I would like to dedicate this volume — the twenty-fourth in the series — to the memory of John Updike, who died on January 27, 2009, and whose contribution to this volume on the "aging writer" was one of the last essays to be published in his lifetime. I'd like to thank Kyle J. Giacomozzi and Matthew Keough for a stimulating interview they conducted with me for *The Bridge*, the award-winning student journal of fine arts published at Bridgewater State College. The topic of this year's Foreword grew out of the challenging questions that they and other members of the journal's staff tossed at me over the course of several hours. As always, the Houghton Mifflin Harcourt staff did everything to bring so many moving parts together in so short a time, and I once again appreciate the efforts of Deanne Urmy, Nicole Angeloro, Larry Cooper, and Megan Wilson. Working on this volume with Mary Oliver was from start to finish a wonderful experience, as was spending time with her in her beloved Provincetown. Though widely known as one of the nation's leading poets, she is also very much at home with the essay and her work has been featured several times in this series. The collection throughout reflects her vivid awareness of the world and the word.

R. A.

Introduction

MY OWN FAVORITE writer of essays is Emerson. Why is this? Because he writes as if I am inside his mind, a mind that is, as Robert Richardson expressed it, "on fire." Because of his delectable sentences. Because of his subjects — the individual spirit and its conduct in this world, as well as the Oversoul. His writings do not thoroughly answer the questions so many of us ask, but often enough such questions cannot be reasoned out entirely. What I feel is an affinity with Emerson's queries. I'm captivated by his suggestive propositions ("hitch your wagon to a star") and find them a blessing, a richness.

But what, anyway, is an essay? Montaigne, who lays claim to inventing the form, stated:

> The world always looks straight ahead; as for me, I turn my gaze inward. I fix it there and keep it busy. Everyone looks in front of him; as for me, I look inside of me; I have no business but with myself; I continually observe myself, I take stock of myself, I taste myself. Others always go elsewhere, if they stop to think about it; they always go forward . . . As for me, I roll about in myself.*

Two centuries later Samuel Johnson offered as his dictionary definition of the essay "a loose sally of the mind." Each of these definitions is intriguing, but neither is anywhere near complete, or definitive. For the essay, like nothing else, has nimble feet and

* Michel de Montaigne, from *The Complete Works*, translated by Donald M. Frame.

sometimes even wings; it keeps up with the times, is ever changing, in style, subject matter, and intent.

To go back to Emerson, I like to think of his admonition that we should each of us lead "an examined life." And often enough the essay is full of personal discoveries, experiences, disclosures, a revelation of the "examined" self. Just as often, though, the essay is full of the excitement of some discovery beyond the self, set loose, as it were, in the world. How wonderful! The single mind with its treasures of ideas, propensities, offering them up to the reader. The writing of essays is a party to which all subjects are invited: humor, pathos, remembrance, declaration, emotions, religious belief, the natural world we have inherited (and not perfectly cared for). Such congeniality and engaging variety are notable in the present collection.

Years ago, when I first knew I was going to leave Provincetown to teach, I had a wish: to take with me from my beloved homeland all the things I loved. So most of my essays became a record of things that had happened to me in the woods and waters of Provincetown. I wrote about the time when I caught, or rather failed to catch, fish; when I ate snapping-turtle eggs; when I hunted for the nest of an owl; when a storm-broken boat heaved its way westward in the waves in front of our house; when I brought a broken-winged gull into the house and he lived with us for two months, as he weakened inevitably, learning to play feather-catch, to delight in our company.

Which illustrates, I think, the marvelous opportunity of the essay; what we receive is not didactic, not even, sometimes, totally believable, but the soul-felt truth from the individual perspective of someone deft in the craft of expression. Nothing else, no other form of writing, is quite like it. The essay is not the world of *Middlemarch,* of Mrs. Dalloway going out to buy the flowers — it is neither less nor more, but different. It is not "Tyger, Tyger" or the felling of the Binsey Poplars — it is neither less nor more, but different.

We speak a good deal these days of the loss of community, and many of us feel that we have lost therefore something very precious. Essays can move us back into this not-quite-lost realm. Tackling a hundred subjects, in a hundred different styles, they are like letters from a stranger that you cannot bear to throw away. They haunt you; they strengthen you.

In the time of all time, the Now, some essay for each of us, be it old or fresh on the page, may turn out to be a most fervent, provocative, and valuable friend.

MARY OLIVER

The Best
AMERICAN
ESSAYS
2009

SUE ALLISON

Taking a Reading

FROM *Mid-American Review*

A YARD, A PACE, a foot, a fathom. How beautiful the language of measurement is, and we're not even talking iambs yet. A fifth, a finger, a jigger, a drop, a dram, a grain, a scruple. A scruple is twenty grains, or twenty barley cornes. It is as small as a pebble. If you have three, you have a dram. First scruples comprise arithmetic degrees and are divided into seconds. A fluid dram takes sixty minims. Add twenty more minims, at minimum, and you have a teaspoon.

My husband's foot is twelve inches long, but mine only seven, making it useless for counting off the length of a carpet or a couch. The yard we have together is bigger than the yard around the house I lived in as a child, and yet is still a yard. If my husband's foot was 660 times what it is, it would be a perfect furlong, but fathom is my favorite. It's how tall my husband is.

A span, a palm, a hand, a nail, an ohm, a knot, a stadion. A stadion was Greek for 622 feet, Roman for 606, not an inch more or less. It was a distance before it was a theater of sport or massacre. The distance between two thumbs is infinite, whether touching or not. A cranberry bushel is bigger than a bushel and a petroleum barrel is bigger than a barrel. What is a bushel and what a barrel when the cranberries are on the bush and the petroleum below ground? A gill is a half of a cup. I have read many recipes that called for half a cup, but none that ever called for a gill, which is never half empty nor half full but all there is when there's a gill.

Carat, candela, caliber, Kelvin, case. A chain is precisely 66 feet divided into precisely 100 links. It is also what is around my neck holding a small diamond heart which I've kept clasped since receiving it some anniversaries ago. It cannot hold a ship to shore, but holds a great deal more. A decibel is barely audible, it taking ten to work up to a light whisper, and who's to say whose whisper we should use. Could I be the Greenwich of sound? An ell does not come before an em. I don't know why you use hands to measure horses. I mean, how could you possibly? My hand or yours? Two hogsheads make a pipe, though the quantity of a hogshead depends on what it is in it, molasses, say, or ale, as well as where it is meted out: London or an ordinary country shire.

A quintal, a quire, a case, a ream. A ream is a lot of paper, sold and purchased blank. Written on, it's a book.

CHRIS ARTHUR

(En)trance

FROM *The Literary Review*

IT WAS WHILE THINKING about the pillars at Shandon that I realized I would never be the sort of writer I used to believe I'd become. I mean the kind who undertakes complete stories, who engineers a beginning, works things through to an ending, and offers readers an experience of apparent wholeness. No matter what the subject, such tales encompass a territory in a manner that suggests it has been adequately covered by the time you leave it. There's a feeling of a journey well prepared for and satisfactorily completed. Words have been packed carefully into whatever cases of style the writer favors. Nothing important is left out. We have everything we need for whatever excursion is embarked upon. A sense of ample provisioning prevails. Step by step we're led toward repletion, resolution, closure.

It is, of course, an illusion — but a wonderful one. Such narratives have an almost narcotic allure. I love to immerse myself in the artificial worlds they offer and it remains a regret that I don't create them myself. Still, there's as little point pining for a genre that doesn't fit your writing as to pretend a sexual orientation that doesn't match whatever sparks your passion.

A writer of the sort I'm not would have been through the Shandon pillars and halfway up the avenue by now, introducing us to key characters along the way and laying out the plot they're going to follow. The jigsaw would be starting to fit together, offering tantalizing hints of the emergent picture. Such authors place the pieces of their story with a precision nicely judged to carry things along at a tempo that will hold the reader's attention. My efforts —

I almost said "alas," but would not have meant it — result in less immediately enticing prospects, though I hope they too can lay claim to holding the attention, albeit with a less comfortable grip. Instead of the strategic assemblage of location, character, and action, the systematic setting of the scene within which things unfold, the piece-by-piece unveiling of the story whose hooked beginning caught us at the outset on the barbs of its intriguing promise, I take single pieces of life's puzzle and lean the weight of reflection upon them till they're pulverized, then ponder the dust particles; how we're wedded to them, how they're threaded through us, how they create unnoticed galaxies in the unlikeliest places.

"Only connect," said the great E. M. Forster. "Only write about what you know," says the old watchword of practical advice for would-be writers. I attempt to disconnect things from the dense mesh of their immediate, camouflaging milieu and examine them with a gaze whose first allegiance, far from being given to the warm familiarity of the known, is rooted in a recognition of the strangeness that attends even the most mundane circumstance. While Forster and writers of his exalted ilk concentrate on the construction of fictions, weaving their delicately spun cocoons of imagined happenings and outcomes on the hard substratum of facts — about India, about manners, about sexuality — I focus on fragments of the substratum itself, trying to tease out the tendrils that are coiled tightly at the heart of every moment, their intricate abundance independent of invention.

Shandon was the County Antrim farm where my mother and her two sisters grew up, and where her eldest sister subsequently raised her own family. We lived nearby and often visited, so it was a place that shaped me too. Its trees and fields and garden were part of the world colonized by childhood. But colonizing is always a two-way process. Shandon's contours gently laid their weight upon our games and imaginings, leaving an invisible imprint on our lives.

I suppose I should at least make some attempt to *describe* the pillars through which I have so far refused to go. Approached in one way, this constitutes no great problem — beyond the usual difficulty of finding words to fit flush with the mind's jutting hoard of pictures. Built of faded redbrick, the pillars were five feet high and acted as thickset entrance markers flanking the avenue leading to the house. It was almost as if whoever built Shandon had dropped a piece of the house about fifty yards away, for the pillars were made of the same material and echoed its style. They gave early warning in miniature of the more massive structure they represented. Each one was capped with a domed, cream-painted slab of concrete which made them reminiscent of giant red-stemmed mushrooms. Perhaps "pilaster" ("a square column, partly built into, partly projecting from a wall") would be a more accurate term, for the pillars were not freestanding but were each attached at one side to a short curve of wall, also redbrick and topped with the same cream hue of painted concrete, thickly applied, like a slab of icing. But technical correctness must yield to common usage. We called them pillars, not pilasters, and so I will continue to name them here. Their attenuated walls ran for no more than eight or ten feet before merging with the mixed shrubs of the uneven hedge that marked most of Shandon's extensive boundary — a tangled line of hawthorn, beech, and flowering currant interspersed with some mature chestnut trees. This outpost of brickwork at Shandon's entrance echoed the hedge's wall of greenery, but in an altogether different key — a linear staccato of squares and right angles set in counterpoint to the curving whorls of leaves and branches.

On their wall-less side, where the avenue flowed between them like a hardened river made of tar, the pillars still bore traces of where wrought-iron gates once hung. But the gates themselves had vanished long before I appeared on the scene to read meaning into their absence. The immediate reason for their removal is prosaic enough. Like iron gates and railings all over Britain, they were removed during World War II to be melted down and reforged into armaments. Beyond this immediate, practical reason, though, the taking away of Shandon's gates provides a symbol for another, and more significant, feature of that moment in history — the way in which it heralded an opening up to outside influences, an increase in the permeability of the boundaries set by family, nation, faith. Shandon, like these other enclosures, could not stay isolated from the modern world. None of our barriers, whether physical, psychological, or cultural, even in so insular a society as Northern Ireland, were able to resist its insistent ingress.

Approached in another way, describing the pillars becomes more problematic. It's like lighting a touch-paper whose unre-

markable fizzling will lead to an explosion of complication. Unlikely as it may seem, fireworks are hoarded in the unsuspected ar-
senal of these little redbrick columns. In this approach, a kind of
cognitive tripwire is laced around all sorts of unseen interrelation-
ships and unexpected connections so that every step toward a description brings things crashing down and colliding together in
combinations that fracture the containment of our ordinary cate-
gories.

A writer of the sort I know I'll never be wouldn't stumble at this
first hurdle of describing Shandon's pillars, but would instead leap
deftly over every tripwire and move on. His or her polished craft
would briskly package a palatable image in a dozen words or less,
something functional, efficient, spare, unencumbered. The pillars
would be treated in a commonsense manner, something to be
taken in en passant. What I see as portals to another world which
have the power to stop me in my tracks, gasping at the miles-deep
lagoon of possibilities they open up, my authorial alter ego would
see as no more than background detail to be glanced at and dismissed.

The pillars and their walls were like giant cupped hands placed
at the roadside. They were held strategically apart at just the right
angle and distance to welcome visitors and shepherd them along
the obvious route — following the curved avenue that wound up
the gentle incline to the house. Instead of herding readers
through Shandon's pillared entrance and moving things quickly
forward to the apparent seat of action — the house as stage for a
score of dramas, the setting in which lives unfold into their rich
spectrum of stories — my focus, perhaps perversely, is on the pillars themselves and the unsuspected other-world they suggest. If,
immediately on entering Shandon's gateless entrance, you turned
hard left or right and pushed your way through the outer foliage of
the dense laurel thickets that grew behind the pillars and their
walls, you would find yourself inside a cool leafy enclosure. The
laurel thickets could be stepped into. At their center was a hollow,
not quite hedge and not quite garden. It straddled the space between boundary and territory. Fallen leaves accumulated over
years matted the ground here, preventing the growth of any grass,
paving the shady heart of the thickets with a soft brown floor that
gave slightly beneath even a child's light tread, releasing an aroma

of earth and rot mixed in with the sweetly cloying anesthetic smell that freshly crushed laurel leaves exude with even greater potency.

The way the pillars were positioned, and the camber of the land leading up to Shandon, meant that the laurel grotto behind the left-hand pillar offered a better vantage point from which both road and house could be observed. Because of this, and because the laurel grew more densely here, this was the side we favored. Behind the pillar and its wall, beneath the green canopy of laurel growing snug within the shielding brick, was one of the special places of childhood. We often played there. The details of our games are long forgotten, but the arena that hosted them remains vividly remembered. This was one of our secret observation posts for spying on the adult world. It was here we found a discarded whiskey bottle not quite empty, a half-smoked cigarette, its butt pinked with lipstick, crumpled pages from a pornographic magazine, once a pair of knickers. Sharp verbal flecks ("fuck," "bastard," "cunt") blew in from the conversations of strangers walking past, providing spoken parallels to these tawdry artifacts. We little suspected that our encounter with such things was part of the incremental process of initiation into the tribe that at once fascinated and bored us.

The pillars were set back from the road, and there was a semicircle of dusty tarmac between it and them, almost as if the road's vein had bulged outward and grown varicose with the pressure of traffic it carried, leaving a kind of asphalt no man's land where cars occasionally turned. From our laurel den we often watched unseen, our presence unsuspected, eavesdropping on people walking by or writing down the registration numbers of cars speeding to and from Lisburn, the bustling market town whose center was only a mile or two from Shandon. The road away from Lisburn led to the airport and to the ferries at the port of Larne, so it was nearly always busy. A rich seam of stories could be tapped into by building on the foundation of those *not* turning in at Shandon's pillars, but passing by, going elsewhere, preoccupied with other homes and families, entrances and destinations, lives entirely unaware of ours. Peeping over the brick, camouflaged by the laurel's foliage, who knows what stories we witnessed so fractionally, or how the different threads of our lives and the lives of those who went by could be joined up to make sense of the history we were all, moment by mo-

ment, weaving together? Setting the intricacies of that mesh of
lives alongside the fortunes of the few protagonists on whom we focus is a good way of remembering how much our sense of things
relies on abstraction, how much our pictures of the world leave
out.

The pillars are gone now, and their walls, and the laurel that nes-
tled behind them. Shandon itself is still there, but lived in by
strangers and occupying only a heavily pruned remnant of its former territory. There are new houses on what used to be its lawns
and tennis court and fields and orchard. All those untidy margins
where hens once wandered freely, pecking amongst the long grass
and weeds, have been flattened, concreted over, made into patios
and parking spaces. Today, looking at the anonymous bungalows
with their tiny manicured gardens spread out on old Shandon's
sprawling territory, it's like seeing a palimpsest of neat equations
pasted over the swirling curlicues of a disheveled, rambling manuscript that once told many tales. I can remember the original
manuscript so clearly that it sometimes feels as if I'm reading the
past and present mixed together — watching the ghosts of unruly
children tearing around open-plan living rooms, climbing damson
trees suddenly growing again in designer kitchens, playing tag
around the shiny vehicles, making daisy chains on driveways where
the grass tennis court used to be. We often chased each other there
with the heavy roller meant for keeping the court's surface even —
though any smoothness we managed to impose was soon ruptured
by the wildflowers that studded the grass with irresistible profu-
sion, however often mower and roller were applied.

So, my description of the pillars is not drawn from life. I can't go
there now with notebook and camera, take their likeness from the
things themselves and come away again to make this wordy shadow
of their substance. Instead, I have to sketch them from the spectral
images my memory offers. I know that memory's grip, however
firm and true it might appear, cannot be relied on to cup things
with the same steady pressure of exactitude that being there af-
fords. Moreover, words find it harder to get a grip on what's invisible than on what the eyes lay out before us, so there's a double slippage to consider in terms of assessing the accuracy of what I say.
I'm no doubt unaware of the real extent of this slippage, but I do
know that memory has filtered out the drabness that a photo

would inevitably show. I always see Shandon's pillars lit by mellow sunlight. Even as it warms my recollection, I know this distillate of a hundred perfect summer days cannot be real. County Antrim's is no Mediterranean climate. Often we played when it was wet and cold. Gray clouds supplied the backdrop more often than the unbroken blue and gold that remembrance now bestows. But showing them suffused by a clemency the local weather rarely offers, picturing them without the shadow of the ordinary, while not "true to life" in the sense of constituting a faithful reproduction of a camera's snapshot, is, at a deeper level, far more accurate than any photograph could claim to be. Memory's version captures a truth about the place, not merely as it *appears,* but as it was felt, played in, dreamed of, as its lineaments intertwined and pulled on mine, delicately adjusting the sails of childhood to catch the breath of meaning that emanates from things — things that, to an adult's rigging, have only the unbreezy weight of the ordinary about them. Memory can offer up the richness of imagining where a photograph would only dole out the thin gruel of the visually literal.

Trying to escape the doldrums of adulthood, the way the grown-up mind too easily falls for the lure of the superficial, the simple, the no-nonsense, the cut-and-dried, and lazily equates what meets the eye with truth, I sometimes picture Shandon's pillars via different perspectives from my own. My hope is that by altering its angle and tempo in this way, perception might be given further purchase and gradually unroll a fuller picture, one that might catch more of the pillars' elusive quality of fullness-beyond-labeling, a quality that nags on the edges of every description and defies each stratagem of words to pin it down. In the same way that shamans take on the guise of animal spirits to guide them through trances, so, more prosaically, I adopt nonhuman familiars to help me see entrances (trance and entrance are, of course, blood brothers), and to notice the pillars that stand even on the humblest of things, marking the start of unexpected avenues.

This imaginative process, whose inevitable anthropomorphism invalidates any claim actually to "see" things as the animal in question might have done, certainly suggests a more richly textured view of the Shandon pillars than does our customary viewpoint. Many horses must have passed between them. How did the brickwork fall upon an equine eye? What shape did they take for a butterfly basking on the pillars' sun-warmed brick? How did they appear to the owl that flew above them one spring night in 1941, a freshly killed mouse clutched in its talons, the sound of German bombers droning overhead? How did they seem to the Shandon dogs, who stopped always at the pillars, venturing no farther, their innate sense of territory acting as surely as any gate? Shifting biological realities like this is, naturally, speculative and unsupported, but it can help free us from that commonest of intellectual constraints — the assumption that our own outlook is the only one, or that it's somehow uniquely authoritative and can be relied on to deliver a veridical picture of the world.

My favorite shamanic familiar in terms of broadening the view of Shandon's pillars, breaking the spell of the familiar and making visible some of the threads that suture the ordinary to the extraordinary, is a kind of temporal kestrel. It hovers above them, immobile, a fixed point, keeping its position constant as, below it, time is made to speed by, rapidly spooling and unspooling toward a far distant future, a far distant past, so that the pillars' present is churned into different focus. This fluttering familiar of the imagination can provide new perceptual footholds that allow me to ascend a little farther up the sheer wall of that most difficult ascent: describing things the way they are.

A writer of the kind I'll never be would view this kind of self-willed temporal dislocation with misgivings. Stories cannot flourish when time is sluiced through the pillars at the speed and volume my feathered familiar can release. Such writers prefer the ordinary tempo of hours-days-weeks-months-years, our customary backdrop of duration cut to allow our fleeting presences to show up, their significance assured by the scale of this familiar screen. They would take us (and I often like to follow) not into the free fall of some sheer shamanic precipice where the dimensions of the drop make all our minuscule doings seem insignificant, but rather into the clipped sure world that prose so readily offers, laying uncomplicated sentences upon the mind as if they could hold the weight of the actual and so safely bear our tread across the abyss of existence.

In this clipped sure world a wealth of stories can be conjured from the raw material of what happened at Shandon, or what could have happened there, as this is shown by the images that appear on our screening scale of mundane time and circumstance. So we might focus on the maids who used to work here, employed via hiring fairs, living in — a small bedroom was provided — and paid the pittance usual at this time, allowed the expected miserly allotment of holidays. The maids were young, single, usually from rural areas, and invariably Catholic. They offered my mother and her sisters a friendly keyhole through which to gaze at the — to them — exotic rituals of this different faith, at once familiar and forbidden. My mother remembers one maid taking her to chapel, aged six or seven. The candles, incense, Latin, realistic depictions of the crucifixion — so different from the austere simplicities of her parents' Presbyterianism — fell upon her mind with such an impact that the image was held there, perfectly remembered, for eighty years. Or, the focus could be made to fall on the army officers billeted at Shandon during the war. One night the household was wakened by the screams of a major's wife. They suspected murder but found her sitting up in bed, terrified, as a bat circled the room and her husband snored beside her. One suspects she would have readily agreed with the philosopher Thomas Nagel's view that "anyone who has spent some time in an enclosed space with an excited bat knows what it is to encounter a fundamentally *alien* form of life." How would that alien creature have "seen" the pillars? What, if any, sense of entrance would it possess? Or, one might chronicle, or create stories from, those family Christmases at Shandon which, for years, acted as a kind of magnet, pulling us back through the pillars from the familial diaspora that was to come (no one envisaged or wanted it) as Ulster's "Troubles" scattered us far from our County Antrim roots.

Anyone who passed between the pillars might be used to snag a line of narrative and take it forward, pulling the attention of readers along behind them. Funeral corteges passed through, embryos enfolded in their mothers' flesh, strangers, cousins, gardeners, laborers, doctors, governesses, tinkers, and suitors, each with their own story, each story adding its featherweight to the enormous tonnage of the human saga. Once, when my mother was ten, an uncle came bloodied to the door for help, his eye spiked and blinded by a thorn while grubbing up a blackthorn hedge. Once, when I was a teenager, terrorists must have passed between the pillars, a furtive nocturnal trespass, to lie in wait for a prison officer who lived in a new house just beyond Shandon's hedge. Mercifully, this attempted killing failed.

Since writers of the sort I'm not aren't constrained by the boundaries of what happened, it would be easy to invent all manner of stories about love and lust, about class and religion, about Englishness and Irishness, war and poverty. Using Shandon's building blocks, a story could be constructed around a youthful lieutenant, fresh from public school, who's torn between a sensually sophisticated maid and the naïve refinement of one of the virgin daughters of the house. It's tempting to succumb to such diversions, to sweep through the pillars dramatically, making an entrance that draws the eye toward the unfolding of some vivid story, baited perhaps with rape or murder or the compelling simplicity of some other violently eye-catching beginning. But, for whatever reason, my interest is set in a key that eschews the racy harmonics of such narratives, even though I'm partial to them and often like to hum along. The entrances that intrigue me lead to less obvious destinations than the Big House with its cast of characters. For me, the pillars don't just suggest the domestic scale of a habitation and its dwellers. They also bring to mind pillars as ancient religious markers erected on the earth to stake some claim to the numinous, to post a reminder of entrances beyond the obvious. These upright markers can be found scattered through the landscapes of many countries. Their style and date may vary; they may have been raised on the occasion of covenant, sacrifice, or worship. But for all their seeming variety, and despite their dense solidity, such pillars serve a similar function — to act as apertures, bore holes, openings, entrances from the seen to the unseen world, reminders that mystery lies just beneath the crust of the quotidian.

In Japan, the gates of shrines are guarded by pairs of stone dogs called *koma-inu*. These sit facing each other at either side of the entrance, creating an invisible barrier that visitors must cross. One dog has its mouth open; the other has its mouth shut. The one with its mouth open is breathing in and is called *A*. The one with its mouth closed is breathing out and is called *Un*. The phrase *A-Un*-no-kokyu ("*A-Un* breathing") has come to describe a relationship between people that's so close they can communicate without using words.

For me, invisible dogs stand at Shandon's pillars, their shared respiration symbolizing the intimate and mysterious connection that exists between the known and the unknown, between the telegraphic attenuations of the names we give things, the descriptions we offer — superficial, partial — and the significance that's coiled intricately within them. Passing between the pillars, I trip on this invisible umbilical of breathy connection and, as I fall, sometimes catch a glimpse of the endless sands of being upon which the mirages of common diction sparkle out their little images. We exist in a world of multiple registers that allow us to move through it in a variety of modes, but we sometimes forget the links between them. The no-nonsense world of facts and figures, at once useful and obscuring (perhaps useful *because* obscuring) skitters its way across a surface created by its own computations. Yet for every *Un* there is an *A*. Even if we are oblivious to it, in the breath of every sentence we inhale dormant complexities, their unnerving plenitude is only temporarily suspended by the icy hold of words; the promise of a thaw of complication-into-wonder remains whenever we pause for reflection.

From my temporal kestrel's vantage point, the land can be seen changing so much across time that it seems like liquid. Not just the gradual rhythm of the seasons and the gentle ripple of plant life as thorn bushes and chestnut trees edge their shoots slowly from the earth, unfolding into the shapes their mature form etches on the mind and parsing time with their annual budding and leaf-fall. Like a living space-probe filming across incomprehensible distances, my kestrel-familiar leaves its camera running so that the recognized small-scale scene soon retreats into the nonbeing that preceded it, the earth claiming back, pulling into its dark fastness, all the trees and fields and roads and houses, replacing them with an unpeopled wilderness of ocean, and before that smoldering lava, and before that an amorphous cloud of debris and gas in space waiting to spark into the particularities of existence. Racing upward through time's amplitude, the pillars and house I know are there and gone in a flash, the people I knew replaced by strangers, our generation grubbed out like a blackthorn hedge to make way for the next one, and the next one following on from that. Sometimes our customary preoccupations, our everyday measures, seem to act like a thorn in the eye, blinding us to the real dimensions of things. Sometimes they seem more like blinkers that stop us catching sight of what would only terrify, that offer a shield against the vertigo of being.

Somewhere in the hovering kestrel's imagined purview there are the first human eyes ever to have looked at this place which, centuries after their individual extinction, would be momentarily marked by the pillars. Somewhere there will no doubt be the last pair of human eyes to harbor the image of whatever exists at these precise coordinates of space long after Shandon, and all memory of it, has completely vanished. And between these pillars marking each end of our species' story, there flows a torrent of individuals, images, experiences too rich for any account to catch beyond the blandest generalization. Go forward, go backward, using Shandon's pillars as a kind of navigation buoy, and you are soon lost in dwarfing distances. We may think we've tamed things with our words. But always waiting, just inside the doorway of the dullest declension, is the portal of the seemingly unlimited. The shape and color of unremarkable redbrick pillars falling on a human retina may seem of little moment. But the pillars bear a cargo heavier by far than anything the eyes can hope to carry. And the retina itself soon unspills from the neat baptism of that label into a story of cells and genes and light juggled across eons as we slowly emerged from the flotilla of creatures that bore life from its veiled beginnings toward our own small part in its unfolding.

In Greek mythology, dreams entered via one of two gates. True dreams came through the Gate of Horn, false dreams through the Gate of Ivory. Looking down from the perspective of my kestrel-familiar, hovering in an imagined temporal updraft as the eons flow by beneath its watching eye, I sometimes think a third gate should be added, somewhere between dreams and waking. This Gate of Laurel is the entrance through which comes a crushing counterweight of fullness, a corrective for all the simplifications and superficiality with which we customarily clad things. It is a gate where the trance of mystery might be joined to those entrances whose thresholds we've grown so used to crossing as we make our way into our variously impoverished visions of the world.

The streetlights used to stop several hundred yards before Shandon's entrance. Once, when she was only nineteen and walking home alone after dark, my mother heard footsteps following behind her. When she slowed down, listening intently, they slowed down. When she stopped, they stopped. When she turned and stared into the darkness, she could make out no figure, but when she walked faster the following steps started up again and went faster too. Heart pounding, she began to run, sure that an assailant was stalking her. In fact, it turned out to be the sound made by her own loose-fitting shoes. Somehow their flip-flop noise sounding out with each step she took seemed more like someone following than the echo of her own paces. When I think about the Shandon pillars now I can hear the noise of another weight of discourse echoing in the wake of memory's gilded pictures. It feels more like the close shadowing of something gargantuan and other than any-thing self-generated, but I'm reminded of my mother's youthful terror and wonder about the depth of deception words may carry in their capacious holds. Perhaps my sense of mysterious entrances implicit in the mundane, entrances that are at once alluring and alarming, is no more than the sound of my own prose running away from its unrecognized echo.

A writer of the type I once wanted to become would have acted as a stricter gatekeeper, controlling the flow of what passed be-tween the pillars of his words. Such a writer would have let through only a manageable cast of characters, actions, dialogue. With such verbal irrigation a rich harvest of stories can be sown. I love such writing and admire the thoroughbred genres in which it flourishes with such sophistication. But I also like the mongrel toughness of the essay, which, standing in the unlikely setting of the hollowed laurel thicket, allows me to resist the closures and conclusions of composition and feel the deluge of the real push against the fabric of the mind until it is engulfed and intoxicated. The sweep of the avenue up the gentle incline toward the house, and the tight turn off the approved route into the laurel thicket behind the left-hand pillar, provides a nice statement of the different ambience of story and essay. Typically, essays occupy the margins, explore liminal spaces, turn back upon themselves, deal with seemingly ordinary things, tolerate meandering and incompletion, estrange the famil-iar. The type of writing I once thought I'd do keeps to broader paths and moves more swiftly toward a dénouement, variously pro-viding the semblance of safe passage via the ingenious handholds that the codes of literary invention and the myths of linearity have variously established.

We each of us pass between the pillar of our first in-breath and the pillar of our last out-breath, the relationship between being and nonbeing as intimately interconnected as that between the endless invisible intercourse of *A* and *Un*. Given the nature of the pillars that mark the beginning and the end of our journey, is it any wonder that, eschewing the terror of the real, we often turn to stories for some comfort? We cannot choose where to go in, do not know when we'll go out, and the attempt to chronicle the nature of our entrance, route, and exit can open up vistas that make the Pillars of Hercules seem toy-like in comparison.

The eighteenth-century Zen teacher known in Japan as Ekai, and in China as Hui K'ai, wrote a famous text, *Wu-men Kuan* (*The Gateless Gate*). This provides commentary on forty-eight classic koans. Zen, he said, has no gates. The key question is, How does one pass through this gateless gate? I hope Master Ekai would not judge the way I've approached Shandon's entrance as being entirely without merit. I make no attempt to close with words the gateless gate that lies between its pillars, a tangible symbol of the portals that await us at the heart of every moment. Instead, I try to see the invisible *koma-inu* that stand there, unleash them from the confinement of the ordinary, and listen, spellbound, to the astonishing susurration of their *A-Un* breathing.

JOHN BERGER

Portrait of a Masked Man

FROM *Harper's Magazine*

I'M SITTING IN A WOOD cabin on the outskirts of the town of San Cristóbal de las Casas, in Chiapas, southeast Mexico, about to begin drawing a portrait of Subcomandante Marcos. Twenty years ago in this town of narrow streets, of houses the color of flowers, of irregular pavements, any Indian walking along a pavement had to step off it to allow a "white" Mexican to continue unperturbed on his way. After the Zapatistas took control of the town, in 1994, this changed. What happens today along the same potholed pavements is a matter of choice and not discrimination.

When I came into the cabin in which Marcos was temporarily living, he asked me where I wanted him to sit. I indicated a chair next to which two Zapatista comandantes — a woman with her six-year-old daughter and an older man — were already sitting. Like this, I reckoned, he'll talk to them and leave me in peace. He looked at me a little ironically, as if reading my thoughts. In peace? Yes, peace is a moment.

Yesterday Marcos had announced in front of several hundred people that he would, for a while, be making no more public appearances, because the threat to the Zapatista communities and their way of life and struggle during the past thirteen years was today so acute that he must re-become the clandestine soldier he had once been to help organize their defense in the mountains. The defense — he reminded the audience — of those who since 1996 had formally renounced any form of armed struggle, but who, if attacked, would stubbornly resist. It seemed that the new Mexican president, Felipe Calderón, and his government, after their fraudulent election in 2006, were calculating that they could shortly proceed to wipe out the Zapatistas, and thus their shining example of disobedience in the face of the tyranny of the global economic order, without provoking widespread protests.

Marcos and the comandantes begin talking, and I begin drawing. The three of them — and the six-year-old girl — are wearing their ski masks. "We wear masks," the Zapatistas once claimed, "to become visible." A strange paradox to consider while drawing a portrait.

Three days ago, in the Zapatista community of Oventic, I was conversing with five of its councilors. These women and men spoke very calmly because they were telling their truths — as distinct from the truth. The calm that accompanies the belief in a single truth is a ruthless indifference. Theirs was a considerate calm. And their masks, far from making their faces less human or less unique, made them more so. I was reading their faces through their eyes, and the messages of eyes are the least controllable of facial expressions and therefore the most sincere.

Speaking of sincerity makes me suddenly think of a photo of a woman who is not wearing a mask. I cut the photo out of the daily newspaper *La Jornada*. Her name is María Concepción Moreno Arteaga. Mother of six boys, whom she brought up alone. Forty-seven years old, living in a village two hundred kilometers north of Mexico City, she earned her living as a washerwoman. Three years ago she was arrested by the Mexican government security forces and thrown into jail on the totally false charge of being involved in the traffic of illegal immigrants. One day María Concepción found herself before six such migrants in rags, who had made it across more than half the country and were pleading for water. So she gave them water and a wedge of something to eat because, given their plight, "there was no way possible to say no."

After being falsely charged she spent more than two years in prison. Her work in prison was the making of logos, labels for free-market clothes. With the few pesos handed over to her for this forced labor, she bought soap and toilet paper to keep clean.

The message of her eyes in the photo is: There was no way possible to say no.

Marcos has large hands with unusually long fingers. Their skin is worn and somewhat callused, their texture like that of a peasant's

hands. When he appears in public he takes on the stance and deliv-
ery of a messenger, and he either carefully and slowly reads the
new message out loud, or else he stands there, embodying it. By
contrast, here in the cabin he's at ease and not counting time. His
limbs hang loosely, like those of a long-distance pilot who has once
again safely landed his aircraft on a short runway. It suddenly occurs to me that he has a slight physical affinity with Saint-Exupéry:
perhaps a comparable diffidence or reticence about his tallness
and size.

Mexico has some of the most extensive silver mines in the world, as
the conquistadors rapidly discovered. It is also a land of mirrors.
Some framed palatial ones many times shattered, and, more extensively, a multitude of fragments, trinkets, sequins, shards of mirror
and mica catching the light. "When we touched the hearts of others, we also touched their sorrows. It was as if we were seeing ourselves in a mirror," the Zapatistas declared in the Sixth Declaration
of the Lacandon Jungle, two and a half years ago.

  Mexico City is perhaps the third-largest metropolis in the world,
with a soaring population of well over twenty million. A city of unbridled consumerism, interlinking rackets, poverty. Entire barrios
run by drug gangs. Residential avenues guarded by private security
guards in bulletproof vests. Colossal pollution. Traffic chaos. The
river Piedad ("Pity") flows east in a monstrous rusty pipeline. Mini-
mal public transportation. There are three "stories" of flyover
roads. Beneath them, without a vehicle, you scurry, as an earwig
does. Here cars have been made as indispensable as lodgings for
those with jobs. The ancient Aztec city of Tenochtitlán has finally
been transformed into a roundabout for the interests of corporate
capitalism.

Each year one million Mexican peasants and indigenous people
are forced by poverty and landlessness to leave their rural homes
and move to the capital or to other cities, while their lands are
taken over by corporate agribusiness.

  Mexico is a migrant country. Fifteen million men and women
work in the United States. Every year they send home about $25
billion. The majority of these workers are without papers and so
are branded as criminals in the United States and treated as such.

  What is happening is a mirror image of what happened in the

Soviet gulag. There, prisoners were forced to work until they dropped from exhaustion; here, workers are hounded as criminals until they become outlaws.

Meanwhile, in Mexico City, millions of questioning glances are exchanged every second, concerning scams, opportunities, jokes, alternatives, routines, honor, or just open, unsettled questions.

"Only for the powerful," the Zapatistas noted, "is history an upward line, where their today is always the pinnacle. For those below, history is a question which can only be answered by looking backward and forward, thus creating new questions."

I'm scrutinizing the eyebrows, the lines on his lower forehead, the circles under the eyes, the way the large nose protrudes against the mask. His physical voice is both distant and persuasive. The written voice is another matter. Contrary to what is usually assumed, a true writer's voice is seldom (perhaps never) her or his own; it's a voice born of the writer's intimacy and identification with others, who know their own ways blindfolded and who wordlessly guide the writer. It comes not from the writer's temperament but from trust.

And as I draw the volume of his head, I wonder how to define, how to put a line around, the place that his voice, as the writer of Zapatista messages, comes from. From where does it speak to the world?

Physically the voice speaks from here, from the rolling and precipitous highlands of Chiapas, today controlled by the indigenous peoples, who have taken back their land to cultivate and who have built schools, village centers, clinics. Yet where does this voice speak from figuratively?

He has just made the young girl laugh. When she laughs, her mask pants like a pup's flank.

I return to the city for an answer to my question. The principal thoroughfare is still, unpredictably, called the Avenida de los Insurgentes! Downtown there are still dozens of streets named after European capitals or countries, because a century ago Mexico thought of itself as a beacon of world progress and revolution.

Almost as many Mexicans go with their families at some time in their lives to look at Diego Rivera's fresco *Epic of the Mexican People* as go on a pilgrimage to the Basilica de Nuestra Señora de

Guadalupe, and they make their visit to this immense painting not
to study art but to recall and ponder their destiny.

I've changed from drawing him with ink to drawing with charcoal,
because it's more tentative, more frayed, more worn. Ink, from the
start, knows what it wants to say; charcoal listens.

No reproduction can give any idea of the force and scale of
Rivera's fresco, which crowns the principal staircase of what was,
until recently, the seat of government, the Presidential Palace. The
comparison often made with Michelangelo's Sistine Chapel is not
far-fetched — but with his *Last Judgment,* not with the ceiling.

Diego, the Elephant, as Frida Kahlo called him, was as ordinary
as any of us. He was sometimes boisterous, sometimes defeatist,
sometimes lazy, often inconsequent. Yet he was transformed when
he felt himself called upon to paint and embody on these walls the
story of the peoples from which he came; then he became conse-
quent to the point of being able to give every detail, every feature,
its particular place in a vast historic destiny. One has the sense at
the top of the staircase that it was a thousand years of history that
invented the colossal painter, not the other way around.

The hundreds of life-size figures from the pre-Columbian civili-
zations, from the street market of Tenochtitlán, from the three
centuries of Spanish colonial exploitation, from the war of independence that ended in 1821 and, most emphatically, from the
century following that war, leading to the revolution of 1910 and
its vision of a different future — all these notorious and anonymous figures are contained together in a vision of such energy and
continuity that, despite the many crying cruelties, it adds up to
something like a fraternal invitation. Each Mexican visitor, walking
down the staircase to leave, has been offered, as it were, a calla lily
from one of the painted baskets of the painted flower sellers.

At the same time — and this is perhaps another reason why I
think of the turmoil of Michelangelo's *Last Judgment* — the political
history of modern Mexico, as laid out on these walls and according
to all that has happened since they were painted, is nothing less
than a gigantic field of broken promises. One sort of enslavement
followed another, new systems of repression and discrimination replaced old ones, modern forms of poverty were invented and im-

posed, more and more natural resources were tapped and stolen by the gringos in the north, and the indigenous peoples were increasingly disinherited. Only Emiliano Zapata's cry *For Land and Liberty!* — before he was murdered in 1919 — continued to ring true.

And so I come to the point. The ravine between the vast field of broken promises and the popular expectations of more justice had somehow to be filled in, and the main political parties, beginning with the PRI (Party of the Institution of Revolution!), have carried this out for seventy years by making rubble of what had once been a political language. Broken promises, broken premises, broken propositions, broken laws. Every principle — except that of self-interest — was emptied of meaning. Political discourse, election campaigns, speeches for the corporate media systematically reduced to the prevarication and diversions of those whom the ancient Greeks termed the *idiotai* (self-seekers), as distinct from the *politai*. The voice of the Zapatista messages, which offer an example of both local and global resistance, comes from this ravine:

> No to trying to resolve from above the problems of our nation, but yes to building from below and for below. We don't believe that the ends justify the means. Finally we think the means are the end. We construct our objective at the same time that we construct the means by which we go on struggling. In that sense, the value we give to the spoken word, to honesty and to sincerity, is great, even though at times we may err ingenuously.

He's watching me drawing and smiles. There are two kinds of smiles (among many others): one that is waiting to hear the payoff line of a new joke, and another that is recalling a joke heard. His is the second.

I was in a village called Acamilpa in the state of Morelos, from which Emiliano Zapata came. *Milpa* means a field of maize in which other plants grow along with the maize and in which many birds, insects, and mammals also coexist. I want to describe an old woman's face that was strangely familiar to me. The woman might have come from my village in the Alps, or is it that age takes us all to the same village? Anyway, it was a Saturday evening and the courtyard of a small farmhouse was full of tables with white linen cloths over them, because it was somebody's birthday and the guests would soon arrive. An accordionist was already playing music. There was a very large acacia tree that would have been there when Emiliano Zapata was a kid. At one table thirteen elders from the surrounding villages were holding a serious meeting to coordinate their plans for civil disobedience and obstruction to prevent their water being diverted and stolen by property speculators. They were speaking in turn, carefully and deliberately. They accepted the music as if it were a dish, simmering, that could be eaten later. The old woman's face was tanned and windswept, and her bright eyes indicated that they were used to looking into the far distance from which winds come. Her long hair, as white as mine, was drawn back from her windswept face and tied in a chignon.

For the birthday party colored balloons had been strung between the house and the acacia tree. And this is what she said to me: "I have lived my life, such as it was given to me to live, and now I think of the future. I think of my grandchildren and their children, and how they will live. We have to resist for their sake. The ones who rule today want to destroy all peasants and every indigenous community because they want to own every seed on earth and every liter of water that comes from our mountains. So we stop their trucks when they come to steal what is ours . . . It's better to die on one's feet than to live on one's knees."

Marcos is wearing a watch on each wrist. One for peacetime, the other for wartime. When the Zapatistas are engaged in a defensive operation, they work according to a changed schedule in case their messages are intercepted.

There are, in any case, occasions that defy either time or any time.

In the town of San Andrés, where in February 1996 the government made a formal agreement with the Zapatistas to recognize the rights of all indigenous peoples, an agreement it never honored, there is the church of San Andrés Apóstol. In the church are a number of statues of the Madonna and of saints who wear sewn and embroidered garments made of cloth.

One midday I stopped there because, as in the village of

Acamilpa, I heard music. The music was ancient and strange. Inside the church were two indigenous young women with babies on their backs and, at a certain distance from them, two men. No priest. The four were singing in polyphony. On the floor of the church were a thousand lit candles, many in glass jars, their flames flickering in the wind that came through a side door left ajar. One of the women, as she sang, was swinging a censer, and the smoke of the incense hung like a mist above the flames that were like flowers. The year, the season, the day, the hour were forgotten details. Until one of the babies cried to be fed and the mother gave him her breast. The other woman was smoothing with her hands a tunic she had brought for the statue of San Andrés; she knew it was time to wash the one he was wearing and to change it.

Meanwhile, the Zapatistas are probably now at risk. Any attacks on them will come from those who shortsightedly believe that their example can be wiped out.

Behind the mask under the large nose, a mouth and larynx that speak from the ravine about hope. I've drawn what I can.

WENDELL BERRY

Faustian Economics

FROM *Harper's Magazine*

THE GENERAL REACTION to the apparent end of the era of cheap fossil fuel, as to other readily foreseeable curtailments, has been to delay any sort of reckoning. The strategies of delay so far have been a sort of willed oblivion, or visions of large profits to the manufacturers of such "biofuels" as ethanol from corn or switchgrass, or the familiar unscientific faith that "science will find an answer." The dominant response, in short, is a dogged belief that what we call the American Way of Life will prove somehow indestructible. We will keep on consuming, spending, wasting, and driving as before, at any cost to anything and everybody but ourselves.

This belief was always indefensible — the real names of global warming are Waste and Greed — and by now it is manifestly foolish. But foolishness on this scale looks disturbingly like a sort of national insanity. We seem to have come to a collective delusion of grandeur, insisting that all of us are "free" to be as conspicuously greedy and wasteful as the most corrupt of kings and queens. (Perhaps by devoting more and more of our already abused cropland to fuel production we will at last cure ourselves of obesity and become fashionably skeletal, hungry but — thank God! — still driving.)

The problem with us is not only prodigal extravagance but also an assumed limitlessness. We have obscured the issue by refusing to see that limitlessness is a godly trait. We have insistently, and with relief, defined ourselves as animals or as "higher animals." But to define ourselves as animals, given our specifically human powers and desires, is to define ourselves as *limitless* animals — which of course is a contradiction in terms. Any definition is a limit, which is why the God of Exodus refuses to define Himself: "I am that I am."

Even so, that we have founded our present society upon delusional assumptions of limitlessness is easy enough to demonstrate. A recent "summit" in Louisville, Kentucky, was entitled "Unbridled Energy: The Industrialization of Kentucky's Energy Resources." Its subjects were "clean-coal generation, biofuels, and other cutting-edge applications," the conversion of coal to "liquid fuels," and the likelihood that all this will be "environmentally friendly." These hopes, which "can create jobs and boost the nation's security," are to be supported by government "loan guarantees . . . investment tax credits and other tax breaks." Such talk we recognize as completely conventional. It is, in fact, a tissue of clichés that is now the common tongue of promoters, politicians, and journalists. This language does not allow for any computation or speculation as to the *net* good of anything proposed. The entire contraption of "Unbridled Energy" is supported only by a rote optimism: "The United States has 250 billion tons of recoverable coal reserves — enough to last 100 years even at double the current rate of consumption." We humans have inhabited the earth for many thousands of years, and now we can look forward to surviving for another hundred by doubling our consumption of coal? This is national security? The world-ending fire of industrial fundamentalism may already be burning in our furnaces and engines, but if it will burn for a hundred more years, that will be fine. Surely it would be better to intend straightforwardly to contain the fire and eventually put it out! But once greed has been made an honorable motive, then you have an economy without limits. It has no place for temperance or thrift or the ecological law of return. It will do anything. It is monstrous by definition.

In keeping with our unrestrained consumptiveness, the commonly accepted basis of our economy is the supposed possibility of limitless growth, limitless wants, limitless wealth, limitless natural resources, limitless energy, and limitless debt. The idea of a limitless economy implies and requires a doctrine of general human limitlessness: *all* are entitled to pursue without limit whatever they

conceive as desirable — a license that classifies the most exalted
Christian capitalist with the lowliest pornographer.

This fantasy of limitlessness perhaps arose from the coincidence
of the industrial revolution with the suddenly exploitable resources of the New World — though how the supposed limitlessness of resources can be reconciled with their exhaustion is not
clear. Or perhaps it comes from the contrary apprehension of
the world's "smallness," made possible by modern astronomy and
high-speed transportation. Fear of the smallness of our world and
its life may lead to a kind of claustrophobia and thence, with apparent reasonableness, to a desire for the "freedom" of limitlessness. But this desire, paradoxically, reduces everything. The life of
this world is small to those who think it is, and the desire to enlarge
it makes it smaller, and can reduce it finally to nothing.

However it came about, this credo of limitlessness clearly implies
a principled wish not only for limitless possessions but also for limitless knowledge, limitless science, limitless technology, and limitless progress. And, necessarily, it must lead to limitless violence,
waste, war, and destruction. That it should finally produce a crown-
ing cult of political limitlessness is only a matter of mad logic.

The normalization of the doctrine of limitlessness has produced a
sort of moral minimalism: the desire to be efficient at any cost, to
be unencumbered by complexity. The minimization of neighborliness, respect, reverence, responsibility, accountability, and self-
subordination — this is the culture of which our present leaders
and heroes are the spoiled children.

Our national faith so far has been: "There's always more." Our
true religion is a sort of autistic industrialism. People of intelligence and ability seem now to be genuinely embarrassed by any so-
lution to any problem that does not involve high technology, a
great expenditure of energy, or a big machine. Thus an X marked
on a paper ballot no longer fulfills our idea of voting. One problem with this state of affairs is that the work now most needing to
be done — that of neighborliness and caretaking — cannot be
done by remote control with the greatest power on the largest
scale. A second problem is that the economic fantasy of limitlessness in a limited world calls fearfully into question the value of our
monetary wealth, which does not reliably stand for the real wealth

of land, resources, and workmanship but instead wastes and depletes it.

That human limitlessness is a fantasy means, obviously, that its life expectancy is limited. There is now a growing perception, and not just among a few experts, that we are entering a time of inescapable limits. We are not likely to be granted another world to plunder in compensation for our pillage of this one. Nor are we likely to believe much longer in our ability to outsmart, by means of science and technology, our economic stupidity. The hope that we can cure the ills of industrialism by the homeopathy of more technology seems at last to be losing status. We are, in short, coming under pressure to understand ourselves as limited creatures in a limited world.

This constraint, however, is not the condemnation it may seem. On the contrary, it returns us to our real condition and to our human heritage, from which our self-definition as limitless animals has for too long cut us off. Every cultural and religious tradition that I know about, while fully acknowledging our animal nature, defines us specifically as *humans* — that is, as animals (if the word still applies) capable of living not only within natural limits but also within cultural limits, self-imposed. As earthly creatures, we live, because we must, within natural limits, which we may describe by such names as "earth" or "ecosystem" or "watershed" or "place." But as humans, we may elect to respond to this necessary placement by the self-restraints implied in neighborliness, stewardship, thrift, temperance, generosity, care, kindness, friendship, loyalty, and love.

In our limitless selfishness, we have tried to define "freedom," for example, as an escape from all restraint. But, as my friend Bert Hornback has explained in his book *The Wisdom in Words*, "free" is etymologically related to "friend." These words come from the same Indo-European root, which carries the sense of "dear" or "beloved." We set our friends free by our love for them, with the implied restraints of faithfulness or loyalty. And this suggests that our "identity" is located not in the impulse of selfhood but in deliberately maintained connections.

Thinking of our predicament has sent me back again to Christopher Marlowe's *Tragical History of Doctor Faustus*. This is a play of the Renaissance; Faustus, a man of learning, longs to possess "all Nature's treasury," to "Ransack the ocean . . . / And search all corners of the new-found world." To assuage his thirst for knowledge and power, he deeds his soul to Lucifer, receiving in compensation for twenty-four years the services of the subdevil Mephistophilis, nominally Faustus's slave but in fact his master. Having the subject of limitlessness in mind, I was astonished on this reading to come upon Mephistophilis's description of hell. When Faustus asks, "How comes it then that thou art out of hell?" Mephistophilis replies, "Why, this is hell, nor am I out of it." And a few pages later he explains:

> Hell hath no limits, nor is circumscribed
> In one self place, but where we [the damned] are is hell,
> And where hell is must we ever be.

For those who reject heaven, hell is everywhere, and thus is limitless. For them, even the thought of heaven is hell.

It is only appropriate, then, that Mephistophilis rejects any conventional limit: "Tut, Faustus, marriage is but a ceremonial toy. If thou lovest me, think no more of it." Continuing this theme, for Faustus's pleasure the devils present a sort of pageant of the seven deadly sins, three of which — Pride, Wrath, and Gluttony — describe themselves as orphans, disdaining the restraints of parental or filial love.

Seventy or so years later, and with the issue of the human definition more than ever in doubt, John Milton in Book VII of *Paradise Lost* returns again to a consideration of our urge to know. To Adam's request to be told the story of Creation, the "affable Archangel" Raphael agrees "to answer thy desire / Of knowledge *within bounds* [my emphasis]," explaining that

> Knowledge is as food, and needs no less
> Her temperance over appetite, to know
> In measure what the mind may well contain;
> Oppresses else with surfeit, and soon turns
> Wisdom to folly, as nourishment to wind.

Raphael is saying, with angelic circumlocution, that knowledge without wisdom, limitless knowledge, is not worth a fart; he is not a humorless archangel. But he also is saying that knowledge without measure, knowledge that the human mind cannot appropriately use, is mortally dangerous.

I am well aware of what I risk in bringing this language of religion into what is normally a scientific discussion. I do so because I doubt that we can define our present problems adequately, let alone solve them, without some recourse to our cultural heritage. We are, after all, trying now to deal with the failure of scientists, technicians, and politicians to "think up" a version of human continuance that is economically probable and ecologically responsible, or perhaps even imaginable. If we go back into our tradition, we are going to find a concern with religion, which at a minimum shatters the selfish context of the individual life, and thus forces a consideration of what human beings are and ought to be.

This concern persists at least as late as our Declaration of Independence, which holds as "self-evident, that all men are created equal; that they are endowed by their Creator with certain unalienable rights." Thus among our political roots we have still our old preoccupation with our definition as humans, which in the Declaration is wisely assigned to our Creator; our rights and the rights of all humans are not granted by any human government but are innate, belonging to us by birth. This insistence comes not from the fear of death or even extinction but from the ancient fear that in order to survive we might become inhuman or monstrous.

And so our cultural tradition is in large part the record of our continuing effort to understand ourselves as beings specifically human: to say that, as humans, we must do certain things and we must not do certain things. We must have limits or we will cease to exist as humans; perhaps we will cease to exist, period. At times, for example, some of us humans have thought that human beings, properly so called, did not make war against civilian populations, or hold prisoners without a fair trial, or use torture for any reason.

Some of us would-be humans have thought too that we should not be free at anybody else's expense. And yet in the phrase "free market," the word "free" has come to mean unlimited economic power for some, with the necessary consequence of economic powerlessness for others. Several years ago, after I had spoken at a meeting, two earnest and obviously troubled young veterinarians approached me with a question: How could they practice veterinary medicine without serious economic damage to the farmers who were their clients? Underlying their question was the fact that for a long time veterinary help for a sheep or a pig has been likely to cost more than the animal is worth. I had to answer that, in my opinion, so long as their practice relied heavily on selling patented drugs, they had no choice, since the market for medicinal drugs was entirely controlled by the drug companies, whereas most farmers had no control at all over the market for agricultural products. My questioners were asking in effect if a predatory economy can have a beneficent result. The answer too often is no. And that is because there is an absolute discontinuity between the economy of the seller of medicines and the economy of the buyer, as there is in the health industry as a whole. The drug industry is interested in the survival of patients, we have to suppose, because surviving patients will continue to consume drugs.

Now let us consider a contrary example. Recently, at another meeting, I talked for some time with an elderly, and some would say an old-fashioned, farmer from Nebraska. Unable to farm any longer himself, he had rented his land to a younger farmer on the basis of what he called "crop share" instead of a price paid or owed in advance. Thus, as the old farmer said of his renter, "If he has a good year, I have a good year. If he has a bad year, I have a bad one." This is what I would call community economics. It is a sharing of fate. It assures an economic continuity and a common interest between the two partners to the trade. This is as far as possible from the economy in which the young veterinarians were caught, in which the powerful are limitlessly "free" to trade, to the disadvantage, and ultimately the ruin, of the powerless.

It is this economy of community destruction that, wittingly or unwittingly, most scientists and technicians have served for the past two hundred years. These scientists and technicians have justified themselves by the proposition that they are the vanguard of progress, enlarging human knowledge and power, and thus they have romanticized both themselves and the predatory enterprises that they have served.

As a consequence, our great need now is for sciences and technologies of limits, of domesticity, of what Wes Jackson of the Land Institute in Salina, Kansas, has called "homecoming." These would be specifically human sciences and technologies, working, as the best humans always have worked, within self-imposed limits. The limits would be the accepted contexts of places, communities, and neighborhoods, both natural and human.

I know that the idea of such limitations will horrify some people, maybe most people, for we have long encouraged ourselves to feel at home on the "cutting edge" of knowledge and power or on some "frontier" of human experience. But I know too that we are talking now in the presence of much evidence that improvement by outward expansion may no longer be a good idea, if it ever was. It was not a good idea for the farmers who "leveraged" secure acreage to buy more during the 1970s. It has proved tragically to be a bad idea in a number of recent wars. If it is a good idea in the form of corporate gigantism, then we must ask, For whom? Faustus, who wants all knowledge and all the world for himself, is a man supremely lonely and finally doomed. I don't think Marlowe was kidding. I don't think Satan is kidding when he says in *Paradise Lost,* "Myself am Hell."

If the idea of appropriate limitation seems unacceptable to us, that may be because, like Marlowe's Faustus and Milton's Satan, we confuse limits with confinement. But that, as I think Marlowe and Milton and others were trying to tell us, is a great and potentially a fatal mistake. Satan's fault, as Milton understood it, and perhaps with some sympathy, was precisely that he could not tolerate his proper limitation; he could not subordinate himself to anything whatever. Faustus's error was his unwillingness to remain "Faustus, and a man." In our age of the world it is not rare to find writers, critics, and teachers of literature, as well as scientists and technicians, who regard Satan's and Faustus's defiance as salutary and heroic.

On the contrary, our human and earthly limits, properly understood, are not confinements but rather inducements to formal elaboration and elegance, to *fullness* of relationship and meaning. Perhaps our most serious cultural loss in recent centuries is the knowledge that some things, though limited, are inexhaustible. For example, an ecosystem, even that of a working forest or farm, so long as it remains ecologically intact, is inexhaustible. A small place, as I know from my own experience, can provide opportunities of work and learning, and a fund of beauty, solace, and pleasure — in addition to its difficulties — that cannot be exhausted in a lifetime or in generations.

To recover from our disease of limitlessness, we will have to give up the idea that we have a right to be godlike animals, that we are potentially omniscient and omnipotent, ready to discover "the secret of the universe." We will have to start over, with a different and much older premise: the naturalness and, for creatures of limited intelligence, the necessity of limits. We must learn again to ask how we can make the most of what we are, what we have, what we have been given. If we always have a theoretically better substitute available from somebody or someplace else, we will never make the most of anything. It is hard to make the most of one life. If we each had two lives, we would not make much of either. Or as one of my best teachers said of people in general: "They'll never be worth a damn as long as they've got two choices."

To deal with the problems, which after all are inescapable, of living with limited intelligence in a limited world, I suggest that we may have to remove some of the emphasis we have lately placed on science and technology and have a new look at the arts. For an art does not propose to enlarge itself by limitless extension but rather to enrich itself within bounds that are accepted prior to the work.

It is the artists, not the scientists, who have dealt unremittingly with the problem of limits. A painting, however large, must finally be bounded by a frame or a wall. A composer or playwright must reckon, at a minimum, with the capacity of an audience to sit still and pay attention. A story, once begun, must end somewhere within the limits of the writer's and the reader's memory. And of course the arts characteristically impose limits that are artificial: the five acts of a play, or the fourteen lines of a sonnet. Within these limits artists achieve elaborations of pattern, of sustaining relationships of parts with one another and with the whole, that may be astonishingly complex. And probably most of us can name a painting, a piece of music, a poem or play or story that still grows in meaning and remains fresh after many years of familiarity.

We know by now that a natural ecosystem survives by the same sort of formal intricacy, ever changing, inexhaustible, and no doubt finally unknowable. We know further that if we want to make our economic landscapes sustainably and abundantly productive, we must do so by maintaining in them a living formal complexity something like that of natural ecosystems. We can do this only by raising to the highest level our mastery of the arts of agriculture, animal husbandry, forestry, and, ultimately, the art of living.

It is true that insofar as scientific experiments must be conducted within carefully observed limits, scientists also are artists. But in science one experiment, whether it succeeds or fails, is logically followed by another in a theoretically infinite progression. According to the underlying myth of modern science, this progression is always replacing the smaller knowledge of the past with the larger knowledge of the present, which will be replaced by the yet larger knowledge of the future.

In the arts, by contrast, no limitless sequence of works is ever implied or looked for. No work of art is necessarily followed by a second work that is necessarily better. Given the methodologies of science, the law of gravity and the genome were bound to be discovered by somebody; the identity of the discoverer is incidental to the fact. But it appears that in the arts there are no second chances. We must assume that we had one chance each for *The Divine Comedy* and *King Lear.* If Dante and Shakespeare had died before they wrote those poems, nobody ever would have written them.

The same is true of our arts of land use, our economic arts, which are our arts of living. With these it is once-for-all. We will have no chance to redo our experiments with bad agriculture leading to soil loss. The Appalachian mountains and forests we have destroyed for coal are gone forever. It is now and forevermore too late to use thriftily the first half of the world's supply of petroleum. In the art of living we can only start again with what remains.

And so, in confronting the phenomenon of "peak oil," we are really confronting the end of our customary delusion of "more." Whichever way we turn, from now on, we are going to find a limit beyond which there will be no more. To hit these limits at top speed is not a rational choice. To start slowing down, with the idea of avoiding catastrophe, is a rational choice, and a viable one if we can recover the necessary political sanity. Of course it makes sense to consider alternative energy sources, provided *they* make sense. But also we will have to reexamine the economic structures of our lives, and conform them to the tolerances and limits of our earthly places. Where there is no more, our one choice is to make the most and the best of what we have.

BRIAN DOYLE

The Greatest Nature Essay Ever

FROM *Orion*

. . . WOULD BEGIN WITH an image so startling and lovely and wondrous that you would stop riffling through the rest of the mail, take your jacket off, sit down at the table, adjust your spectacles, tell the dog to lie *down*, tell the kids to make their *own* sandwiches for heavenssake, that's why God gave you *hands*, and read straight through the piece, marveling that you had indeed seen or smelled or heard *exactly* that, but never quite articulated it that way, or seen or heard it articulated that way, and you think, *Man, this is why I read nature essays, to be startled and moved like that, wow.*

The next two paragraphs would smoothly and gently move you into a story, seemingly a small story, a light tale, easily accessed, something personal but not self-indulgent or self-absorbed on the writer's part, just sort of a cheerful nutty everyday story maybe starring an elk or a mink or a child, but then there would suddenly be a sharp sentence where the dagger enters your heart and the essay spins on a dime like a skater, and you are plunged into waaay deeper water, you didn't see it coming at *all*, and you actually shiver, your whole body shimmers, and much later, maybe when you are in bed with someone you love and you are trying to evade his or her icy feet, you think, *My God, stories do have roaring power, stories are the most crucial and necessary food, how come we never hardly say that out loud?*

The next three paragraphs then walk inexorably toward a line of explosive Conclusions on the horizon like inky alps. Probably the sentences get shorter, more staccato. Terser. Blunter. Shards of sentences. But there's no opinion or commentary, just one line fitting into another, each one making plain inarguable sense, a goat or even a senator could easily understand the sentences and their implications, and there's no shouting, no persuasion, no eloquent pirouetting, no pronouncements and accusations, no sermons or homilies, just calm clean clear statements one after another, fitting together like people holding hands.

Then an odd paragraph, this is a most unusual and peculiar essay, for right here where you would normally expect those alpine Conclusions, some Advice, some Stern Instructions & Directions, there's only the quiet murmur of the writer tiptoeing back to the story he or she was telling you in the second and third paragraphs. The story slips back into view gently, a little shy, holding its hat, nothing melodramatic, in fact it offers a few gnomic questions without answers, and then it gently slides away off the page and off the stage, it almost evanesces or dissolves, and it's only later, after you have read the essay three times with mounting amazement, that you see quite how the writer managed the stagecraft there, but that's the stuff of another essay for another time.

And finally the last paragraph. It turns out that the perfect nature essay is quite short, it's a lean taut thing, an arrow and not a cannon, and here at the end there's a flash of humor, and a hint or tone or subtext of sadness, a touch of rue, you can't quite put your finger on it but it's there, a dark thread in the fabric, and there's also a shot of espresso hope, hope against all odds and sense, but rivetingly there's no call to arms, no clarion brassy trumpet blast, no website to which you are directed, no hint that you, yes you, should be ashamed of how much water you use or the car you drive or the fact that you just turned the thermostat up to seventy, or that you actually have not voted in the past two elections despite what you told the kids and the goat. Nor is there a rimshot ending, a bang, a last twist of the dagger. Oddly, sweetly, the essay just ends with a feeling eerily like a warm hand brushed against your cheek, and you sit there, near tears, smiling, and then you stand up. Changed.

DAVID JAMES DUNCAN

Cherish This Ecstasy

FROM *The Sun*

THE PEREGRINE FALCON was brought back from the brink of
extinction by a ban on DDT, but also by a peregrine falcon mating
hat invented by an ornithologist at Cornell University. If you can't
buy this, Google it. Female falcons had grown dangerously scarce.
A few wistful males nevertheless maintained a sort of sexual loitering ground. The hat was imagined, constructed, then forthrightly
worn by the ornithologist as he patrolled this loitering ground,
singing *Chee-up! Chee-up!* and bowing like an overpolite Japanese
Buddhist trying to tell somebody goodbye. For reasons neither scientists nor fashion designers entirely understand, this inspired the
occasional male falcon to dive onto the ornithologist's head, fuck
the hat, and fire endangered sperm into the hat's hidden rubber
receptacle. The last few females were then artificially inseminated
so that their chicks could be raised in DDT-free captivity. The
young produced in this way saved the peregrine from extinction —
a success story from the annals of human meddling, one as rare as
debacles like DDT are common.

The same year that I was researching a novel about birds entering extinction while my first marriage was doing the same, I wrote
a long, intimate letter to the Cornell ornithologist. That he was a
stranger perhaps explains the intimacy, strangers being preferable
to friends when things as personal as marriages are falling to ruin.
That he'd managed to save a species explains my blind trust. It's
been decades since I wrote the letter, and I didn't keep a copy.
Memory fixates on times of intense passage, but also mythologizes
them. Allowing for this paradox, here is everything I remember
about my letter to the ornithologist:

I got right to it, asking if he would be so kind as to use the enclosed self-addressed, stamped envelope to send me a diagram of his unimaginable hat or, better, a photo of said hat with his head in it, enduring furious, wing-beating coitus. I explained that I was a novelist and bird lover, promised that my interest was sincere, and said that no detail of his work could be too inconsequential for my purposes. I asked, for instance, whether, in addition to the Buddhistic bowing, he had to walk in a suggestive manner to lure down the hat's, so to speak, opposite sex. And if so, I added, could he describe this walk to me so that, should occasion arise, I could reproduce it in the vicinity of a wife who'd grown dangerously scarce.

Though this kind of praise may at first seem a stretch, I confessed to the ornithologist, I want you to know that I admire you not only because you've helped save a magnificent species but because I, far more than most, know what it is to have a wild bird achieve orgasm on my head. *Listen,* my letter and I whispered: A few evenings ago I was sitting on a lonely, moss-covered veranda I'd once considered a sort of sexual loitering ground, hurting, but praying, but hurting, but praying (perhaps you know the drill), when a lust-crazed male red-shafted flicker chased a female under an eave not four feet over my head, mounted her, and pierced her so profoundly that her wings went limp and hung down toward me like two exquisite garments she was compelled by passion to remove. She went so limp she couldn't fly. Do you see the beauty in this? She relinquished her defining power. She hung, beak open, eyes open, cheeks crimson, passion-shattered, till I was reminded of the too-great-for-Catholics saint Meister Eckhart. *The greater the nudity, the greater the union,* he preached to Christ-impassioned Rhine Valley women by the thousands, scaring Rome's crimson-beanied finest so christless they waited till the *meister* had died, then invaded the Rhine, clubbed and dissected his still-living sermons, silenced or burned Christ's profoundly pierced lovers, and excommunicated the nudity and wings.

Those two flickers so smote me that, late the same night, while my wife was out dancing, two dream flickers flew into my room and fused like a feathered halo o'er my head, and though not a wing or talon touched me, their passion poured in and in and in till it summoned, from some lost chasm of bliss miles inside me, the most ecstatic nocturnal emission of my life. I awoke, I told the ornithologist, passion-shattered in blackness, sensing wings. And suddenly knew: *I am never alone.* Knew, to be as scientific as I can about this, that *I am loved.* With no one and nothing there to show it. This invisible, ecstasy-producing, neither-avian-nor-human love then gave me the strength, right there in the blackness, to relinquish the defining power of marriage and accept my wife's wish to leave me.

So I can't help but wonder, I wrote the ornithologist: *Have you felt it?* This unspeakable, more-than-human love? Transfixing you via a magnificent male falcon during a nighttime visitation perhaps? Or out in the field, singing and bowing in your preternaturally receptive hat?

In Dostoyevsky's novel *The Brothers Karamazov,* I told the ornithologist, Father Zossima tells Alyosha, "All is an Ocean. All flows and connects so powerfully that if, in this life, you manage to become more gracious by even a drop, it is better for every bird, child, and animal your life touches than you will ever know. Start praying to birds in an ecstasy! Cherish this ecstasy, however senseless it may seem to people!" So I do. In a desolate, even life-threatening time, a pair of love-inflamed flickers transpierced and remade me as surely as your *chee-ups!* and Buddhist bowing and hat have remade the peregrine. I'll thank wild birds, and you too, forever for that. I trust that you now see why a small photo of the hat, in this time of personal passage and great gratitude, would serve as a kind of holy icon for me.

The Cornell ornithologist never answered my letter. And he was wise, it turned out, not to do so: for into the vacuum created by his lack of an answer wild birds flew, and have never stopped answering. Like the forty-three Vaux's swifts that dropped like dead leaves from an autumn dusk into my cold black chimney, grew still, but then thrummed in their sleep, close by the astonished ear I kept putting to the stove vent, as only eighty-six swift-wings can thrum, nonstop through the night. Or like the small black hole in the ice of a desolate, frozen river at which I happened to be gazing when out popped a lone water ouzel who, after a single deep knee-bend, burst into ecstatic, desolation-defying song.

Or like the still-smaller black hole in a leafless, frost-blasted cottonwood against which a heartbroken friend, Max, happened to lean on a Montana winter's walk, and out of which burst, like bees from a June hive, more than a hundred pygmy nuthatches, bequeathing Max, just that fast, an acceptance of heartbreak from which grace, like honey, began to flow. Or like the fourteen Hungarian partridges my rancher friend Tom flushed from buckbrush after a blizzard in twenty-below, who half circled a gulch so frigid Tom feared they'd freeze in midair, only to slam headfirst, wings tight to their bodies, thirty miles an hour, into a fresh snowdrift a hundred yards above him, *ffufuf!fuff!fuff!uf!fuf!uff!*, to spend the night tucked in twenty-above powder, bequeathing Tom, like a love poem the next day, fourteen tiny snow caves, the insides of which shone with the cold's own luminous blue.

Or like the lone female loon who mistook a wet, moonlit interstate for water and crash-landed on the truck-grooved pavement of the fast lane; loon to whom I sprinted, as a convoy of eighteen-wheelers roared toward her, throwing my coat over her head so she wouldn't stab me, pulling her to my chest as I leapt from the concrete; loon who, when she felt this blind liftoff, let out a full, far-northern tremolo that pierced, without stabbing, my coat, ribs, heart, day, life. All is an Ocean, she and Father Zossima and the avian choir keep singing as into black holes in trees, truck routes, river ice, frigid hearts, ecstatic birds keep dropping. Till even alone and in darkness, with no special hat, clothes, or wings to help me fly up and feel it, I find myself caught in the endless act of being loved.

PATRICIA HAMPL

The Dark Art of Description

FROM *The Iowa Review*

I WAS COMING DOWN the last lap of my most recent book, a memoir about my mother and father, and I was painfully aware of just how specific every bit of writing is, full of choices and chances, not theoretical at all, not the business of sweeping statements or smart ideas about "form" or "genre" or anything remotely theoretical. Just subject-verb-object and the hope of meaning.

Two nights away from the finish of my book, I was working late. I looked away from the computer screen for a moment and there was my dog staring at me intently. She was on the verge of speech. I could see it. *Come to bed.* Her eyes said this clearly. It was almost two A.M. and for the past four hours I'd been changing commas to dashes and then back again to commas with the obsessive focus only a fanatic can sustain.

You've become a crazy person again, I said right out loud. The dog padded away.

The great short story writer J. F. Powers was once stopped by a colleague in the corridor at their university. The man asked him how things were going. Powers allowed that it had been a tough day — "I spent the morning trying to decide whether to have my character call his friend 'pal' or 'chum,'" he said.

That's where I often find myself — thinking how important the choice of "pal" or "chum" is, how whatever truth writing lays claim to resides in a passion for just such quite mad distinctions. This monomania is what a friend of mine calls the six-hundred-pound gorilla of a book. Once the six-hundred-pound gorilla gets hold of you, you're his (or hers). "Those last weeks of finishing a book are a world in themselves," she said. "I think that gorilla is the reason most of us write — it's a real high, but it's also a subconscious agreement not to be available or even normal for as long as it takes."

But as soon as you — or I, anyway — break away from the gorilla's embrace of a particular book, those big, rangy theoretical questions begin to make their approach again. Maybe this is especially true of memoir, the odd enterprise of "writing a life" that has captivated our literary life for the past two decades or so. We tend to think of the novel as the classic narrative form — ever evolving, but familiar, its stately provenance long the preserve of academic interest and the center of trade publishing. Whereas the memoir seems new or somehow "modern," a rather suspect literary upstart. And therefore a form that invites interrogation.

But strictly speaking, autobiography is a genre far older than the novel and is hard-wired into Western literary history. Perhaps from that first injunction of the oracle at Delphi — *Know thyself* — Western culture has been devoted to the exploration of individual consciousness and the unspooling of individual life.

That commandment to *know thyself* was central to antiquity. Plato uttered a version of it; Cicero used it in a tract on the development of social concord. It was such a pillar of cultural, even spiritual value that in the early Christian period Clement of Alexandria felt compelled to claim that the saying had been borrowed by the Greeks from Scripture, thus binding the two developing spiritualities, pagan and monotheistic, together in a seamless endeavor.

Closer to modernity, Goethe is supposed to have said with a shudder, "Know thyself? If I knew myself, I'd run away." And André Gide probably expressed this revulsion best: "Know thyself! A maxim as pernicious as it is ugly. Whoever observes himself arrests his own development. A caterpillar who wanted to know itself well would never become a butterfly."

But the strongest indictment of the form I have ever encountered came from a student in Indiana who had been conscripted by his Freshman Comp teacher to attend a reading I gave some years ago. He sprawled in his chair with his baseball cap on backward, his eloquent body language making it clear he was far, far away. Can't win them all, I decided, and carried on, my eye straying back to him like a tongue drawn to the absence of a just-pulled tooth.

During the Q&A I fielded the decorous questions the students posed. And then, suddenly, apparently in response to something I'd said, my antihero sat bolt upright and was waving his hand urgently, his face alight with interest. Ah, a convert. I called on him, smiling.

"I get it," he said. "Nothin's ever happened to you — and you write books about it."

He was right, of course. And in pronouncing this acute literary critical remark, he touched on the most peculiar aspect of the rise of the memoir in our times — namely, that fundamentally it isn't about having a more interesting life than someone else. True, there is a strand of autobiographical writing that relies on the documentation of extraordinary circumstances, lives lived in extremity, often at great peril. But such memoirs have always been part of literary history. What characterizes the rise of memoir in recent times is precisely the opposite condition — not a gripping "narrative arc," but the quality of voice, the story of perception rather than action.

The self is not the subject of memoir, in this kind of book, but its instrument. And the work of the self is not to "narrate" but to describe. There is something fundamentally photographic about memoir, photographic rather than cinematic. Not a story, but a series of tableaus we are given to consider. No memoirist is surprised by the absences and blanks in action, for another unavoidable quality of autobiography as I am thinking of it — as lyrical quest literature — is that it is as much about reticence as it is about revelation.

It is often remarked that the advent of the movies and the ever faster pace of modern life have conspired to make description a less essential part of prose narrative in our own times. We don't need to be told what things look like — we are inundated with images, pictures, moving or static. In this view, we need the opposite of the photographic quality so beloved of nineteenth-century descriptive writing in which the landscape is rolled out sentence after sentence, the interior of a room and the interior of the character's mind meticulously presented.

We require writing, instead, that subsumes description, leaps right over it to frame episode and to create the much-sought-after "narrative arc." The motto — even the mantra — of this narrative model is of course the commandment of introductory fiction writing workshops: *Show, don't tell.*

But as recent memoir writing shows, descriptive writing abounds. And it proves, finally, not to be about the object described. Or not only. Description in memoir is where the consciousness of the writer and the material of the story are established in harmony, where the self is lost in the material, in a sense. In fiction of the show-don't-tell variety, narrative scenes that "show" and dutifully do not "tell" are advanced by volleys of dialogue in which the author's presence is successfully obscured by the dramatic action of the dialogue of his characters. But in description we hear and feel the absorption of the author in the material. We sense the presence of the creator of the scene.

This personal absorption is what we mean by "style." It is strange that we would choose so oddly surfacey a word — style — for this most soulful aspect of writing. We could, perhaps more exactly, call this relation between consciousness and its subject "integrity." What else is the articulation of perception?

Style is a word usually claimed by fashion and the most passing aesthetic values. But maybe that's as it should be, because style in writing is terribly perishable. It can rot — that is what we mean when we recognize writing to be "precious," for example. But at its best and most essential, style is the register between a writer's consciousness and the material he is committed to wrestling to the page. It is the real authority of a writer, more substantial than plot, less ego-dependent than voice.

In 1951, Alfred Kazin published his memoir of his boyhood in Brooklyn, *A Walker in the City,* the book that establishes modern American memoir. The critic Leslie Fiedler admired the book but was also frustrated by it. It "perversely refuses to be a novel," he said with some annoyance, as if Kazin's book, deeply dependent on descriptive writing, were refusing to behave. And it was. It was refusing to obey the commandment "Show, don't tell."

When you read "The Block and Beyond," a much-anthologized chapter from Kazin's memoir, it is impossible to discuss the main characters and certainly not its plot or even its narrative structure. It is a rhapsodic evocation of a place and time. And once read, it is impossible to forget, as indelible and inevitable as a poem.

What Kazin was able to do — what every memoirist can attempt — in liberating himself from the demands of show-don't-tell narrative was to enter into reflection, into speculation, into interpretation, and to use the fragment, the image, the vignette, rather than narratively linked scenes, to form his world and his book. He was able to show *and* tell. To write a story and write an essay — all in the same tale, braided and twined together. The root of this double power lies in description.

I was one of those enthralled teenage readers of long nineteenth-century English novels. I toiled my way through dense descriptions of gloomy heaths and bogs to get to the airy volleys of dialogue that lofted back and forth down the page to give me what I wanted: Would Jane and Mr. Rochester . . . or would they not? Would Dorothea Brooke awaken — would Mr. Lydgate? I didn't relish the descriptive passages; I endured them. Just as Jane and Dorothea endured their parched lives, as if these endless descriptive passages were the desert to be crossed before the paradise of dialogue and the love story could be entered.

Yet all this description was, after all, the *world* of the book — not simply because it gave the book "a sense of place," as the old literary cliché puts it. It wasn't a "sense of place" I cared about in these passages, but the meeting place of perception with story — the place where someone *claimed* the story, where I could glimpse the individual consciousness, the creator of the scene. The person pulling the wires and making Jane and Dorothea move. I was looking, I suppose, for a sign of intimacy with the invisible author. That "dear reader" moment so familiar in nineteenth-century novels — think of Thackeray pausing to have a chat with the reader — with you! — about how to live on nothing a year. Think of George Eliot breaking off to describe the furnishings of Dorothea's ardent mind.

Henry James is probably the crown prince of nineteenth-century describers, a flâneur of the sentence, a lounge lizard of the paragraph, taking his own sweet time to unfurl an observation, smoking the cheroot of his thought in the contemplative after-dinner puffery of a man who knows how to draw out the pleasure of his rare tobacco. Or — because James himself never hesitates to pile up opposing figures of speech until he has sliced his thought to the refracted transparency he adores — maybe I'll just switch meta-

phors and say that James sits mildly at his torture apparatus, turning the crank in meticulously calibrated movements as the reader
lies helplessly strained upon the rack of his ever-expanding sentences, the exquisite pain of the lengthening description almost
breaking the bones of attention. In short (as James often says after
gassing on for a nice fat paragraph or two on the quality of a Vene-
tian sunset or the knowing lift of a European eyebrow glimpsed
across a table by an artless American ingénue), in short, he loves to
carry on.

Carrying on, I was discovering, is what it is to describe. A lot. At
length. To trust description above plot, past character development, and even theme. To understand that to describe is both
humbler and more essential than to think of compositional im-
ponderables such as "voice" or to strain toward superstructures
like "narrative arc." To trust that the act of description will *find*
voice and out of its streaming attention will take hold of narration.

By the time I was considering all of this, I had passed from being
a reader and had become that more desperate literary type — a
writer trying to figure out how to do it myself. I had no idea how to
"sustain a narrative" and didn't even understand at the time (the
late 1970s) that I was writing something called "a memoir." Yet
when I read *Speak, Memory* by Vladimir Nabokov and later read his
command — *Caress the detail, the divine detail* — I knew I had found
the motto I could live by, the one that prevailed over "Show, don't
tell."

Perhaps only someone as thoroughly divested of his paradise as
Nabokov had been of his boyhood Russia and his family, his native
language and all his beloved associations and privileged expectations, could enshrine the detail, the fragment, as the divinity of his
literary religion, could trust the truths to be found in the DNA of
detail, attentively rendered in ardent description. The dutiful observation that is the yeoman's work of description finally ascended,
Nabokov demonstrated, to the transcendent reality of literature, to
metaphor itself.

Nabokov was asked in an interview if his characters ever "took
over." He replied icily that *his* characters were his galley slaves.

Yet when it was a matter of locating the godhead of literary endeavor, even a writer as unabashedly imperious as Nabokov did not
point to himself and his intentions but to the lowly detail. *Caress the*

detail, the divine detail. Next to grand conceptions like plot, which is the legitimate government of most stories, or character, which is the crowned sovereign, the detail looks like a ragged peasant with a half-baked idea of revolution and a crazy, sure glint in its eye. But here, according to Nabokov, resides divinity.

Henry James put his faith in something at least as insubstantial. "If one was to undertake to . . . report with truth on the human scene," he wrote, "it could but be because notes had been from the cradle the ineluctable consequence of one's greatest inward energy . . . to take them was as natural as to look, to think, to feel, to recognize, to remember." He considered his habit the basis of literature and called it "the rich principle of the Note."

Such "notes" are of course details, observations. Description. In attending to these details, in the act of description, the more dynamic aspects of narrative have a chance to reveal themselves — not as "action" or "conflict" or any of the theoretical and technical terms we persist in thinking of as the sources of form. Rather, description gives the authorial mind a place to be in relation with the reality of the world.

It was surely this desire for the world — that is, for the world's memoir, which is history — that drew me to memoir, that seemingly personal form. And it was to description I tended, not to narrative, not to story. Maybe the root of the desire to write is always lost — properly lost — in the nonliterary earth of our real lives. And craft, as we think of it, is just the jargon we give to that darker, earthier medium.

I know it was my mother who was the storyteller in our house. I was her audience. Her dear reader, in a way. I dimly — and sometimes bitterly — understood that nothing much was happening in our modest midwestern lives, yet I clung to the drama with which she infused every vignette, every encounter at the grocery store.

And when I sought to make sense of the world that kept slipping away to the past, to loss and forgetfulness, when I protested inwardly at that disappearance, it was to description I instinctively turned. Coming from a background in poetry and therefore being a literalist, it didn't occur to me to copy other prose writers. If I wanted to learn to write descriptively, I needed — what else? — pictures.

I took myself off to the Minneapolis Institute of Arts and

plunked myself down in front of a Bonnard. I wrote the painting. Described it. I went home and looked at a teacup on my table — I wrote that too. Still-life descriptions that ran on for several pages. I wrote and wrote, describing my way through art galleries and the inadvertent still lifes of my house and my memory, my grandmother's garden, her Sunday dinners.

To my growing astonishment, these long descriptive passages, sometimes running two, three pages or longer, had a way of sheering off into narrative after all. The teacup I was describing had been given to me by my mother. And once I thought of the fact that she had bought these cups, made in Czechoslovakia, as a bride just before the Second World War, I was writing about that war, about my mother and her later disappointments, which somehow were, and were not, part of this fragile cup. Description — which had seemed like background in novels, static and inert as a butterfly pinned to the page of my notebook — proved to be a dynamic engine that stoked voice and even more propelled the occasional narrative arc. Description, written from the personal voice of my own perception, proved even to be the link with the world's story, with history itself. Here was my mother's teacup, made in Czechoslovakia before the war, and here, therefore, was not only my mother's heartbreak, but Europe's. The detail was surely divine, offering up miracle after miracle of connections out of the faithful consideration of the fragments before me.

We sense this historical power at the heart of autobiographical writing in the testaments from the Holocaust, from the gulag, from every marginal and abused life that has found the courage to speak its truth, which is often its horror, to preserve its demonic details — and in so doing has seen them become divine. Nadezhda Mandelstam, Anne Frank, Primo Levi, to name only a very few. In time we will surely see such documents from Guantánamo and the unknown places of extreme rendition.

The history of whole countries, of an entire era and even lost populations, depends sometimes on a little girl faithfully keeping her diary. The great contract of literature consists in this: you tell me your story and somehow I get my story. If we are looking for another reason to explain the strangely powerful grip of the first-person voice on contemporary writing, perhaps we need look no further than the power of Anne Frank's equation — that to write one's life enables the world to preserve its history.

But what of lives lived in the flyover? Lives that don't have that powerful, if terrible, historical resonance of radical suffering. Ordinary lives, in a word. Alfred Kazin's life — or yours. And certainly mine in middling Minnesota in the middle of the twentieth century. Why bother to describe it? Because, of course, all details are divine, not just Nabokov's. In fact, perhaps the poorer the supposed value, the more the detail requires description to assure its divinity.

Which brings me to, if not a story, at least a fragment, a vignette. Early in my teaching life, I went (foolishly) through a killer snowstorm in Minneapolis to get to my university office because I had student conferences scheduled. By the time I arrived, the university had closed and the campus was empty, whipped by white shrouds of blizzard snow, the wind whistling down the mall. I sat in my office in the empty building, cursing my ruinous work ethic, wondering if the buses would keep running so I could get home.

Then a rap on my office door. I opened it and there, like an extra out *of Doctor Zhivago,* stood my eleven A.M. appointment, a quiet sophomore named Tommy.

He looked anxious. He was really glad I was there, he said, because he had a big problem with the assignment. I had asked the students to write short autobiographies. "I just can't write anything about my life," he said miserably, his head down, his overshoes puddling on the floor.

I waited for the disclosure. What would it be — child abuse, incest, what murder or mayhem could this boy not divulge? What had brought him trooping through the blizzard to get help with his life story? How would I get him to student counseling?

"See, I come from Fridley," he said, naming one of the nowhere suburbs sprawling drearily beyond the freeway north of Minneapolis.

I stared at him. I didn't for a moment comprehend that this was the dark disclosure, this the occasion of his misery: being from Fridley meant, surely, that he had nothing worth writing about.

There it was again — nothin' had ever happened to him and I was asking him to write about it.

"I have good news for you, Tommy," I said. "The field's wide open. Nobody has told what it's like to grow up in Fridley yet. It's all yours."

All he needed to do was sit down and describe. And because the detail is divine, if you caress it into life, you find the world you have lost or ignored, the world ruined or devalued. The world you alone can bring into being, bit by broken bit. And so you create your own integrity, which is to say your voice, your style.

GARRET KEIZER

And Such Small Deer

FROM *Lapham's Quarterly*

Santiago

About a dozen years ago my wife and I planted a hedge of twenty-
seven arborvitae trees along the border of our backyard, which, although our house sits on nineteen acres of fields and woods, is also
the back border of our property. A sloping hayfield with a realtor's
dream of panoramic views lies directly behind us, so the hedge was
our attempt to secure privacy for the future. The nurseryman who
sold us the shrubs assured us they were the best species for our purpose and climate. I measured and marked the planting sites, called
in "Chink" Norris (whose possibly racist nickname I've not looked
into any more than I have the nurseryman's credentials) to come
with his small backhoe and dig the holes. As advised, I faithfully watered and fertilized each tree throughout the first year, with results
that were everything I'd been promised: dense, hardy, and luxuriant, a towering bulwark of green.

Thus began an episode of great vexation and buffoonery in my
life, known and (I have no doubt) merrily recounted in local circles as the tale of "Garret and his trees," or as my wife puts it, "Garret and the deer." It so happens that we live next to one of the
county's most extensive "deer yards," those areas of canopied
woods to which the deer retire in winter, making networks of
deeply furrowed tracks and foraging as best they can until there's a
declared winner in the yearly foot race between spring and starva-
tion.

It also happens that deer find arborvitae a delicacy, related to the cedar that they also love, but thicker and more succulent. By the second winter they'd found and attacked my trees. I fought back, not with a vengeance — I stopped short of that — but with something close to obsession. I erected fence structures that made our backyard look like a scene from the Somme. I played recordings of wolves howling, recordings of me howling. I fired pistol shots at random hours of the night. I hung or sprinkled repellents of blood meal, urine (mine), and deodorant soap. Hearing that deer were repelled by the scent of human hair, I asked some hairdressers to set aside their sweepings in a bag with, as the saying goes, my name on it.

Joan Didion once wrote, commenting on a folk remedy for hysterical distress, that it is difficult to feel like Catherine Earnshaw in *Wuthering Heights* with your head in a Food Fair bag. It is also difficult to imagine you are Santiago in *The Old Man and the Sea* when you're stuffing sachets of cut-up pantyhose with human hair. But often I thought of the old fisherman, whacking the sharks with his club as his labor and his dream were devoured in front of his eyes.

As any game warden will tell you, if deer are hungry enough they will get through anything, which this year included an electric fence hooked to a charger supposedly powerful enough to deter elephants. So the farmer who'd helped me rig it up assured me. What he did not tell me, because he did not know, was that the insulating snowpack would prevent an animal from completing the circuit with the ground. In came the deer like a school of piranhas. This was shortly after a man from Connecticut purchased the hayfield behind our house for a price few of my neighbors could have afforded and none of them could believe and set about measuring the foundations of a house.

Gatsby

Nature teaches us economy and art, tenacity and grace, but all by analogy to itself. "Eyes front, please," it says, tapping the blackboard with its teeth and claws. What it gives us for homework, though, is futility.

"Boats against the current, borne back ceaselessly into the past" is how Fitzgerald puts it in *The Great Gatsby*. Only an American would be so naïve as to think he is talking solely about an American dream. It is American only insofar as America retains the memory of contact with a wilderness that invites dreams but makes no covenant with them. The boat borne back into the past is, in its most elemental form, the corn bitten back to the stalk. The wheat beaten down by the hail. As soon as Jonah sits down under a gourd vine, a worm starts eating his shade. Earlier a whale had tried eating him.

We sense the same futility in history. The enduring cliché that history repeats itself implies a comparison to the cyclical patterns of nature. Writing in 1933 about the rising fascist movements, Leon Trotsky said, "Today, not only in peasant homes but also in city skyscrapers, there lives alongside of the twentieth century the tenth or the thirteenth." At the same time as the deer were devastating my hedge, President George W. Bush vetoed a bill that would have outlawed waterboarding. Torquemada redux. At our town meeting last March an angry electorate defeated a barebones school budget for the first time in a dozen years. People said derogatory things about teachers, about children receiving special education, that I had not heard in more than twenty years. The telemarketers I'd driven back over the borders of our dinner hour resumed their evening raids. Like weeds and whiskers, everything grows back. And what you want to grow — the saplings, the school music program, some notion of a humanistic civilization — is eaten down to the root.

Several years ago I spotted two farmers squatting at the top of the hayfield behind our house, looking intently at the ground. I wondered if they had driven the baler over a rabbit or a snake. Instead, they were puzzling over the first traces of a rare infestation of army worms, so called because they advance in a line. A freak in the weather had called them out like Huns onto the steppes. They ate the hayfield from top to bottom, they ate our back and front lawns. They crossed the road, in such numbers that cars were sliding in the black and green gore of their bodies, and proceeded to eat the pastures beyond.

All is vanity, said Ecclesiastes. He planted vineyards, gardens, and fruit trees, but decided that all was vanity. Anyone who lives close to the woods envies him for making as good a go of it as he did.

Goya

Futility does not excuse, but perhaps explains, the cruelty with which we have sometimes treated the natural world. In 1814 the naturalist John James Audubon watched as a farmer climbed into a pit where he'd trapped a family of wolves. He severed their hamstrings, dragged them out, and set his dogs on them. Audubon records the scene without censure. During the same winter wolves had destroyed nearly all of the farmer's sheep and one of his colts. His vengeance was not atypical. American homesteaders burned wolves alive and dragged them to death behind horses. They wired shut their mouths and genitals and set them loose. Socialized in packs where submission bought mercy, the wolves mostly cowered.

My parents were merely efficient when the gypsy moths descended on New Jersey in my childhood. I can still see my father holding a long torch up to the ghostly tents, the black bodies writhing in the flames. Those I gathered by hand my mother dropped into a coffee can of gasoline. Out of sight under the pine tree where I played, I hung their living bodies noosed on strings like a scene out of Goya. At night, standing in the yard very still, you could hear their mouths munching the foliage, eating our trees.

One year a game warden told me I could "take one down" if the deer continued with their destruction. I held back. Harried beyond scruple, I asked the question again last winter. This time the answer was no. I was tempted but held firm. Even without fear of God or the law — and I happen to fear both — I feared the neighbors. A wounded deer limping over the snow "out of season," its bloody tracks easily traceable, would have branded me a pariah, worse than a defender of school budgets. Though the autumn finds our woods choked with hunters, local people have a deep and paradoxical affection for the animals that is probably as old as the hunt itself.

On the walls of a cave at Les Trois Frères in the Pyrenees stands the upright figure of a man in a deer skin, antlers mounted on his head. Sometimes called "The Sorcerer," he is estimated to be fifteen thousand years old. Whatever his archetypal relation to Satan or to Santa Claus, he is even more easily identified as the ancestor of those carved red men stuck outside cigar stores and the buxom figureheads affixed to the prows of whaling ships (the soldiers sent by Kublai Khan on a futile mission to conquer Japan used captured Japanese women for the purpose, threading tackle through slits cut into their hands) — to man's totemic adoration of the creatures he hunts down and devours.

The meter reader gawks at my damaged hedge, the trees like cat-eaten cartoon fishes, the fine bones of the desiccated branches curved toward the green scaly heads. He chuckles in spite of himself. "I shouldn't laugh," he says. His face betrays his fondness. The little scamps.

In the fall he'll shoot one through the heart with a four-bladed arrow or a high-velocity bullet, string it up, flay and disembowel it. For Christmas his children will give him and their mother matching silk-screened sweatshirts with the image of a buck and doe.

Job

"Behold now behemoth, which I made with thee." Thus says God to Job. He may be talking about a hippopotamus. Job wants some kind of explanation for his pain, for the seeming futility of his shattered life. But when God reveals himself, he starts talking about animals. None of them are domesticated. The ostrich, the mountain goat, behemoth and leviathan — all are creatures with no use and little resemblance to the lives of women and men. It seems that nature was not made for Job. He has his place in it, but it is not *his* place. His suffering can be no more comprehensible to him than a hippo's dung-broadcasting tail.

In the light of Job's theophany, the oft-professed love of nature, ardent and all-embracing, is the highest form of hubris. It is a claim to see the creatures of this world as only God can see them.

The deer have no such delusions. A woodsman friend of mine tells me that you can approach a deer, according to a ruse he first heard from an Abenaki Indian, by putting your arms and hands behind your back — that is, by hiding those terrifying features that do not exist among the other quadrupeds. "Behold the human, which I made with thee. His head is blunt but his arms are most terrible."

I take a book out of the library to learn the ways of white-tailed deer. It is not as though they belong to another planet. The bucks make a strange, Elvis-like curl of their lips when they sense a doe in estrus. Except during the rut, the males and females live in separate groups, as some think the Neanderthals might have done, the males coming around now and then to the females' tidier caves to trade meat for sex. An old doe dominates the younger females in the deer yards and will drive away the bucks when neither she nor the weather is in heat. With their sharp hooves deer have been known to kill rattlesnakes.

Like most people, I find the deer beautiful to watch, but this winter they have started to look ugly to me. Before going to bed, but after I've switched on the boom box with the Alaskan wolf howls, I shine a spotlight into the hedge, and there is a large doe with red glowing eyes, her neck swollen like a cobra's.

Some biblical commentators say that leviathan is a crocodile. My deer book says that the alligators of southern swamps and bayous probably take an occasional deer. "He maketh the deep to boil like a pot." I entertain the fantasy of a winter-hardy alligator on a leash. Twelve feet long and faster than an ostrich. From time to time I let him loose. Over the snow he scuttles as the scattered deer sink down into it. The challenge of living close to wild animals, I decide, is not all that different from the challenge of living close to human beings: how to keep the exertion of preserving your sanity from making you nuts.

Poor Tom

One day during the height of the carnage, I realize that I have received no fewer than five phone calls from people who are suffering from different forms of mental illness. I am not a psychologist. I am simply a man with a certain appeal. Some middle-aged men with literary professions are irresistible to leggy graduate students who like to wear black; I happen to be irresistible to people on psychotropic drugs. Just as well, I think, since I am happily married and because it grounds me to converse with men and women who know on the most tenuous level what it means to feel "a little better today," what courage it takes to fling that modest claim at the sharp fangs of futility. I remind them to take walks. "Don't neglect to get outdoors," I say. My hands are almost too numb to hold the phone, still so frozen they are from repairing the fortifications that the deer have broken through yet again.

The madman and the pretend madman were stock characters on the Elizabethan stage. Banished Edgar in *King Lear* pretends he is mad, the only recourse of a sane man in a world beginning to rave. He calls himself Poor Tom o' Bedlam. He eats "mice and rats and such small deer," though he would have been of no use to me, since he probably means deer in the early English sense of any wild animal. A rat was once "a deer." My friends often hear me define a deer as "a rat with long legs." Poor Tom's a-cold. Poor Tom's going just about crazy from these varmints. Poor Tom has an incoming call from a person on loxapine.

After I hang up, I say to my wife, "These people who called tonight, those deer in the back, they are all hungry. This is all about hunger."

This is hardly an epiphany. But for some reason, saying those words, thereby connecting the deer's voraciousness to my callers' yearning for friendship and to my own yearning for privacy — the more elemental forms of hunger being too alien to my well-provisioned life — causes a palpable shift in my attitude. I go from being painfully obsessed to being insufferably didactic.

The whole world is hungry, I keep saying. The natural world is hunger itself. Even the cruelty of the wolf killers was traceable to hunger, to what happens to one's children when all the sheep are taken. I know nothing about living in harmony with nature. Harmony with nature is the conqueror's old cant, a slave master's fond illusion of happy slaves. It is the romantic wreathed with daisies, touring the Lake District on a spring fling from Chelsea. Shakespeare knew more when he wreathed wildflowers around heads that were losing their minds: Ophelia's, Lear's. He was closer than Wordsworth to the wild. Those settlers who went mad in their sod houses on the prairie were closer still.

It is not harmony I need to think about, but hunger: the basic moral conundrum of how to feed the hungry without being eaten oneself. Any higher is Christ — "Take, eat. This is my body which is given for you" — or the Buddha, who in an earlier incarnation is supposed to have offered himself as a meal to a starving mother ti-

ger. For all I know, in an even earlier incarnation, he was an arborvitae tree.

Sisyphus

And still I might have shot one. I might have chanced it. There are
people on these back roads who are hungry too, and I fancied leaving a carcass in the littered dooryard of somebody's slouching
trailer. Late at night, the doe eyes fixed with a light beam in the
time-honored method of the poacher, a close, clear shot — who
would have to know? It was my wife who reminded me that for this
to have any lasting effect, I would have to kill the whole herd. I
would have to hate my struggle with the deer enough to end it with
their annihilation.

The opposite of struggle is not peace but total war. War is the attempt to end struggle once and for all. Rub out the competition.
The old Pax Romana. Flatten the hill of Sisyphus and blow up his
stone with a one-megaton bomb. "Get er done," as the rednecks
blazon on their trucks; "get closure" as their classier neighbors like
to say. Idealism taken to the extreme is always genocide: the pure
race, the utopian state, the rocking chair perched atop the mass
grave. "They make a wilderness," Tacitus wrote of the Roman imperial policy, "and call it peace." You can destroy a wilderness and
call it peace too.

In other words, when in my despair I said, "No matter what I do,
I can't seem to win," I was making the right point without entirely
getting it. Or, rather, I was close to the point, which is that the essential human task is not winning the struggle but raising it to the
highest possible plane.

I believe in chivalry more than in harmony. I believe in loving
the enemy more than in peace. If chivalry is dead, so are we. By
chivalry I mean a willingness to parley. A disdain for violence
against any creature temporarily under one's thumb. A tendency
to rate courage only a little higher than generosity in one's code of
honor. An approach that puts the loveliness and dignity of means
— and what an environmentalist would call the sustainability of
means — on a par with and even above their efficacy. For some two
hundred years the samurai class of feudal Japan foreswore fire-
arms, though the Japanese were aware of them and were expert

gunsmiths. (Sixteenth-century matchlocks of Japanese make were still used by soldiers as late as 1904 in the Russo-Japanese War.) Predictably, the samurai didn't like the devaluation of their courage in hand-to-hand combat, but they also didn't like the posture that firing a matchlock required. It offended the sensibilities of a culture in which nearly every gesture had aesthetic criteria. Put simply, the samurai thought they looked stupid. More pacifistic than Gandhi, the Amish are actually closer to samurai than any road warrior you're likely to see looming in your rearview mirror. They have figured out that a man looks less stupid holding the reins of a buggy than he does gripping a cell phone in the cockpit of an SUV. As for a man taking down a deer (even in his head) with a rocket launcher, we will leave that to speak for itself.

A chivalrous approach to nature is one of greater labor, risk, and elegance. It seldom permits victory. It does admit pleasure. Think of it as raising the battle of the sexes to the plane of a betrothal. Eyes gone moony under his protruding brow ridge, Neanderthal man proposes a new social contract. With these spareribs, I thee wed. It will be more work in some ways, more compromise, but it will do wonders for his posture. He will look less stupid.

Ishmael

"You look like a whaler," my wife says, as I stand in my snowshoes gripping my telescoping pole saw with its crescent-shaped blade and the long pull rope to operate the pruning knife. I am going into the woods to cut down cedar fronds for the deer to eat, to knock down any frozen apples that may still be clinging to the trees. Sensible in their evolution, deer eat by roving, giving the bits they've nibbled time to grow back by the time they return. Like browsing deer, I will plot my cuttings along a wide circle. Like thwarted electricity, I will find my way home.

I have gone this way before. I used to buy sacks of deer feed (pellets and corn kernels dipped in a kind of molasses) and sled it into the woods until that became illegal (not good for the deer tummies, they said) and I could no longer buy the food. I went this way many years ago when I decided that I would homeschool our daughter, when I decided that it was more ennobling to write lesson plans for a year or two than to harangue taxpayers and get on principals' backs. I suppose I went this way when I planted the trees in the first place. More work, more cost, but better than dreading the acquisition of a neighbor. It's just that the Sisyphean stone I've been rolling has to be adjusted now; there's a new depression on the hill.

My wife is too kind to mention the whaler I was starting to resemble before I took up this arboreal harpoon. About him Melville writes, "Ahab had cherished a wild vindictiveness against the whale . . . [for] in his frantic morbidness he at last came to identify with him, not only all his bodily woes, but all his intellectual and spiritual exasperations. The White Whale swam before him as the monomaniac incarnation of all those malicious agencies which some deep men feel eating in them, till they are left with half a heart and half a lung." "Call me Ishmael" is my way of saying, Please don't let things get to the point where you'll need to call me Ahab.

The name of the narrator of *Moby Dick* comes from the Bible, where it belongs to "a wild ass of a man" whose hand is ever against his enemies', and theirs against his. Ishmael's life is one of perpetual struggle. Ishmael is the Celt, but Ahab is the Roman, riding the *Pequod* like a chariot toward an imperial — and impossible — peace. He has a victory to win. Ishmael merely has a job to do, a story to write. Call me Ishmael. Call me a schlemiel, but next year we're putting up a wooden privacy fence. The deer can have the bottoms of the trees, hidden like the neighbors from our view; the unreachable bushy crowns will adorn the top of the fence. My whaling wall.

Not that I look down on Ahab. His grievance cuts to the bone and all the way through. "The horror! The horror!" as Conrad puts it — the futility most of all. Still, I would say to anyone who wants a moral here, some compensation for all this essayistic jumping around, that if a white whale should get your leg, resist the dream of his blowhole spouting blood, of hearing the old whalers' cry of "Chimney's afire!" That chimney is on your house.

Get a good prosthetic device, a circle of friends who know better than to talk too much about the sea, and, if the vineyards have not been utterly nibbled away, a few bottles of wine. Eat, drink, and be chivalrous, for tomorrow you die. As does the whale.

VERLYN KLINKENBORG

Our Vanishing Night

FROM *National Geographic*

IF HUMANS WERE truly at home under the light of the moon and stars, we would go in darkness happily, the midnight world as visible to us as it is to the vast number of nocturnal species on this planet. Instead, we are diurnal creatures, with eyes adapted to living in the sun's light. This is a basic evolutionary fact, even though most of us don't think of ourselves as diurnal beings any more than we think of ourselves as primates or mammals or earthlings. Yet it's the only way to explain what we've done to the night: we've engineered it to receive us by filling it with light.

This kind of engineering is no different from damming a river. Its benefits come with consequences — called light pollution — whose effects scientists are only now beginning to study. Light pollution is largely the result of bad lighting design, which allows artificial light to shine outward and upward into the sky, where it's not wanted, instead of focusing it downward, where it is. Ill-designed lighting washes out the darkness of night and radically alters the light levels — and light rhythms — to which many forms of life, including ourselves, have adapted. Wherever human light spills into the natural world, some aspect of life — migration, reproduction, feeding — is affected.

For most of human history, the phrase "light pollution" would have made no sense. Imagine walking toward London on a moonlit night around 1800, when it was Earth's most populous city. Nearly a million people lived there, making do, as they always had, with candles and rushlights and torches and lanterns. Only a few houses were lit by gas, and there would be no public gaslights in the streets or squares for another seven years. From a few miles away, you would have been as likely to *smell* London as to see its dim collective glow.

Now most of humanity lives under intersecting domes of reflected, refracted light, of scattering rays from overlit cities and suburbs, from light-flooded highways and factories. Nearly all of nighttime Europe is a nebula of light, as is most of the United States and all of Japan. In the South Atlantic the glow from a single fishing fleet — squid fishermen luring their prey with metal halide lamps — can be seen from space, burning brighter, in fact, than Buenos Aires or Rio de Janeiro.

In most cities the sky looks as though it has been emptied of stars, leaving behind a vacant haze that mirrors our fear of the dark and resembles the urban glow of dystopian science fiction. We've grown so used to this pervasive orange haze that the original glory of an unlit night — dark enough for the planet Venus to throw shadows on Earth — is wholly beyond our experience, beyond memory almost. And yet above the city's pale ceiling lies the rest of the universe, utterly undiminished by the light we waste — a bright shoal of stars and planets and galaxies, shining in seemingly infinite darkness.

We've lit up the night as if it were an unoccupied country, when nothing could be further from the truth. Among mammals alone, the number of nocturnal species is astonishing. Light is a powerful biological force, and on many species it acts as a magnet, a process being studied by researchers such as Travis Longcore and Catherine Rich, cofounders of the Los Angeles–based Urban Wildlands Group. The effect is so powerful that scientists speak of songbirds and seabirds being "captured" by searchlights on land or by the light from gas flares on marine oil platforms, circling and circling by the thousands until they drop. Migrating at night, birds are apt to collide with brightly lit tall buildings; immature birds on their first journey suffer disproportionately.

Insects, of course, cluster around streetlights, and feeding at those insect clusters is now ingrained in the lives of many bat species. In some Swiss valleys the European lesser horseshoe bat began to vanish after streetlights were installed, perhaps because those valleys were suddenly filled with light-feeding pipistrelle bats. Other nocturnal mammals — including desert rodents, fruit bats, opossums, and badgers — forage more cautiously under the permanent full moon of light pollution because they've become easier targets for predators.

Some birds — blackbirds and nightingales, among others — sing at unnatural hours in the presence of artificial light. Scientists have determined that long artificial days — and artificially short nights — induce early breeding in a wide range of birds. And because a longer day allows for longer feeding, it can also affect migration schedules. One population of Bewick's swans wintering in England put on fat more rapidly than usual, priming them to begin their Siberian migration early. The problem, of course, is that migration, like most other aspects of bird behavior, is a precisely timed biological behavior. Leaving early may mean arriving too soon for nesting conditions to be right.

Nesting sea turtles, which show a natural predisposition for dark beaches, find fewer and fewer of them to nest on. Their hatchlings, which gravitate toward the brighter, more reflective sea horizon, find themselves confused by artificial lighting behind the beach. In Florida alone, hatchling losses number in the hundreds of thousands every year. Frogs and toads living near brightly lit highways suffer nocturnal light levels that are as much as a million times brighter than normal, throwing nearly every aspect of their behavior out of joint, including their nighttime breeding choruses.

Of all the pollutions we face, light pollution is perhaps the most easily remedied. Simple changes in lighting design and installation yield immediate changes in the amount of light spilled into the atmosphere and, often, immediate energy savings.

It was once thought that light pollution only affected astronomers, who need to see the night sky in all its glorious clarity. And, in fact, some of the earliest civic efforts to control light pollution — in Flagstaff, Arizona, half a century ago — were made to protect the view from Lowell Observatory, which sits high above that city. Flagstaff has tightened its regulations since then, and in 2001 it was declared the first International Dark Sky City. By now the effort to control light pollution has spread around the globe. More and more cities and even entire countries, such as the Czech Republic, have committed themselves to reducing unwanted glare.

Unlike astronomers, most of us may not need an undiminished view of the night sky for our work, but like most other creatures we do need darkness. Darkness is as essential to our biological welfare, to our internal clockwork, as light itself. The regular oscillation of waking and sleep in our lives — one of our circadian rhythms — is nothing less than a biological expression of the regular oscillation of light on Earth. So fundamental are these rhythms to our being that altering them is like altering gravity.

For the past century or so, we've been performing an open-ended experiment on ourselves, extending the day, shortening the night, and short-circuiting the human body's sensitive response to light. The consequences of our bright new world are more readily perceptible in less adaptable creatures living in the peripheral glow of our prosperity. But for humans, too, light pollution may take a biological toll. At least one new study has suggested a direct correlation between higher rates of breast cancer in women and the nighttime brightness of their neighborhoods.

In the end, humans are no less trapped by light pollution than the frogs in a pond near a brightly lit highway. Living in a glare of our own making, we have cut ourselves off from our evolutionary and cultural patrimony — the light of the stars and the rhythms of day and night. In a very real sense, light pollution causes us to lose sight of our true place in the universe, to forget the scale of our being, which is best measured against the dimensions of a deep night with the Milky Way — the edge of our galaxy — arching overhead.

AMY LEACH

You Be the Moon

FROM *A Public Space*

THERE IS AN ALTITUDE above every planet where a moon can
orbit forevermore. In millions of miles of ups and downs, there is
one narrow passageway of permanence. If a moon can reach this
groove, it will never crash down like masonry nor drift away like a
mood; it will be inalienable; it will circle its planet at the exact
speed that the planet rotates, always over one site, like the Bad-
lands or Brazzaville or the Great Red Spot, so that the planet
neither drags the moon faster nor slows it down. Moons not
locked into this synchronous orbit are being perturbed either up
or down.

The law is stringent about this; there are no clauses; and all
moons are dutiful followers of the law. But, as all good followers of
the law discover in the end, unless you happen to roll onto a track
precisely 18,254 miles above your planet, the law ejects you or
dashes you down. One moon in our solar system has achieved
synchronous orbit, being pledged forever to its planet — Pluto's
moon Charon. The other 168 moons have not.

Mars has two small moons whose names mean "panic" and "terror." Phobos looks like a potato that experienced one terrible, and
many average, concussions. Phobos hurtles around Mars every
eight hours, which is three times faster than Mars rotates, which
means Mars pulls it back and slows it down. Slowing down makes a
moon lose height; in the end Phobos will smite its planet, or else
get wrenched apart by gravity into a dusty ring of aftermath. Mars's
other moon, Deimos, is a slow and outer moon; an outer and
outer moon; someday it will be a scrap moon, rattling around in

the outer darkness, where drift superannuated spacecraft and ex-hausted starlets.

So fast moons slow down and slow moons speed up, and only during excerpts of time do planetary dalliances appear perma-nent. Our moon through many excerpts — the Moon — is a slow moon. Thus it is speeding up, thus it is falling up, coming off like a wheel, at one and a half inches per year. Let us now reflect upon the Moon; for the Moon has long reflected upon us. To get an idea of the relationship between the Earth and the Moon and the Sun, find two friends and have the self-conscious one with lots of atmosphere be the Earth and the coercive one be the Sun. And you be the Moon, if you are periodically luminous and sometimes unobservable and your inner life has petered out. Then find a large field and take three steps from the Earth, and have the Sun go a quarter mile away.

For an idea of how long your light takes to reach Earth, sing one line from a song, such as "Sail on, my little firefly," and that is how long moonlight takes. The Earth can sing the same line back to you, to represent earthlight. "Sail on, my little firefly." As for the Sun, he should sing as lustily as sunlight; have him discharge the song "I Gave Her Cakes and I Gave Her Ale," which is eight minutes long, which is how long sunlight takes to reach the Earth. Also the Earth may sing to the Sun, and the Sun to the Moon, and the Moon to the Sun, songs of representative length.

Now keep singing and everybody spin and the smaller two of you orbit the next largest rotundity. Now as you, the Moon, go around the Earth, do not circle perfectly, as if you were a mill horse, or an idea. You are not an idea; you make the Earth's heavy blue waters heave up and down! Circle asymmetrically, then, like a small coplanet; truly you and the Earth *both* orbit the center of your com-bined mass, called the barycenter. Of course, if you and the Earth were equal in bulk, the barycenter would lie exactly between you; you and the Earth would pass your lives in social equilibrium, like the rooster and the pig on the carousel. However, as the Earth is eighty-one times more massive than the Moon, the barycenter is eighty-one times closer to the Earth: thus the barycenter is *inside the Earth,* though not at its *center.* This means that the Earth orbits a point inside itself. The Earth is a self-revolver, nodding slightly to the swooping Moon.

Now the Earth does not *look* eighty-one times as massive as the Moon — in fact it is just four times as wide. To address this perceptual difficulty we will interrupt our lunar reenactment and consult philosophy. Let us refer to our index of philosophies and select one known as Interiorism, which says that truth is to be known by introspection. To discover why the Earth acts so central and the Moon so obsequious, let us not measure yards but consider inward differences. The Earth is not gigantic and the Moon is not slight, but the Earth has a core and the Moon does not. Or rather, if the Moon has a core, it is undetectably small and inert, like a frozen mouse.

How do we know that the Moon has a mousy core? Who has ever really been a Lunar Interiorist? Here we shall invent a philosophy and call it Imaginative Exteriorism, wherein by looking at the exterior, we *imagine* the interior; for the face often tattles on the heart, and an empty surface may bespeak an empty center (though this is not true of alligator eggs). The Moon has a stony face, while the Earth's face is a slaphappy burlesque, screaming flocks of peacocks here, and cloudbursts there, and spriggy merriment everywhere. Such an exhibition is possible only if inside itself the Earth has a core whose nickel density enables the planet not only to sport a moon but also to hold on to tiny flighty molecules. For these bouncing shimmying molecules are Earth's genius, and they are harder to keep than moons. Cloudland has a core of adamant.

On behalf of those who feel vacant and uninhabited, to whom nothing occurs, who look up day and night from chalky dust into unrefracted blackness, who watch their plush, blue-headed neighbors yielding splashy gullies and snow devils and excitable vespiaries and backsliding pinnipeds and heady cauliflowers and turtle centuplets and rosy squirrelfish swarming through Rapture Reefs — on behalf of unprofitable individuals everywhere, is the Moon ordained to ever be a shabby waste of rubbled regolith? Could it never scrabble together a genius like the Earth's?

What about molecule trustees, like the Sun? The solar wind blasts a plasma of particles throughout the solar system; could not some of these particles accrue upon the Moon? For not *all* atoms are wiggle-away; xenon, for example, is heavy and slow. It would make a nicely noncombustible atmosphere, of glowing lavender hue, and would make sound possible, albeit slow, so everyone's voice would drop several octaves and everyone would sound like walruses. And xenon is an anesthetic, so inhabitants would be blithe and amenable to dentistry. But the wind that bringeth the elements taketh them away; the atmosphere on the Moon is thinner than the thinnest vacuum we can contrive.

Haloes cannot be affixed to the head with pins and clips. Marañón forests, hosting spinetail birds and purple-backed sunbeams and gray-bellied comets and velvet-fronted euphonias and long-tailed weasels, cannot be administered from without. Glory cannot be administered from without. Glory will only coalesce on a body wherein throbs a fiery, molten, mad-stallion heart so dreadfully dense, so inescapably attractive, that it matters little the circumference of the frame.

Of course if your heart is *too* fervent, you will become an attractive incinerator, like the Sun, glorious but no pleasure boat. The glory of the Sun is violent and uninflected; its features are all flames and its sounds are all explosions. The Sun is so loud, like a million bombs all the time, that fine-spun sounds cannot be heard, like birds wading or figs tumbling or the muttering of mathematicians. On the Sun all private qualities disappear into the main loud yellowness.

Nothing makes a sound on the Moon and nothing ever could: not a harpsichordist, not a shattering tureen of mangel-wurzel stew, not the pebble-sized meteoroids that whang down at seventy-eight thousand miles an hour and heat the ground so hot it glows like a little piece of star; not the huge meteoroids that fracture the bedrock, forming craters two hundred miles across, creating new rings of mountains, making the Moon to tremble on and on — since it doesn't have a sturdy core, the Moon is very convulsible; once atremble, it stays atremble. But it fractures and trembles and glows in absolute silence, for sound is like birds and cannot travel without air.

From looking at its face we had inferred that the Moon's heart is small and dead; but this is not to say that its face has no properties; not even the most stuporous face has no properties. The moonscape is pleated and rumpled, with rills and ridges and craters and crevices and darknesses and brightnesses. Except for some meteor-made bruises, though, its features have not changed for three billion years; they are memorials of an ancient vim. Once the Moon was welling up from inside, jutting into volcanoes from the force of its own melting, cracking at the rind from its deep inner shifts. Now it wears the same glassy expression eon after eon, like a taxidermied antelope. The Moon is a never-brimming eye, a never-whistling teakettle, and it shadows the very flower of planets.

There are several kinds of orbits in the orbit catalogue. One is an interrupted orbit, which describes the path of a dumpling flung from a window, the ground being the interrupter of the dumpling's orbit. Another is known as an open orbit, where an unaffiliated traveling object gets pulled to another body, curves around it, and flies away, never to return, like a minute. It is just a gravitational encounter and it merely redirects the object. The other kind of orbit is where a rock, after ages of streaking obliviously past acquisitive black holes and great gassy moon-catchers like Jupiter, happens to come close to a small motor-hearted globe, close enough to feel its influence, to be drawn closer, to make a circle around it, and another and another, and never thereafter to stop, not for billions of years. Once it was its own, and now it is a foundling. This wrapping of the one around the other is called a closed orbit.

In truth, the beginning of the Moon is a secret. Maybe a piece of Earth broke off and went into orbit, maybe the Moon was begotten by a terrible collision, or maybe it really was a drifter snatched from its onward way. However the Moon began, here is how the Moon will finish: in a billion years the Earth will have nudged it far enough away that it will look 15 percent smaller; in three billion years it will look smaller still; in five billion years the Sun will become a red giant and swallow its children up. The Earth's involvement with the Moon will not last long enough to end.

The disposition of the universe — that crazy wheelwright — designates that we live on a wheel, with wheels for associates and wheels for luminaries, with days like wheels and years like wheels and shadows that wheel around us night and day; as if by turning and turning, things could come round right. For the moment, if you are still in the field of feathery grass where you were playing the Moon, you might look back at your footprints. The Sun spins in place so his path is just a point; and the Earth leaves a long ellipse around the Sun; but your path is a convoluted zigzag, for you loop around a looping planet. Your trajectory is something like the trajectory of sea ducks. Little harlequin sea ducks swim over the oscillating waves of the sea, diving down into the cold, gray-green waters to unfasten limpets and blue mussels from their rocks, swinging back up into the rough winter waves, the sea itself rolling up and down under the spell of the sailing Moon.

MICHAEL LEWIS

The Mansion: A Subprime Parable

FROM *Condé Nast Portfolio*

I WAS LOOKING TO return to New Orleans, where I'd grown up, to write a book. The move would uproot my wife and three children from California, and I felt a little bad about that. They needed a place to live, but places to live in New Orleans are hard to find. Ever since Hurricane Katrina, the real estate market there has been in turmoil. Owners want to sell, buyers want to rent, and the result is a forest of For Sale signs and an army of workers commuting from great distances.

At the bottom of every real estate ad I saw was the name of the same agent. One woman ruled the market, it seemed, and her name was Eleanor Farnsworth. I called her and threw myself on her mercy. She thought my problem over and then said, "I only know of one place that would work for you." She'd suggested it to Brad Pitt and Angelina Jolie, she said, before selling them their more modest place in the French Quarter.

That shouldn't have been a selling point; it should have been a warning. I should have asked the price. Instead, I asked the address.

As soon as I saw it, I knew it — the mansion. The most conspicuously grand house in New Orleans. As a child, I'd ridden my bike past it two thousand times and always felt a tiny bit unnerved. It wasn't just *a* mansion; it seemed like the biggest mansion on the street with all the mansions, St. Charles Avenue, an object of fascination for the tourists on the clanging streetcars. But it was hard to imagine a human being standing beside it, much less living inside it, and as far as I could tell, none ever did. There was never any sign of life around it; it was just this awesome, silent pile of pale stone. The Frick Museum, but closed.

Inside, it was even more awesome than outside. It was as if the architect had set out to show just how much space he could persuade a rich man to waste. The entryway was a kind of ballroom, which gave way to a curved staircase, a replica of one in the palace of Versailles. The living room wasn't a kind of ballroom; it *was* a ballroom, with $80,000 worth of gold on the ceiling. The bedrooms were the size of giant living rooms. The changing rooms and closets and bathrooms were the size of bedrooms. There were two of everything that the rest of the world has one of: two dining rooms, two full kitchens, two half kitchens. Ten bathrooms and seven bedrooms.

I didn't ask the price — I was renting — so I didn't know that the last time it changed hands it had sold for close to $7 million, and was now valued at $10 million. I imagined how it would feel to live in such a place. What it wouldn't feel like, clearly, was anything close to being in the other houses in which I'd lived.

Upper middle class — that's how I've always thought of myself. Upper middle class is the class into which I was born, the class to which I was always told I belonged, and the class with which, until this moment, I'd never had a problem. Upper middle class is a sneaky designation, however. It's a way of saying "I'm well-off" without having to say "I'm rich," even if, by most standards, you are. Upper-middle-classness has allowed me to feel like I'm not only competing in the same financial league as most Americans — I'm winning! Playing in the middle class, I have enjoyed huge success.

In this house, I now glimpsed the problem with upper-middle-classness: it isn't really a class. It's a space between classes. The space may once have been bridgeable, but lately it's become a chasm. Middle-class people fantasize about travel upgrades; upper-class people can't imagine life without a jet. Middle-class people help their children with their homework so they'll have a chance of getting into Princeton; upper-class people buy Princeton a new building. Middle-class people have homes; upper-class people have monuments. A man struggling to hold on to the illusion that he is upper middle class has become like a character in a cartoon earthquake: he looks down and sees his feet being dragged ever farther apart by a quickly widening fissure. His legs stretch, then splay, and finally he plunges into the abyss.

This house, and everything it represents, stands on the more appealing side of the chasm. "It's perfect," I said.

Every few days, I Googled the house and stared at it. Then a funny thing happened: it began to shrink. Sure it's big, I told myself, but houses come bigger. The White House, for instance. I told my wife and children only that I'd found a house with a swimming pool and enough bathrooms for everyone to have his or her own. Which is to say, they really had no idea what they were getting into. How could they? It didn't occur to them that not only would they have their own bathrooms, they'd need to decide before dinner which of the two dining rooms to eat in — and afterward, which of the three dishwashers to not put their dishes in. To believe it, and to grasp its full upper-class implications, they'd need to see it.

On the day we move in, we're all stuffed together, *Beverly Hillbillies* style, in a rented, dirty, gold Hyundai Sonata. For fun, as I drive up and down St. Charles Avenue, I ask them to guess which of these improbably large houses is ours.

"That one?"

"No."

"That one!"

The exercise turns giddy. Each house is bigger than the last. The girls squeal in the back seat and press their noses against the windows, while their mother, in the front, does her best to remain calm. We pass in front of the mansion and they look right past it. The thing takes up an entire city block, and somehow they can't see it. It's too implausible. It's not a home. It's a mint.

We circle around the block and approach from the rear, the Sonata rolling up the long driveway and coming to a stop beneath the grand stone porte-cochère. "*This* is our new house?" asks Quinn, age eight.

"This is our new house," I say.

She begins to hyperventilate.

"Omigodomigodomigod!"

My small children plunge from the rental car into the driveway. They leap up and down as if they've just won an NBA championship. By the time we get inside, they're gasping. They sprint off to inspect their new home.

"There's another floor!"

"Daddy! There's an elevator!"
My children love me. They have a house with an elevator.

In all the public finger-pointing about the American real estate bust, surprisingly little attention has been paid to its origin. There's obviously a long list of people and ideas that can share in the blame: ratings agencies, mortgage brokers, big Wall Street firms, small Wall Street firms, Angelo Mozilo, Alan Greenspan. Every few weeks, the *New York Times* runs a piece exposing some new way in which a big Wall Street firm has exploited some poor or middle-class family. The rich people on Wall Street blame their bosses. The brokers at Merrill Lynch blame Stan O'Neal; the traders at Bear Stearns blame Jimmy Cayne. Everyone blames Countrywide. But all of this misses the point: however terrible the sins of the financial markets, they're merely a reflection of a cultural predisposition. To blame the people who lent the money for the real estate boom is like blaming the crack dealers for creating addicts.

Americans feel a deep urge to live in houses that are bigger than they can afford. This desire cuts so cleanly through the population that it touches just about everyone. It's the acceptable lust.

Consider, for example, the Garcias. On May 30, the *New York Times* ran a story about a couple, Lilia and Jesus Garcia, who were behind on their mortgage payments and in danger of losing their homes. The Garcias had a perfectly nice house near Stockton, California, that they bought in 2003 for 160 grand. Given their joint income of $65,000, they could afford to borrow about $160,000 against a home. But then, in 2006, they stumbled upon their dream house. The new property was in Linden, California, and, judging from its picture, had distinctly mansion-like qualities. Its price, $535,000, was a stretch.

Then, of course, the market turned. The Garcias failed to make their mortgage payments and couldn't sell their original house. They owed the bank about $700,000 and were facing eviction. The mistake supposedly illustrated by the Garcias' predicament was that they held on to their former home in Stockton as an investment. The moral: Americans are in their current bind because too many of them saw houses as moneymaking opportunities.

But the real moral is that when a middle-class couple buys a house they can't afford, defaults on their mortgage, and then sits down to explain it to a reporter from the *New York Times,* they can be confident that he will overlook the reason for their financial distress: the peculiar willingness of Americans to risk it all for a house above their station. People who buy something they cannot afford usually hear a little voice warning them away or prodding them to feel guilty. But when the item in question is a house, all the signals in American life conspire to drown out the little voice. The tax code tells people like the Garcias that while their interest payments are now gargantuan relative to their income, they're deductible. Their friends tell them how impressed they are — and they mean it. Their family tells them that while theirs is indeed a big house, they have worked hard, and Americans who work hard deserve to own a dream house. Their kids love them for it.

Across America, some version of this drama has become a social norm. As of this spring, one in eleven mortgages was either past due — like Ed McMahon's $4.8 million jumbo loan on his property — or in foreclosure, like Evander Holyfield's $10 million Georgia estate. It's no good pretending that Americans didn't know they couldn't afford such properties, or that they were seduced into believing they could afford them by mendacious mortgage brokers or Wall Street traders. If they hadn't lusted after the bigger house, they never would have met the mortgage brokers in the first place. The money-lending business didn't create the American desire for unaffordable housing. It simply facilitated it.

It's this desire we must understand. More than any other possession, houses are what people use to say, "Look how well I'm doing!" Given the financial anxieties and indignities suffered by the American middle class, it's hardly surprising that a lower-middle-class child who grows up in a small house feels a burning need to acquire a bigger one. The wonder is how an upper-middle-class child who grew up in a big and perfectly enviable house is inexorably drawn to a mansion.

When you move into a house you cannot afford, the first thing you notice is everything that you suddenly need — things that, before you arrived, you didn't even want. The dressing room was a microcosm of our mansion's ability to instruct. It wasn't a closet, but a room as big as the master bedroom we'd left behind in California. Even after my wife had stored her countless pairs of shoes, there was more than enough space for all of my stuff. Three weeks later, I noticed a door near the master-bedroom suite that I hadn't seen before; it was like a magical door that someone had carved into the wall while I slept. What could it be? I opened it to find . . . another huge dressing room! Inside, I could have fit every stitch of clothing I owned, three times over. It seemed weird to just leave it empty, but I didn't have anything left to put in it, so I closed the door and pretended the room wasn't there. But the thought occurred: Maybe I need more clothes.

The pool was another example. Because we moved in during the winter, we didn't pay that much attention to it at first. Had we bothered to dip our fingers in, we'd have discovered that it was not merely heated but was saltwater. It was a full six weeks before we really even noticed the pool house. Full bathroom, full kitchen, shiny new Viking range, and a fridge stuffed with twenty-four bottles of champagne. For a few weeks I felt that all of this was excessive. Then one day I became aware of the inconvenience of having to walk, dripping wet, from the pool back into the main house. This is what you need a pool house for — so you can make the transition from water to dry land without the trouble of walking the whole fifteen yards back into the house and climbing a long flight of stairs to the giant dressing room. From that moment on, it seemed to me terribly inconvenient to *not* have a pool house. How on earth did people with pools, but no special house adjacent to them, cope?

The problems posed by the mansion were different from the problems posed by most other houses. How to locate loved ones, for instance. There's been no room inside any home I'd ever lived in from which, if I yelled at the top of my lungs, I couldn't be heard in every other room. The mansion required a new approach to human communications. Standing inside the mansion and screaming at the top of your lungs, you knew for certain that your voice wasn't reaching at least half the house. If you wanted to find someone, you could run around the house, but that took ages and presupposed that the other person was not similarly wandering in the void. A trek up the Himalayan staircases quickly became the subject of an elaborate cost-benefit analysis. How badly do I really want to find my six-year-old daughter? How much does my one-year-old son's diaper really need to be changed? After a while, it seemed only natural to my wife to begin with the assumption that her husband could not be found. Even when she knew for a fact that I was somewhere in the house, she'd begin her search with a phone call. She'd call my cell when I was two flights up and she'd call my cell when I was a room away. One afternoon she called my cell twenty minutes after I had come home with our three children and had gone looking for her to take them off my hands.

"Where are you?" she asked.

"I'm in the house taking care of the kids," I said, a little indignantly.

"Well, you can't be watching them very closely," she said, "because I'm in the house taking care of the kids."

Even though you couldn't find anybody, all sorts of people could find you. People stumbled into other people's spaces and terrified them. The house was so vast that the sound waves that normally precede the arrival of a living creature got lost. And so while there was, in theory, a great deal of privacy, there was, in practice, none. The mansion came with a gardener, a pool man, a caretaker, and a housekeeper. Any one of these people might turn up anyplace, anytime. The housekeeper, a sweet woman, came twice a week. She developed a habit of turning up over my right shoulder without warning and, as I stared helplessly at my computer screen, booming, "How's that book of yours coming along??!!!"

"Ah!" I'd yell, and leap out of my chair.

"Always writing, writing, writing!" she'd say with a laugh. (Writing in the mansion never ceased to be inherently comical.)

Money was another problem. It was suddenly going out faster than it was coming in. When I'd finally gotten around to asking the real estate agent what the mansion cost to rent, she'd said — in the most offhand tone, as if it were the least important thing about the house — "I'll have to see, but I think it's around thirteen." Thirteen. The extra digits are just assumed. One reason is that no one can bring themselves to actually utter the sentence: "Your rent will be thirteen thousand dollars a month."

Thirteen thousand dollars a month is not the rent I was raised to pay. When I let it slip to my mother what I'd be paying, she just said, "Oh, Michael," in exactly the same tone she'd have used if I'd informed her that I'd just run over the neighbor with a truck or been diagnosed with pancreatic cancer. Thirteen thousand dollars a month might be a record rent in New Orleans, but it was really just the ante.

We'd been there only three weeks when the first bills arrived. Utilities were $2,700. That turned out not to include water, which was another $1,000. Think of it: $1,000 a month for water you don't drink. (The drinking water came in truckloads from a spring-water company.) How did we use so much water? you might reasonably ask. The answer is, we didn't. The mansion did. The pool, the fountains, the sprinklers that came on in the wee hours to keep the great lawn lush and green — all were suddenly necessary. So, it turned out, was cable, at $800 a month. Who was I to argue? I wasn't even entirely sure how many televisions we had. Nine, at least. I thought I'd found the last of them when, two months after we'd arrived, I opened a cabinet and found another.

Walking into the mansion after school one day, my younger daughter, Dixie, asked, "Daddy, what's a Daddy Warbucks?" She'd caught a ride with a new friend's babysitter, who didn't know where we lived. Instead of giving the babysitter directions, the friend's mother had just said, "They live in the Daddy Warbucks house."

The first request for money came exactly eleven days after we arrived. A former schoolmate was calling on behalf of our high school; its fundraising department had somehow learned that I'd not only moved back to town but had moved into the mansion. My old school friend had a number in mind, somewhere between $25,000 and $100,000. Two days later, we had another old friend to dinner and — in hopes that she'd spread the word — I spoke of my amazement that anyone thought we could fork over 100 grand on a whim. "It's funny you should say that," she said. She'd just spoken with the director of a New Orleans museum, who had also heard we'd moved into the mansion. "He's trying to figure out the best way to approach you," she said.

We'd become an engineering problem.

Late one night the doorbell rings. There on our great stone porch is a man, obviously down on his luck, doing his best to appear subservient.

"I was just wondering if you have anything," he asks.

"Have anything?" I ask back.

"Some work that might be done, you know."

It's a feudal exchange right out of the eleventh century. Vassal calling on lord with the mutual understanding that lord owes vassal employment. The only thing missing is the offer of a freshly slaughtered rabbit.

A couple of months into our stay, we all sit in the formal dining room, under the gilded ceiling and the crystal chandelier, eating packaged tortellini off paper plates. We are Cuban peasants in late 1959 who have just moved into a Havana mansion on the heels of the rich owner, who has fled in terror from the revolution. Dixie, then five, blurts out, "I hate it when people say, 'Oh, I love your house,' because then I have to say, 'It's not my house.'" To which Quinn adds, "Yeah, I hate it when people say, 'You must be rich.'"

This was new. My children had taken to their new splendor like ducks to water. They'd see the St. Charles streetcar rolling past, and the tourists gawking and pointing at their new house, and their first reaction was not to cringe but to perform. They'd throw on their most princess-like dresses and run out front and dance around the malfunctioning marble fountain, pissing water in all the wrong directions, and wave to the commoners. One morning, as Quinn descended the staircases, overdressed for school, she announced, "I need to look good. I'm the girl who lives in the mansion."

But after a few months, the charm of pretending to be something they know they are not is wearing off.

There's a moment in the life of every American child when it dawns on him or her that the divvying up of material spoils is neither arbitrary nor a matter of personal choice, that money is a tool used by grownups to order and rank themselves, and that the easiest way to establish those rankings is through their houses. At first, everyone's house appears more or less the same; at any rate, you don't spend much time dwelling on the differences. But then one day someone's house is either so much humbler or so much grander than anything you've ever seen that you realize: A house is not just a house. It's one of the tools people use to rank me.

Children are basically Communists. Seeing other children's material prosperity, they follow their first instinct, which isn't to understand it or stew about it. It's to ask for some of it — to get invited to the mansion. As far as I knew, my children had never given much thought to what their house said about them and their place in the world. They'd been friends with rich kids and poor kids, without dwelling on the differences. That had just changed.

I resist the urge to explain how their misery might be good training for grown-up American life; how we are, quite obviously, a nation of financial impostors, poised to seize the first opportunity to live in houses we cannot afford; and how, if they want to fit in, they'll need to learn to handle the stress. They will have to learn these important lessons for themselves.

Instead, I turn my attention to survival. The mansion was not satisfied with making us uneasy. It wanted us out. It preferred us to leave quietly, without a fuss. But if we didn't, it was prepared to get violent.

The first inkling of this came one lazy Sunday afternoon. I was fathering my one-year-old son by teaching him how best to watch an NBA game — which is to say, in high-def with surround sound. Our bliss was disrupted by the cry of a small child. It was muted, as if someone were calling out from inside the walls. It *was* from inside the walls. Our girls, with their ten-year-old cousin, were trapped inside the elevator, which had mysteriously jolted to a stop. I tried to yank the metal gate off its hinges to get into the shaft, but failed. It wouldn't have mattered anyway, as they were between floors. For a good twenty minutes, I grunted and groaned and sweated and pretended that this wasn't anything I couldn't handle. Then I called the caretaker, who gave me the number of the man who had made the elevator work in the first place. By some miracle, he was around and willing to drive the twenty miles from his house to ours on a Sunday. Two hours later, the girls, sobbing melodramatically, were sprung. The elevator man turned to me and said, "I'm surprised you let them in there."

"Why?"

"She didn't tell you about the cat?"

No one told me about the cat that had been riding up in the elevator with its billionaire owner. As they ascended, the cat had jumped out of the owner's arms and stuck its head out of the metal gate. Its head had been chopped off.

I shut down the elevator.

A few days later, the phone rang. "We want to let you know that we received a message from the equipment-supervision device on your control panel," said the voice on the other end of the line. The what on the what? The mansion, I learned, was equipped with tiny cameras that enabled it, in effect, to watch its inhabitants. One of these, apparently, had malfunctioned. I went into the basement, found the video-control panel, and yanked out as many plugs as I could find.

The next afternoon, the house felt chilly. I hunted down the many thermostats and turned them back up, from the 68 degrees to which they'd somehow plummeted, to 72. The house ignored the request; no matter what I did, it remained at exactly 68 degrees. My skin became the world's most sensitive thermometer, an expert on the state of being 69 degrees, because the moment the house would reach that temperature, all hell would break loose — one, then another, and then a third of the massive air-conditioning units that sat outside would begin to purr. Every now and again, I'd feel a brief tingle of warmth, a premonition of climate change, but that moment was always followed by the roar of engines and a correction.

The day after I tried to change the mansion's temperature, early in the morning, the alarm went off. Then the phone rang. It was the alarm company, wanting to know our password. I gave it to them. "I'm sorry, we don't have that as a password," said the lady on the other end of the phone, and then, as I begged and pleaded ("No, please, no! Let me try again!"), she quickly hung up.

Moments later, two squad cars with lights flashing sped into our driveway. Four police officers leapt out and banged on the front door. The mansion had phoned the cops at exactly the moment I appeared most shockingly arrestable: wearing only underpants and a T-shirt, hair sticking up in six different directions, and without a trace of evidence that I belonged there. I grabbed Dixie ("Daddy, I don't want to go! What if they arrest me too?") and pulled her close to me, as a kind of human shield.

"Sir, we're responding to an alarm signal."

"It was obviously a mistake. Sorry to trouble you."

Silence.

"We're just renting the place."

The police drove away, more slowly than they'd arrived. But they weren't the problem. The house had a mind of its own, like one of those old horses you find at dude ranches. You begin with the as-

sumption that you are in control of the beast. Then you try to
guide it as much as two feet off the assigned path, and it resists and
takes control of the steering. You are left feeling ashamed of whatever cowboy pretense you had to begin with.

I investigated the history of our property. It was built in 1912 by
an entrepreneur named E. V. Benjamin, whose son, raised in the
mansion, became eccentric enough for a small group of interested
residents of New Orleans to create a gathering called the Benjamin
Club, whose sole purpose was to swap stories about him. The house
then moved into the hands of another very rich man, J. Edgar
Monroe, who had made the bulk of his fortune from taking over
the Canal Bank. When the bank was closed by the federal government during the Great Depression, he had himself appointed the
bank's liquidator, repaid its shareholders, and then bought up a
huge chunk of the leftover shares for pennies.

Monroe went on to buy not only this house but also Rosecliffe,
the Newport mansion used in the filming of *The Great Gatsby*. He
was famous for telling anyone who would listen how much money
he had given away to charity. After he donated a music building to
Loyola University New Orleans, he insisted that the school mount
a plaque on one of its walls with an inscription he wrote:

J. EDGAR MONROE HAS DONATED TO CONSTRUCTION OF THIS
BUILDING $1,000,000.00 (ONE MILLION) IN CASH. MY SECRE-
TARY HAS STRONGLY URGED ME TO MAKE A PLAQUE OF
THIS DONATION SO THAT THE STUDENTS OF THE MUSIC
SCHOOL AND THE PUBLIC WILL KNOW OF THIS GIFT. FATHER
CARTER, PRESIDENT OF LOYOLA UNIVERSITY, ACKNOWLEDGED
RECEIPT OF FOUR $250,000.00 CHECKS, OR $1,000,000.00.
MR. MONROE HAS GIVEN OVER ONE HUNDRED MILLION DOL-
LARS ($100,000,000.00) TO ORGANIZED CHARITY OF WHICH
THE LARGEST SHARE WAS GIVEN TO LOYOLA UNIVERSITY.

When Monroe's wife, Louise, died in 1989, the old man wrote
her obituary. It opened with a paragraph or two about the de-
ceased, but then quickly moved on to detail her husband's incredible generosity. "Mr. Monroe is still living and is 92 years of age," he
wrote. "He has been very generous and has given over one hundred million dollars to organized charity . . ." and so on. He too
died in the house a few years later.

Until the mid-1990s, the house had been owned by men who

could comfortably afford it. They didn't need the house to prove how rich they were; everyone knew how rich they were. The moment the house became troubled was the moment someone who couldn't afford it moved in — a man who was using it to slake his own thirst for status. He was a lawyer.

Lawyers are upper middle class. But this lawyer grabbed the saddle horn of magnificence and hung on for dear life — until the day in 2004 when he was bucked off. There in the dust he lay, exposed — in the New Orleans *Times-Picayune* — for defrauding his law partners. His firm defended big companies from class-action suits. To make the kind of money he needed to live in this house, the poor guy had resorted to allegedly cutting secret deals with plaintiffs' lawyers. He reportedly gave up his law license to avoid being formally charged.

The mansion made him do it — that's what I thought when I heard the story. As sordid as his behavior was, I'm incapable of feeling toward him anything but sympathy. He wanted this mansion, he bought this mansion, and then he discovered that the mansion owned him.

The next owner was a woman. She'd grown up middle class in New Orleans, and in her youth had driven past the mansion and fantasized about owning it. Then she'd married an oil-and-gas billionaire who gave her the house as a surprise for her birthday.

The billionaire's wife proceeded to spare no expense in redoing it exactly as she wanted. She spent $250,000 on gold to touch up the gilt fringe of the moldings and the ceiling medallions. I spoke with the interior decorator she hired. It was this man who grasped the inappropriateness of a mere lawyer owning this house. "They tried to shrink it," he said to me one day. "They painted the walls taupe; they had canopies over the beds to make a room within the room. They tried to make it homey." The billionaire's wife succeeded in undoing that. The taupe returned to white, the canopies fell, and the gilding on the ceiling soon gleamed like new. Several million dollars later, she had the mansion looking as she wanted it to look, which was more or less like Versailles. Luckily for her, birthday presents are not community property, because by the time she was finished touching up the house, her husband was divesting himself of her. No matter what the settlement came to, the property belonged to her outright. But she was not happy.

And neither was her mansion. When we moved in, she'd been

trying to sell it for the $10 million or so she had put into it. Characteristically, the house was refusing to give her the money back. It resented people trying to sell it, just as it was beginning to resent people who can't afford it.

Now it was expressing that resentment. It committed an act that, for a New Orleans house in summer, is tantamount to eviction. All by itself, with the temperature outside rising into the low 90s, it shut down its air conditioning. I do not mean that any of its eleven air-conditioning units broke. A broken unit can be repaired. The repairmen came and went, shaking their heads. There was nothing they could see that was wrong with even one of the mansion's massive air compressors. The problem was deep inside the walls, perhaps in the wiring. The ballroom, interestingly, was still 68 degrees, but the bedrooms were now 83. The house not only had microclimates, but also a unifying theme. The grand public spaces continued to be pleasant and comfortable, as if the mansion, in chasing us out, had no interest in sullying its public reputation. Only its putatively private spaces — bedrooms, bathrooms — were uninhabitable. Amazingly, it could be 83 degrees and humid in one room and 68 and dry in another — on the same floor. For the first time inside a house, it occurred to me that it might rain.

And so we fled, back to where we'd come from: the upper middle class. Obviously this presents new problems. Even as my children grew weary of pretending they were richer than they are, they became accustomed to living as the rich do. On the way back to California, my wife drove Quinn, who'd just turned nine, across the Southwest and then up the coast. They came to Hearst Castle and stopped to take the guided tour. A few minutes into it, as they stood in one of William Randolph Hearst's many bedrooms, the guide asked if anyone had a question. My child raised her hand. The guide smiled indulgently and called on her.

"Why," Quinn asked, "is it so small?"

BARRY LOPEZ

Madre de Dios

FROM *Portland*

I ENTERED A JESUIT prep school in New York City at the age of
eleven and later finished two degrees at the University of Notre
Dame. During those years in the city, I served regularly as an altar
boy at Low Mass and also at Catholicism's most complex public
ceremonies, including the solemn High Easter Mass, when the pas-
chal candle is ritually prepared and light begins to fill the cavernous dark of a cathedral, ending the purple-shrouded silence of
Good Friday and Holy Saturday. At the Masses at which I served, I
felt no doubt or cynicism about what I was doing. Whatever my
moods might have been, I believed and understood that I was in
the presence of a great mystery.

As a freshman and sophomore at Notre Dame, I attended Mass
three or four times a week. No matter what pangs of adolescence I
might have been feeling then, and they were in my case severe, or
whatever family troubles I might have been embroiled in, I felt the
support and consolation of this Catholic ritual and the theology
beneath it. Catholicism, though, was not a religion I was formally
born to. I was baptized in the Church at the age of five, the son of a
Roman Catholic father and a Southern Baptist mother. Soon afterward my father, a bigamist, abandoned my younger brother, me,
and his spouse to return to his other wife and son. My mother —
inexplicably, it would seem later — insisted on raising my brother
and me as Catholics, though she herself would never convert. She
supported us as a teacher and, years later, told me that the Catholic
schools in California's San Fernando Valley back then were better
than the public schools. Maybe for her that was all there was to it.

In college, I came to see that the Jesuits had encouraged in me a more metaphorical than literal understanding of Catholic liturgy, and that they had also encouraged me to develop an informed, skeptical attitude toward organized religion in general. The Jesuit approach to spiritual life was famously cerebral, but, importantly for me, theirs was a tradition also at ease with mysticism as a path to God. By the time I was thirteen — my mother had gotten remarried by then, to a twice-divorced Roman Catholic who moved us from California to New York — I had found a spiritual home in Catholicism. I reveled in Catholic iconography and ritual. I was fascinated by the difference between the regal Jesus of religious institutions and the historical Jesus. And I was a diligent student of the overarching Catholic history of medieval Europe (though not very well informed about the foul underbelly of the Crusades or the behavior of the Borgia popes).

At the end of my senior year in high school, I accompanied my classmates to a Jesuit retreat house at Cornwall on Hudson, New York. I was fixated at the time on leading a life like that of Teilhard de Chardin, the Jesuit paleoanthropologist, a life of inquiry into secular and sacred mystery, and a life of service to God and man. We spent three days in prayer, silence, and contemplation (as the Jesuits characterized it), in order to become more certain each of us was taking the right next step as we prepared for college. I hoped to return to the city convinced that my future lay with the Jesuit order, but that was not what happened. I felt no calling. I entered, instead, the University of Notre Dame, declaring aeronautical engineering as my major.

It turned out that aeronautical engineering was not my calling either. By the middle of my freshman year, with some pointed advice from my physics professor, I came to see that I was enthralled not with the mechanics of engineering but with the metaphors of flight, with Icarus's daring and the aerial acrobatics of tumbler pigeons, which I had raised in California after my father left. I moved over to the College of Arts and Letters, and there took up writing, photography, and theater. At the time — the mid-sixties — every Arts and Letters undergraduate was required to take four years of philosophy and four years of theology. As the reading and classroom discussion in these particular courses went successively deeper, my understanding of the lives of mystics like Theresa of

Ávila and John of the Cross expanded, along with my curiosity about what ordinary daily life was like for people like Francis of Assisi and Martín de Porres.

During my graduate and undergraduate years at Notre Dame, if I prayed in public at all, it was usually at a grotto on campus, a shallow shelter of fieldstone built into a slope between the campus's two lakes. A statue of the Mother of God stood there on a pedestal above a barrier of wrought-iron pickets. It was flanked and fronted by dark wrought-iron stands on which racks of votive candles burned in deep red and dark blue glass vessels. The Grotto, as it was called, was lit day and night by these hundreds of flames. The flickering yellow light, swept regularly but rarely extinguished by gusts of wind and so arranged as to not often be extinguished by rain or snow, represented for me the elusiveness of what had attracted me and others to organized religion, to that sphere of incomprehensible holiness which, in the Western imagination, stands beyond the reach of the rational mind. On some frigid nights when I knelt there, alone in the effervescent swelling of candlelight holding the darkness at bay, I felt a streaming convergence of inert stone, gleaming light, weather, and shadowed trees, all of it presided over by an unperturbed and benevolent Queen of Intercession, a woman hearing my prayers.

I drifted away from Catholicism in my junior and senior years, though without anger or denouncement. Most of the friends I made at Notre Dame broke with the Church during their time there, but I did not experience the fury they felt, the sense of betrayal they described. (We were a decided minority at the school, listening to Bob Dylan in our dorms and protesting against the Vietnam War in our Carnaby Street bell bottoms.) My friends imagined themselves trapped in a risible and suffocating superstructure of religious doctrine, cut off from the very empirical experiences that could make for a full life. The Church, in their view, was asking them to embark on lives that had already been led.

I drifted away because the religion I sought was, finally, not to be found at Notre Dame. The environment in which we learned was not just exclusively male; hardly a single Protestant attended class with me, let alone an agnostic or Jew. No philosophy but that which had produced the culture of the West was examined. We were middle-class white youths, being taught to perpetuate our religious and economic values throughout the world. We were largely innocent of the world, however, so innocent it should have scared us.

When I graduated, I took a job with a publishing house in New York, but the question of both my vocation and my religion remained unsettled. A few months into my employment I asked for a week off and traveled to Kentucky, to make a retreat at Gethsemani, the Trappist monastery near New Hope where Thomas Merton lived. I wanted to address one more time the possibility of a religious life. This monastery, with its daily routine of liturgy and manual labor — it was a working farm — seemed a right place for me, a Cistercian community in the tradition of the French Carthusians and Benedictines. As attractive as I found the lives monks led there, however, the answer for me still seemed to be no.

In the decades following that decision to look elsewhere, I was fortunate to be able to travel often and widely, from Greenland to Tierra del Fuego, from Tajikistan to Namibia, from Poland to Tahiti. Much of what I would see, to employ a noun popular in some Catholic circles when I was young, was the culture of heathens, though these foreign epistemologies and metaphysics always appeared to me to be recondite and profound on reflection. In traveling with Alaskan Eskimos, with Kamba tribesmen in Kenya, and with Warlpiri people in the Northern Territory in Australia, I found a spirituality and a capacity to engage with mysticism that I have come to think of as universal among people. The utility and strength of these ways, of course, are often obscured by the ordinary failure of every human society to live up to its own expectations. How a particular society reconciles its history of seemingly intractable failures, its strains of injustice and irreverence, with its spiritual longing for perfection is, to me, a succinct expression of its religion.

In those many years of travel, long after I had lost touch with my Catholic practice, I continued to rely, anyway, on the centrality of a life of prayer, which I broadly took to be a continuous, respectful attendance to the presence of the divine. Prayer was one's daily effort to be incorporated within that essence. I continued to believe, too, in the immanence of the Blessed Mother, for me a figure of compassion and charity, a female bodhisattva (not meaning here to slight either strict Catholics or Buddhists). She was simulta-

. neously a figure rooted in my religious tradition (including the tradition of the Black Madonna, of which the Church of my youth never spoke) and a figure who transcended religion. Like her son, the battered Jesu nailed to a gibbet at Golgotha, she did not need a religion to inspire belief in her existence. Further, if one had any imagination, she did not need the papal bulls of Pius IX and Pius XII to gain credibility in the eyes of either a devout Catholic or an apostate.

I have felt the presence of the Blessed Mother only twice. I was in the northern part of the Galápagos Archipelago once, in 1989, passing just to the north of Isla San Salvador late on a May afternoon, when I saw a slight disturbance on the shoreward water, about a mile away. Just inside Buccaneer Cove, the low rays of the setting sun were catching what seemed to be the vertical strikes of blue-footed boobies diving for fish. The repeated splashes, however, were occurring only at one spot. With a pair of ten-power binoculars I finally made out a herd of sea lions trapped in a net.

We were on a course for distant Isla Genovesa, and I knew the captain might not want to detour. I located our guide, Orlando Falco. I gave him the glasses and he quickly confirmed what I thought — sea lions drowning in a net set illegally by local fishermen, who intended to use the carcasses as bait to catch sharks. The sharks would have their fins cut away and then be turned loose to drown. (Over the past few days, we had seen four or five definned sharks washed up on Galapagean beaches.) The fishermen were selling the shark fins — another illegal act — to buyers aboard Asian factory ships who, as it happened, were supplying them surreptitiously with the expensive nets and other fishing gear.

Orlando was conflicted. He said the captain, who was his employer, would be very reluctant to get involved in what would appear to be a judgment about the livelihood of other men on the islands, illegal or not; and he would not want to get caught up in Galápagos National Park politics. Nevertheless, we went to the bridge and he argued our case. The captain glared briefly at Orlando, then changed course.

Once the *Beagle III* was anchored in the cove, Orlando and a crewman lowered a motor-powered, fourteen-foot panga into the water and, with four other tourists traveling aboard the *Beagle,* we approached the sea lions. Some of them were trussed so tightly in the net's green twine that their eyeballs bulged from their heads. To get a short breath one animal, closely bound to three or four others in a knot, might have to force the others underwater, only then to be driven underwater itself by another animal struggling to breathe. The high-pitched whistles and explosive bellows of animals gasping for air rent the atmosphere in the cove again and again. Their desperation and sheer size made an approach in the small panga dangerous, but we had no choice now. Orlando and I braced ourselves to work on the port side. Two people leaned out on the starboard side, to balance the boat. The crewman kept the lunging jaws of the sea lions away from us with an oar blade, and Orlando and I went after the net with our knives.

I ran a hand under the constricting mesh, pulled it toward me, and began cutting. In their efforts to climb into the panga — they were biting frantically at the port gunwale to gain purchase — the animals threatened to pitch both of us overboard. How they had survived until now, I couldn't begin to understand. Braced hip-to-hip, Orlando and I cut away at the twine, trying not to nick the sea lions' flesh. It was full dark now on the equator, where dusk is brief. A second panga arrived with flashlights from the *Beagle* and stood away after handing them over. The light beams swept wildly through the night, catching the mesh pattern of the net, pink mouths, white canines, and the glistening conjunctivas of the sea lions' eyes. Orlando and I nicked our forearms and hands, and our shins cracked repeatedly against the boat's gunwale.

In the heaving chaos something yanked at the hilt of my knife — a sea lion flipper, the net — and it was instantly gone. Snatched into the night. Without it I could not continue to help. I was briefly paralyzed, then swung around to help Orlando. Someone was bailing the panga around my feet. Like a tightrope walker I reached out to maintain my balance. When I closed my empty hand in the dark air above the water, it closed around the haft of the knife. Orlando, adjusting his stance to accommodate me, saw the knife appear in my hand. He looked at me without expression and then fell back to work. Orlando and I became aware then that whenever our hands touched an animal, the moment it felt a knife sliding between the twine and its skin, it went limp, while the sea lions next to it continued to bawl and thrash. With this help from them we were able to work more quickly.

In the weak beams of the flashlights, though we could not be certain, it seemed we finally freed about fifteen animals, all but one of which swam slowly away. Before we left, Orlando and I pulled ourselves hand-over-hand along the entire length of the float line all the way to the anchor buoy, cutting the net's mesh to shreds.

Back aboard the *Beagle*, everyone save Orlando and I stepped into the main cabin for a late dinner. The two of us sat on the open deck in silence, barefoot, our T-shirts and shorts soaked. Orlando, a young Argentine, was not a man particularly reverent about anything, certainly not mystical. In the deck lights we could see that our shins were turning black-and-blue, that the small cuts on our hands and arms were swelling shut from the saltwater.

I said, "Did you see what happened with the knife?"

"La Madre de Dios," he said, staring into the night.

Later that evening, unrolling my sleeping pad on the *Beagle*'s deck, I recalled a single one of her many appellations: Mediatrix of Graces.

The other time I felt the Blessed Mother near, it was not another man's observation that I accepted without hesitation, a moment when something made perfect sense. It was thirty-six years earlier. I was eight years old, trapped in a pedophile's bedroom. This man, who first sodomized me when I was six, went on doing this until I was eleven. He enjoyed the complete confidence of other adults in our community. He commanded their respect as a medical doctor. I was a rag doll in his bed, an object he jerked around to suit himself. He had carefully arranged the many fears of my childhood life — insecurity, lack of physical strength, a desire to do the right thing — to create a cage. I could not see any way out.

That afternoon, gazing into the shabby bedroom in catatonic submission, I saw the Blessed Mother, a presence resolved in the stagnant air. She was floating barefoot a few inches above the floor, clothed in a white robe. Over her head she wore a pale blue veil. Her hands were extended toward me. She said, "You will not die here." I took her to mean that something else lay beyond this. As bad as it could still get, she seemed to be saying, she would be there.

The Queen of Heaven, I might have thought then. And would say now.

Faint Music

FROM *Harvard Review*

WITHOUT A DOUBT it's a family affliction. I believe the trait comes from my mother, who once collapsed in the veterinarian's waiting room at the mere thought of our cat being palpated. My brother and sister have also had their share of woozy moments. But I'm undoubtedly the champion when it comes to the phenomenon known as vasovagal syncope.

The process begins with a sudden drop in blood pressure. This drop is a steep one: after all, if the blood issuing from your heart wasn't immediately channeled into the arteries, it would be capable of forming a small gusher, six or seven feet in height. But in certain situations, your nervous system can play havoc with the whole setup by dumping a shot of acetylcholine into your bloodstream. This hormone makes your veins and arteries dilate like mad. Your blood pressure plummets, and you end up with what the *New Gould Medical Dictionary* describes as a "temporary suspension of consciousness from cerebral anemia" — i.e., a dead swoon. No blood in the brain.

Fainting is dramatic, it elicits sympathy, it suggests a sensibility so tender, so receptive to the flood tide of emotion, that the fainter must black out from sheer feeling. Or perhaps not. Perhaps it's less romantic than that.

The date is August 20, 1909. Three travelers are having lunch in Bremen. They will soon board the *George Washington*, pride of the Norddeutsche Lloyd, and sail off for their first visit to the United States. Killing time over coffee, one of the travelers, Carl Gustav Jung, keeps talking about an archaeological dig in northern Germany where workers have unearthed prehistoric remains. One of the other travelers, Sigmund Freud, takes his companion's chatter as a barely concealed death wish against himself. Bang: Freud hits the canvas.

Three years later, in November 1912, the same thing happens again. At a psychoanalytic powwow in Munich, Freud argues with Jung over the publication of psychoanalytic articles that omit Freud's name. Jung defends himself. The argument grows heated. Then, according to one witness: "I remember thinking, [Freud] was taking the matter rather personally. Suddenly, to our consternation, he fell on the floor in a dead faint. The sturdy Jung swiftly carried him to a couch in the lounge, where he soon revived."

I wonder what Freud saw as he regained consciousness. Presumably he gazed up into the face of the sturdy Jung and recognized his anointed prince and antagonist. When I fainted in my doctor's office back in 1989, I remained unconscious on the office floor for a full minute. This caused some alarm. Finally I opened my eyes. A few inches above me floated a broad face with a short Mennonite-style beard. The lips above the beard were moving, and the words I made out were these: "Do you know who I am, Mr. Marcus?"

I didn't. The million and one facts that made up my consciousness — the facts that were me, in a sense — floated out of reach. I was nobody.

Then I was me again. I recognized my doctor, he of the brisk yet kindly manner and the fishing prints on the walls. I tried to sit up and almost fainted again. There was blood on the floor, blood in my scalp, and the nurse was telephoning my wife.

"The ambulance is on the way," the nurse told my doctor.

Ambulance? I had come in because I was experiencing heartburn. Patiently I submitted to the EKG, joking with the nurse as she affixed the suction cups. I was weighed, measured, I raised an obedient finger when the doctor pricked my sole with a toothpick. Given my perennial queasiness with medical stuff, I sometimes felt woozy. Yet I was proud of my performance. I had stayed upright even when the doctor prodded my abdominal wall for a hernia.

"Cough," he said. I coughed.

The moment of truth came during the rectal examination. I bent over the white-enameled examination table, the doctor inserted his gloved and Vaselined fingers, probed, and my blood pressure plunged. As I collapsed, my head struck the edge of the table, opening a deep gash.

I use that phrase, "the moment of truth," in its colloquial, semi-meaningless sense. But perhaps it's worth dwelling on what truth, if any, was being disclosed. Was that particular portion of the exam humiliating? Was there simply too great a sense of violation? On other occasions I've blacked out when blood was drawn, or when a doctor discussed with me the (unlikely) chance of my having prostate cancer, or, once, when I was sitting in a restaurant in Brattleboro, Vermont, reading a description of gangrene. I wonder if those were also moments of truth. I wonder if, given sufficient scrutiny, every moment is.

My assumption is that my blackout in 1989 was psychologically triggered — that it was a moment of avoidance, evasion, terror — and I'm forever trying to tease from it some essential fact about myself. I'm trying to learn from it. Still, I read in a medical journal called *Consultant* that it's actually quite common for patients to pass out from "gastrointestinal or genitourinary stimulation," which fits the bill quite nicely. So perhaps my literary, Freud-driven expectation that this is a meaningful event — one of those "royal roads" to the unconscious, or at least an on-ramp — is misguided. Perhaps there's no meaning here at all.

I insisted that I could walk out to the ambulance, which in any case would be carrying me only two or three blocks. At the hospital some persuasive ER assistant stuck me in a wheelchair and steered me from floor to floor in search of an empty bed. This is how my wife caught up with me: seated, chalk-white, terrified of whatever was going wrong.

That was the whole point. The doctor hadn't confided in me exactly why he was sending me to the hospital. Someone needed to sew up the gash in my head, of course, but it was clear that my minute-long blackout had aroused concern. What kind of concern? To me it suggested epilepsy, brain fever, neural damage. It confirmed my long-standing suspicion of my own body, which I always saw as ripe for malfunction, unreliable, with hidden glitches and snarls in its system. Think of all those moving parts, those liquids and gels, the miles of tubing and nervous circuitry. Think of the heart, which is hollow, or the paper-thin membrane of the eardrums. Everything inside us is fragile, treacherous, accident-prone. It's a wonder we don't all die sooner.

I know. Surely a doctor's son, raised in a studiously empirical household, the possessor at age six of a midget microscope, should have a less fearful attitude toward the human body. But there are many ways of assimilating your father's mental furniture, including the outright repudiation of it.

The nurses installed me in a bed with an excellent view of the East River. My heartburn, which had brought me to the doctor's office in the first place, was soon diagnosed as pericarditis, a minor inflammation of the membrane lining the heart. Nothing a few pills wouldn't fix. In the meantime, my irritated heart produced a friction rub; young doctors flocked from every corner of the hospital to press their stethoscopes to my chest, sometimes several at a time.

Over the next three days the hospital ran a battery of tests on me. Every half hour, or so it seemed, a nurse came to draw blood from my arm. I was wheeled and then allowed to walk to various diagnostic sites, and such was the quality of my nervousness that I hardly remember a single one.

My wife visited every day. My friends came as well, and as the test results came back and it became increasingly clear that I wasn't ill, I began to grow uncomfortable with visitors. I felt obliged to entertain them, to make them laugh; I also imagined that they could see through the sham and figure out that I wasn't an authentic invalid. I wasn't sick. I lolled in bed all day in my paper gown, pondered the menus the nice Jamaican nurse brought me, and stayed up late reading *Prosatori del novecento,* a textbook of Italian fiction. I enjoyed sexual fantasies about some of the female doctors, which usually began with one of them listening to my friction rub with her stethoscope. I was faking it.

Faking it is very much to the point in any discussion of fainting. Indeed, fainting might be called the Malingerer's Friend, allowing the so-called victim to avoid any physical or emotional unpleasantness. Fainters absent themselves. They create missing moments. Let's remember that syncope is not only a medical term, but a grammatical and musical one; it involves chopping letters or notes from the middle of a phrase to shorten it.

I wasn't, of course, faking it when I plunged to the ground at the doctor's office. I lost control; and I did disappear for nearly a minute. My syncopated consciousness went into hiding as I lay on the linoleum, leaking blood.

I was eight years old the first time I fainted. I was at a friend's house, and a bee stung me on the back of the neck. I had felt nothing but a slight pinch and the bug was soon wiped away and flushed down the toilet, but since I looked pale I was urged to call my mother. As I told her what had happened, I felt myself blacking out, sinking to the floor, vaguely aware that I was still gripping the receiver.

Perhaps I was allergic to the bee sting — the only one I've ever gotten, although to this day I have a phobia about bees, wasps, and other insects. But the image of an eight-year-old boy in Keds crumpling to the ground while he describes his injury to Mommy seems to return us to Freudian territory. Note the umbilical image of the phone cord. Note the sting itself, with its skin-piercing suggestion of penetration.

Call me fanciful. Still, I'm afraid these undertones are hardly dissipated by the second fainting incident I can recall, which practically reeks of the family romance. This took place one weekend morning while we were gathered in the kitchen to eat breakfast. My mother stood at the stove making French toast, which she had already served to the kids; my father, seated at the table, was cutting a bagel with a sharp bread knife. Contrary to every principle of kitchen safety, he was holding the bagel in his hand and cutting inward, and eventually he made a neat, shallow incision in his palm. The blood was profuse.

Being a hematologist, my father didn't panic: this was just business as usual. But my mother stopped flipping French toast and collapsed to the floor. I, inspired by the blood and my mother's collapse and the powerful odors of syrup and sugar rising from my plate, slumped forward. My forehead went into the syrup. I heard a roar — it seemed to me that I was being clutched beneath the armpits and whirled around — and then my father shook me back into consciousness. He had already attended to my mother.

Still think I'm fanciful? Then listen to this. Out of curiosity I asked my mother when her first fainting episode had occurred.

She paused, thought it over, and came up with the following. At age thirteen, she went to visit her father in the hospital, who only the day before had had his appendix removed. Aside from her father, still conked out from the anesthesia, the only other person in the room was a nurse, who was busy changing the dressing on the patient's incision, which hadn't quite closed. For some reason the nurse had to leave the room. At this point, she asked my mother to hold the soiled dressing in place until she returned. My mother complied. Standing over her dazed father, gingerly holding a used bandage over a hole in his lower abdomen, the thirteen-year-old grew lightheaded. I assume the nurse returned before she hit the floor.

Freud: "The loss of consciousness, the 'absence' of the hysterical attack, is derived from the fleeting but unmistakable loss of consciousness which can be observed at the climax of every intensive [and autoerotic] sexual gratification."

If my attacks are derived from some sexual taproot, then what's going on at the eye doctor's? The dizziness hits me when that glowing blue filament — a test, I think, for glaucoma — is steered directly into my pupil. The room is dark, the doctor makes small talk to distract Mr. Sensitive, and before long I say, "I think I'm getting woozy." Promptly the doctor pops open an ammonia capsule and waves it beneath my nose, which makes me feel like a Victorian woman with the vapors. It works. Consciousness flies back into my brain.

To lessen my embarrassment, the ophthalmologist assures me that I'm not the only fainter among his patients.

"It's not uncommon," he says, using that consolatory phrase that usually means one in a million or maybe two million. "In fact, a very well-known woman novelist has fainted while sitting in this exact same chair."

So we're back to the artistic thing. A susceptibility to experience, emotion, to every frequency on the existential bandwidth. Like Mozart, I tell myself, who experienced fainting episodes in 1791, shortly before his death.

I've thought about it, and I've come to ascribe Mozart's fainting to the impossible pressure of all that music on the inside of his skull. That flimsy chamber wasn't designed to house a fraction of what it did: the galloping tempos, the transparent woodwind figures and clarinet parts, the punchy D-minor trombone chords.

The last act of *Don Giovanni*. The K. 626 Requiem. Those two sor-
rowful notes that begin *Masonic Funeral Music*. Beauty, sublimity,
and (this being Mozart) toilet humor. The overspill is what made
him black out.

There's even a bit of corroborating evidence. As Mozart lay on
his deathbed, roughing out the parts for the Requiem, he often
summoned his friend Süssmayr to explain how the work should be
performed. On one occasion he tried to clarify the role of the
drums, "and was observed in doing this to blow out his cheeks, and
express his meaning by a noise intelligible to the musician." Here
is the very picture of music — highly pressurized music — escaping from the composer's skull, the way air might from a tire.

Still, there's always a naysayer around to pin the blame on physi-
ology. The current scoop on Mozart's fainting, I read in *Neurology*,
is that he experienced a few nasty spills during the preceding year.
One of these gave him a subdural hematoma — a blood-filled
swelling inside his head — and from time to time the hematoma
switched off his consciousness like a lamp. The proof is a skull displayed in the Mozarteum museum in Salzburg, which shows the
appropriate dings and dents. This memento was donated by an
anatomist named Josef Hyrtl, who got it from a gravedigger, who
got it from his predecessor on the job, who claimed to have super-
vised the composer's burial. Sounds pretty suspicious to me.

Music and fainting do seem to travel in pairs. Take the case of
Frank Sinatra, who crashed to the floor in midphrase during a
1994 concert at the Mosque Auditorium in Richmond. (The interrupted song was "My Way.") An assortment of doctors and para-
medics in the audience rushed to the stage, where the singer lay
unconscious at the foot of his barstool. He remained in that condition, pale and cool of skin, for a full minute — just as I did! Then,
to the rapturous response of the crowd, he came to, and asked for
a wheelchair. His vital signs were normal. He resumed his tour
eleven days later in Tulsa.

Sinatra's faint was certainly linked to his feeble health. But
youth, too, is susceptible. Not long ago, for example, more than
four hundred German girls passed out at a New Kids on the Block
concert. A pair of Berlin doctors interviewed the victims and made
their diagnosis.

The problem, though, is that they excluded all those psychological factors I'm so intrigued by. Were the Teutonic teenyboppers overcome by the charisma of the performers or by the white-washed funk blasting out of the speakers? Nah. Drs. Lempert and Bauer chalked it up to lack of food and oxygen. Their conclusions about what they call "the multifactorial pathophysiology of rock-concert syncope" are so full of cut-and-dried pragmatism they make me feel like a mystic. It's the body, they believe, not the psyche that insists on shutting down for station identification.

Body and mind. I admit that I'm probably segregating the pair in a way that's not very useful, making them into a good cop/bad cop team, playing favorites. I want my fainting to lead me someplace, to some ectoplasmic address. And yet I'm not sure I even believe in this ethereal elsewhere. I think that consciousness — mine, yours, and Mozart's — vanishes at the moment we die. Even if a gravedigger with an eye for the main chance happens to save our skull, there's nothing in there. The plug has been pulled. The ten billion neurons stop firing, the one million billion synapses go dead, and you vanish. No afterlife.

That sounds like a credo even my father could endorse. Still, I'm not a complete materialist. I don't believe that identity is merely the slosh of chemicals in our skulls, or the simple snap, crackle, and pop of electrical impulses. These processes enable us to feel joy and sadness, love and desire and resignation, but even if they are inseparable from such feelings, they are not identical with them — not any more than those two notes, those two exhalations, at the beginning of *Masonic Funeral Music* are identical with two little black marks on a sheet of paper. The physical world falls short. And that leaves room for something: mind, consciousness, maybe even soul. I know this. And I know that knowing it is not the result of some cerebral rheostat being twiddled in the right direction. There is a sense of self that floats slightly above and to the left of the body, tethered to it like a kite, staying nervously aloft at all times. When you faint, the kite dips, but it doesn't crash.

Meanwhile, I can't stop dragging Freud into this, despite his role as the secularist par excellence. It was Freud who preached that everything had meaning, but that we ourselves assembled this meaning after the fact.

In a sense, Freud's first great case study, *Dora: An Analysis of a*

Case of Hysteria (1905), was brought about by a fainting episode. The eighteen-year-old patient, who later drove Freud nuts by terminating her treatment early, had already displayed a smorgasbord of symptoms: migraines, depression, nervous cough, shortness of breath, and mutism. These disturbed her parents, but not enough to drag her into psychoanalysis. That took a dose of syncope. "One day," recounts Freud, "after a slight passage of words between [the father] and his daughter, she had a first attack of loss of consciousness — an event which was subsequently covered by an amnesia — [and] it was determined, in spite of her reluctance, that she should come to me for treatment."

Hearing Dora's story, Freud finds meaning everywhere. He skims it from her symptoms, her dreams, her hesitations and inconsistencies. The significances overflow; they can scarcely be contained by the hapless analyst, who's meanwhile busy explaining to his reader why it's okay for him to talk dirty to this teenager in order to cure her illness. Oh, to be the subject of one of those case studies! To have Freud choose a pseudonym for me, which would immediately become part of the history of Western thought, and to be described, with fin-de-siècle discretion, as

a young man from the town of P——, who was stricken with a series of hysterical "absences." The patient, to whom I shall refer as Little Ernst, had experienced these attacks as early as his eighth year, in the course of which he was stung by a bee, *Apis mellifera*. Many of these attacks struck the patient while he was being examined by a physician. Others have occurred in conjunction with some glancing contact with the medical arts. Since Ernst's father was himself a physician, I immediately ventured a suggestion that this might have an important bearing upon his malady. This line of inquiry will surprise no one who has read my *Studien über Hysterie,* in which Dr. J. Breuer and I put forth a psychological theory of hysteria. In this case, I suspected that a conflict of affects regarding his father was contributing to Ernst's fainting episodes.

To my question, the patient gave his customary answer: "I very much doubt it." Yet he at once went on to relate an anecdote about his father, concerning the latter's fondness for tinned tunafish at lunchtime, which I took as a confirmation of my suggestion. Thus does the unconscious convey its treasures to us, traveling over backwaters and tributaries when the main channel has been blocked . . .

And so on and so forth, *und so weiter,* laminating my life with meaning until it seems I can hardly sneeze without adverting to some earlier event or thought or heated exchange, or perhaps some Primal Sneeze, which was itself a displacement of a tickling sensation in some other part of my body.

According to Freud, not a single molecule of experience is squandered. It all goes back into circulation, which means that the past never ends, never recedes, but continues to play onstage while your life extends in front of it like an ever-lengthening proscenium. And since nothing is lost, nothing is meaningless, either.

It's easy to poke fun at this picture, in which every moment of existence is bagged and tagged for later study. Despite my spiritual affinities, however, I can't help but tip my hat to all that significance. Like Freud, I can't go anywhere without it.

After a few days in the hospital, my impersonation of an invalid wore thin, and I was sent home. My chest pains were gone. No further fainting episodes followed the one at the doctor's office, and none of the tests revealed a thing about why I might have lost consciousness. I was a healthy man.

Still, my mother-in-law agreed to hang around the house for a couple of days while my wife was at work, to make sure I didn't keel over on my way to the refrigerator. I was pleasantly embarrassed about the whole arrangement. I didn't faint, though. And to be honest, these episodes have grown less and less frequent since then.

There have been moments when I've felt the early warnings — starting with the iris effect you see in old movies, which progressively darkens things around the periphery until all you're left with is a pinpoint in the middle. Sometimes, instead, there's a sense that the whole scene is getting darker, acquiring a sepia tint, as if my surroundings were being coated and recoated with layers of Old Master varnish. Then it's the sounds that start to go. At first, conversations seem quieter, and I imagine that they're taking place over a greater distance, and then I'm convinced that I'm in a cavernous room, like a train station, with a dim and dismal lighting arrangement overhead: missing bulbs, low voltage, exposed wiring everywhere. If I had any sense I'd lower my head between my legs, to get some blood flowing into my brain. But although I know I'm about to faint, and don't want to, I'm not coherent enough for this quick fix. If I'm lucky, I manage to move away, take a few deep breaths, and collapse into a chair. Then I come to.

This is exactly what happened a few months ago, when my two-year-old son was getting an ultrasound exam at a nearby hospital. He has a rare disorder that puts him at risk for abdominal tumors, so every few months we find ourselves in the darkened exam room, anxiously watching the technician glide the probe back and forth over his belly. The picture, of course, is merely an echo. Yet we find ourselves peering at the images as if the screen were a window through which we will be able to observe our son's health and happiness, or his illness, his deterioration.

"Uh-huh," says the technician, freezing one particular image and shooting a photo.

We never ask the technicians much, since it's not their job to interpret what they see. But in these circumstances, every flicker of curiosity can be very frightening. My son is getting restless on the gurney. My wife and I are singing songs to him or telling him stories. Suddenly I'm afraid that my son will die before I do.

"The taste of death is already on my tongue," Mozart told his sister-in-law only a few hours before he died. What he tasted I don't know, but perhaps my experience with vasovagal syncope — a dress rehearsal for our final loss of consciousness — has given me the faintest of ideas. The dark room grows darker around me. I'm forced to squat, then to leave the room. The waiting area is bright; pale and blinking, I sink into one of the deep red chairs and collect myself. The other patients lower their magazines and look at me. Okay. With my soul bobbing back into view, I return to the exam room, where the smiling doctor is explaining what the pictures mean.

JILL McCORKLE

Cuss Time

FROM *The American Scholar*

MY DAD OFTEN TOLD a story from his days as a mail carrier when he confronted a little boy no more than five perched up in a tree in a yard severely marked by poverty and neglect. The kid looked down with dirty face and clothes and said, "Whatcha want, you old son of a bitch?" We laughed at his aggressive assertion, but there was something sad and tender in it, too. There was the recognition of his own reality and the hope that his anger and toughness might in time lead him to a better place.

One day when my son was eight, he came into the kitchen while I was cooking and said: "You put bad words in your books, don't you?" No doubt he had overheard my mother, who often tells people who ask about my work: "Well, you'll never find her books in the Christian bookstore."

I said that sometimes — when character and situation called for it — I did use *strong* language, that I couldn't imagine a realistic portrait of human nature, particularly in our contemporary society, without it.

"So can I do that?" he asked, and of course I told him absolutely — that when he writes a short story or novel, he will have all the freedom in the world to do so.

He pulled a ripped sheet of notebook paper from behind his back. "Would you like to hear the first of my book?"

This was when I stopped what I was doing and gave him my full attention, boy in Red Sox shirt and baggy jeans — his uniform of many years. "Now," he said. "Keep in mind that this is a fourteen-year-old girl who is being made to marry a guy she's never even

met and she's mad." I could only assume he had read or heard
something in school to inspire this — stories of another culture
used to enlighten and remind us of our basic rights and free-
doms and how important they are. He paused, giving a very serious look before clearing his throat, shaking the paper, and beginning.

*"Goddamnit why would I want to marry that piece of shit boy? I'm damn
mad as hell."*

He stopped and looked at me, waiting for my response. It was
one of those important parental moments, recognized as it is happening, so I took a few seconds. "Well," I said. "You certainly have
captured her anger and frustration." He nodded, a look of great
satisfaction on his face, and wandered back to where he was playing video games. Needless to say I confiscated that piece of paper
and carefully placed it in the box of treasured writings I have saved.
It is right in there with a letter he wrote his sister claiming he had
"Shitey conselars" at a camp he was unhappily attending.

A year or so before this took place, I had given him permission
to have what we called "cuss time." It began when I realized that he
was silently mouthing a lot of new vocabulary while riding in the
car or drawing. He saw me see him one day, and he was embarrassed, so I told him I knew that urge to test a word and how important it is to do so. Thus the origin of cuss time. Every day for
five minutes, usually right after school, he could say anything he
wanted. He liked to bounce on the already beaten-up leather sofa
while saying the words, sounds emitted as his feet left the cushion.
It was a kind of Trampoline Tourette's — "hell," "bitch," "doo-doo"
— and I'll confess I was always happy that we were never interrupted by UPS or a friend stopping by. What I found particularly
endearing is that in his world, all words that were considered inap-
propriate for public voice weighed exactly the same. "Fart" and
"fuck" and "fanny" were equals. "Shit" and "ass." When the kitchen
timer rang, all cussing ended until the next day.

I found it liberating to watch his liberation. I was a kid who had
gotten my mouth washed out with soap regularly, and all that ever
did — other than leave me foaming and gagging — was to make
me furious and determined to say everything even more. It's one
of the most basic laws of human nature, isn't it? The more we are
denied something, the more we want it? The more silence given to

this or that topic, the more power. All you need do is look to the binge-drinking or eating-disorder cases that surround us, the multitudes of church sex scandals, to show that the demand for abstinence or any kind of total denial of thought or expression or action can often lead to dangerous consequences. When we know we *can* choose to do this or that, we don't feel as frantic to do so, to make a sudden move or decision that might be the worst thing for us.

When our words and actions are filled with possibilities and potential, we are more likely to weigh out the options. I am convinced that the anticipation of cuss time — the *freedom* of cuss time — kept my son from being overheard by some person in authority who might have had no choice but to reprimand him and assign punishment.

"Potential" is a powerful word. I remember feeling so sad when my children turned a year old and I knew, from reading about human development, that they had forever lost the potential they were born with to emulate the languages of other cultures, clicks and hums and throat sounds foreign to me. For that short period of time, a mere twelve months, they could have been dropped anywhere in the world and fully adapted accordingly. But beyond this linguistic loss, we are at risk of losing something far greater each and every time we're confronted with censorship and denial. Perfectly good words are taken from our vocabulary, limiting the expression of a thought or an opinion. I recently read about high schoolers who are not allowed to use the word "vagina." And what should they say instead? When you read about something like this (just one recent example of many), you really have to stop and wonder. Is this restriction because someone in charge thinks vaginas are *bad?* I once had a story editor ask me not to use the word "placenta." I wanted to say: "Now tell me again how you got here?" *Oh, right, an angel of God placed you into the bill of the stork.*

Word by single word, our history will be rewritten if we don't guard and protect it, truth lost to some individual's idea about what is right or wrong. These speech monitors — the Word Gestapo (speaking of words some would have us deny and forget) — attempt to define and dictate what is acceptable and what is not.

Lenny Bruce, while pushing the First Amendment as far as it can go, famously said, "Take away the right to say 'fuck' and you take away the right to say 'fuck the government.'" And maybe that's *really* what all the rules are about — power and control — someone else's over you. Though I felt the impulse to tell my son cuss time was a secret of sorts, "our own little game," I stifled the urge, knowing what a dangerous and manipulative thing the use of a "secret" can be. Besides, any suggestion of denial of the act would have worked against everything I was trying to give him. Of course, it wasn't any time at all before several little boys started asking to ride the bus home with him. "Can I do cuss time?" they pleaded. I sadly had to tell them the truth: they were not of legal age and so cuss time was something only their own parents could give them.

I have often thought what a better, more confident person I would have been if only I had grown up with cuss time instead of soap licking.

My first public reading from my work was when I was twenty-five years old. At the end, as I stood at the podium speaking to people, I noticed an elderly woman slowly making her way down the aisle. I waited for her to reach me only to have her shake a finger in my face and say, "And you look like such a nice girl!" Unfortunately, I was still conditioned to want her to believe that I *was* a nice girl, conditioned to care more about what other people thought of me than what I thought of myself. It was only after the fact that I felt angry, that I wanted to go back and ask if she was even paying attention to what I was reading about — a situation of hurt humans expressing their feelings. I wanted to say "You have every right to your opinions and thoughts, but that doesn't make you *right*." I wanted to say "Fuck you," and even knowing it would have been completely out of character for me to do so, I like knowing that I *could* have.

By limiting or denying freedom of speech and expression, we take away a lot of potential. We take away thoughts and ideas before they even have the opportunity to hatch. We build a world around negatives — you can't say, think, or do this or that. We teach that if you are safely camouflaged in what is acceptable and walk that narrow road — benign or neutral words, membership in institutions where we are told what to think and believe — then you can get away with a lot of things. You can deny who you are and all that came before you and still be thought of as a *good* person. And what can be positive in that? In fact, what is more positive than a child with an individual mind full of thoughts and sounds and the need to express them who has the freedom to discover under safe and accommodating conditions the best way to communicate something? In other words, you old son of a bitch, I say *Let freedom ring!*

KATHRYN MILES

Dog Is Our Copilot

FROM *Ecotone*

COULD EVERYTHING WE know and love (or hate) about evolution depend upon a singularly pampered Victorian terrier? Perhaps not entirely. Then again, probably more than you might think.

Admittedly, Polly was no average dog. Sure, she looked ordinary enough — about fourteen inches tall, just shy of twenty pounds, and possessing a thin, athletic frame. She had a wiry white coat, built more for functionality than elegance. Even still, her face, what with its intelligent eyes, overturned ears, and slight beard, endeared her to Charles Darwin. She was rumored to be both clever and indulgent, consenting to any number of silly tricks for the amusement of visitors. She liked walks but loved curling up in her bed more. She was skilled at eliciting sympathy and engendering affection. She pined when her favorite human was away. In many ways, she was a typical family pet.

But she was also so much more. Polly was a direct descendant of a dog named Trump, who in turn was best known as being the first fox terrier owned by Parson John Russell. The parson was a man's man; he loved to hunt, and even after taking religious orders, he preferred to be called Jack by those who knew him. When he wasn't chasing foxes or administering the Eucharist, Jack Russell liked to experiment with dog genetics or, more specifically, coordinated breeding intended to bring out the most desirable traits in his terriers. He was surprisingly skilled at this pastime — so skilled, in fact, that he is credited with creating one of the first acknowledged dog breeds through speciation, or the process whereby one species is diverged into several. The dog world applauded his efforts by giving all members of this breed the moniker Jack Russell terrier.

Perhaps not surprisingly, Darwin was intrigued by Russell's tinkering in speciation. Darwin was also utterly enamored of the dogs that resulted — including our protagonist, Polly, whom Darwin adopted for his daughter Henrietta. Henrietta liked Polly just fine, but there was never a real connection between the two. So, when Henrietta set off for her new life as a married woman, she left Polly in the care of her doting father. As much as Darwin missed his daughter, he seemed more than pleased with his consolation prize.

Darwin adored dogs. In fact, he had managed to entwine just about every major relationship of his life with the existence of a dog. As a young boy, for instance, Darwin often felt oppressed by his regulated home life. According to his own account, on one day when he felt particularly confined, he became so frustrated he beat a puppy, thinking it would give him a sense of power. It didn't. Instead, it filled him with regret and a lifelong tenderness for the species. Meanwhile, he found other, less harmful modes of exerting sway in a relationship, like deliberately wooing his sister Caroline's dogs, vying for their affection as a way of making a sister jealous. It wasn't until college that Darwin found a dog of his own: a pointer he named Sappho, perhaps as a quiet emotional overture toward his cousin William Darwin Fox. For years Charles had adored William — and William's dog, Fan. He also loved the affection he could draw out from the latter and, in turn, the attention that he garnered from the former. During an extended stay with Charles, William repeatedly awoke at night to see that Charles had persuaded Fan to leave William's bed in favor of his own. William politely suggested that Charles find an unclaimed canine companion of his own.

And so he did in Sappho, who soon became Darwin's bosom confidant. Even after his friendship with Fox cooled, Darwin's affinity for Sappho — and dogs in general — remained strong. After Sappho, a parade of canines came in and out of Darwin's life: dogs by the name of Spark, Nina, Dash, Czar, Pincher, Snow, Bob, Bran, Ponto, and Shelah all shared his home. But the real love of his life — at least as far as puppy love is concerned — was Polly.

Part of Darwin's fascination with Polly was undoubtedly her deliberate breeding. But there were softer reasons for his interest, too. Polly proved to Darwin that dogs possess emotion and can feel. Thirteen years after the publication of *The Origin of Species,* he would point to the terrier's affection as further proof of both behavioral inheritance and the connection between humans and so-called lower animals.

Polly was no less taken with Charles Darwin. The dog accompanied him on his daily walks and was the only living creature permitted to lounge in his very private study. Darwin's son Francis described their relationship as one of mutual adoration. Polly would perform tricks only if asked by Charles; she would wait pensively at home while he toured for his books and his health; she would "go wild with excitement," according to Francis, when Darwin returned. Immediately upon his arrival, Darwin was said to bypass his family in order to greet Polly by pressing their faces together and whispering sweet nothings into her wiry ears. Darwin's wife, Emma, found this intimacy incomprehensible and wryly noted that an entire book could be written about it. "I think [Polly] has taken it into her head that [your father] is a very big puppy," Emma wrote to her daughter. "She is perfectly devoted to him; will only stay with him and leaves the room whenever he does. She lies upon him whenever she can, and licks his hands." Darwin, Emma also reported, returned the affection tenfold.

I love this fact about Darwin. I first discovered it when, like millions of other museumgoers, I visited the Darwin exhibit created by the American Museum of Natural History, which also toured the country. There I read the well-crafted placards and stood respectfully before the framed plant samples taken during the voyage of the *Beagle.* They were everything a display ought to be: lovely, informative, reverent. But they did not captivate me — at least not like Darwin's re-created study at Down House, which appeared near the end of the exhibit and waited quietly behind thick velvet ropes. Most of the other museumgoers walked right past this muted tableau. I almost skipped it too, until something caught my eye. There, next to a plain wooden writing desk and Regency mahogany chair, sat a small basket: a bed for a terrier-sized dog. With raised sides and a fleecy interior, it was precisely the kind of thing one might buy today at a big-box store specializing in impulse purchases for the doting pet owner. Darwin's study, like Polly's coat, was far more remarkable for its functionality than its elegance. He preferred furniture of the metaphoric sort: chairs that could be used to fetch books on upper shelves; divans that could hold coats as well as lounging readers. The inclusion of a small wicker bed, then, seemed uncharacteristically indulgent. This gave me pause. Could Darwin have belonged to that growing modern klatch of munificent pet owners? The sort who monogram sweaters for their dachshunds and buy frozen yogurt for their huskies? Really?

As it turns out, Darwin not only belonged to this set; he all but invented it.

Even knowing Darwin's biography, one finds it easy to forget that he had an emotional affinity for dogs and other domestic animals. His intellectual inheritance tends to overshadow the parts of life that were both sensitive and loving. Opponents of evolutionary theory like to posit a man tortured by his godlessness and the empty life it created; proponents often depict him as the archetypal eminent Victorian — staid and distantly contemplative. Neither offers an obvious venue for face-licking and fawning pet names. Besides, when we do talk about Darwin's interest in animals, we tend to emphasize his fascination with more mysterious creatures, like finches and tortoises, coral and barnacles. Or his continued interest in beetles, ants, and other creepy-crawlies. That's fair of course: all of these animals contributed to Darwin's sense of animal development and classification. Nevertheless, much of the theory underlying *The Origin of Species* is based not on the wild catalogue of animals he observed during his time on the *Beagle,* but rather on what he saw in animals closer to hearth and home. Of these, dogs proved particularly useful in his study.

But why?

Darwin never said specifically. However, we can wager a guess or two. First, dogs provide a bridge between what we know about the wild and the domestic. Their existence is one of tension: we deliberately invite them into our households, and yet we ask them to retain some semblance of their untamed selves. We want them to guard against intruders, to use their instinctual hunting capabilities, to adhere to pack mentalities. Then, at the end of the day, we want them to rest by the fireplace, play with the children, or hop in the car and enjoy a good ride around town. We are looking for a kind of metaphysical toggle switch between natural and cultivated.

Dogs provide it. That was particularly true in 1859, when *Canis lupus familiaris* was still very much a species in transition.

Two thousand years prior to *The Origin of Species,* Aristotle outlined several dog breeds in his *History of Animals,* including the Molossian, the Laconian, the Maltese, and the working sheepdog. This paltry number of dog breeds did not increase all that significantly over the next two millennia. In fact, Britain's first dog show (held, quite conveniently, in 1859) recognized just fourteen classes, all of which were some variation on pointers or setters. Nevertheless, the very definition of dog — with all of its possible permutations — was changing radically during the mid-nineteenth century, thanks to the growing interest in dog fancy. Suddenly dogs were far more than working animals: they were amusing hobbies, good friends, beloved members of many middle-class homes. As a result, the Victorian era witnessed an explosion in dog breeding and the creation of specific dog types, particularly of those dogs willing to exist as lap pets or entertaining indoor diversions.

This couldn't have happened at a better time for Darwin. His theory of evolution had found theoretical verification in his observations of other domestic animals, including pigeons, sheep, and even camels. None, however, showed the variety of traits witnessed in the dog. Darwin knew this, and he directed his inquiry accordingly. He began keeping a grisly assortment of greyhound fetuses, bulldog bones, and other unmentionables in his study. From this amalgamation of house pets and vivisected fetuses, Darwin found what he could not locate during his time on the *Beagle:* a systematic understanding of trait inheritance. Take, for instance, Polly, who was once accidentally burned on her back. When hair returned to the site of the wound, it was red instead of white. This change, Darwin proclaimed to his family, was proof of pangenesis: Polly's father, a red terrier, must have shed cell particles dictating attributes like fur color. These particles then must have remained latent during Polly's fetal development and arisen only now, as secondary growth characteristics.

Through this and other observations, Darwin was certain he had found the intergenerational verification he could not locate in *Beagle* ports of call. But I think dogs provided a more subjective benefit to Darwin's theory, too. The Victorians suffered from a self-professed collecting mania. From butterflies and beetles to spools and soup spoons, no assortment of curios was too inconsequential. By the time Darwin began his inquiry into the origin of species, designer dogs had become the newest, hottest thing to collect — and they were a lot more fun than insects wiggling on a pin. Victorians loved their increasing dog permutations at least in part because, like the young Darwin, they saw in dog attributes something they could control. Want a more effective otter hunter? Breed only those dogs showing chase prowess. Need a smaller dog for your London flat? Pair up the runts of two litters. Want utter adoration? Take the most gregarious, emotive animals and encourage a carnal love fest. Voilà! You've created your ideal dog.

This freedom appealed greatly to the Victorian culture as a whole. No one cried foul or screamed hubris — at least no one did loudly enough to make the annals of history. Darwin must have been aware of his epoch's penchant for dogs; he also understood that this love affair softened public approval for his ideas about the descent of genetic attributes. And why not? Breeding dogs was an increasingly popular pastime, an effective way to get the animal you wanted. So if a naturalist could quietly explain how you came into possession of your King Charles spaniel, or merely suggest that the creation of said spaniel was not so unlike your own arrival on this earth, maybe that might make the evolutionary pill a little easier to swallow.

In dogs Darwin found acceptable proof of human hubris: we can change a species. And if we can, then why couldn't nature, or why couldn't even that species, change itself? As far as Darwin was concerned, it could — and it did. All the time. But how?

Darwin couldn't say for sure. And the issue continued to plague him with more questions than answers. How did Polly relate to the family's larger, mixed breed, named Bob? Or to the greyhounds and bulldogs he had studied so fastidiously for *The Origin of Species*? And furthermore, what did the appearance of such breeds mean for the future of biology and ontology? Wouldn't it be so very interesting, he opined in *Origin*, if we could clear up this canine conundrum, "if, for instance, it could be shown that the grey-hound, bloodhound, terrier, spaniel, and bulldog . . . were the offspring of any single species. Such facts would have great weight in making us doubt about the immutability of the many very closely allied and natural species." Surely showing as much would solve these mysteries.

But proof of this connection remained elusive for Darwin. Instead, he conceded that different breeds must have evolved from different canids. In the years after the publication of *Origin*, Darwin maintained that Polly might best be considered a descendant of a fox, while Bob seemed more likely the relative of a dingo or jackal. The greyhounds and bulldogs in his study might have descended from wolves or coyotes or even some previously unknown species. He maintained this theory of descent — and the affection for *Canis familiaris* — right up until his death, in 1882.

What's become of this theory — and Darwin's beloved species — since then? For starters, we've disproven the theory of pangenesis and replaced it with a developing understanding of DNA. As for Darwin's multiple-progenitor theory of dog evolution, our contemporary iterations keep changing. In 1993, the American Society of Mammalogists, in conjunction with the Smithsonian Institution, concluded that wolves and domestic dogs maintained enough similarities to be considered part of the same species. They then applied the more nuanced distinction of "subspecies" to the domestic dog, changing its name from *Canis familiaris* to *Canis lupus familiaris*.

This was no act of mere semantics. Instead, it acknowledges the belief that dogs, through a combination of natural and artificial selection, descended from wolves. Most ethnologists now contend that ancient wolves accomplished this feat by self-selecting into two distinct groups. According to a study by Raymond and Lorna Coppinger, two of the leading experts on dog evolution, those wolves with less fear of humans and more interest in an easy meal started hanging around early settlements. The ones who didn't care for this kind of life stayed away. Eventually, these groups formed two different breeding pools. That's when there began to be serious differences in appearance and behavior. The self-domesticating wolves looked to settlement dumps for their meals, and the less concerned they were about humans, the bigger the meals they enjoyed. The more food they consumed there, the more energy they had for reproduction. Eventually, those wolves showing the friendliest and most engaging responses to humans were invited to continue their meals in our homes and common areas. By the time the Victorians arrived on the scene, these meals had become bacchanalian feasts.

And if you thought Victorians were indulgent about this invitation, consider our own behaviors. While Polly may have been perfectly content with a wicker bed and daily biscuit ration, these luxuries undoubtedly seem spartan to many contemporary dogs. Visit one of any number of online pet-supply sites and you'll see what I mean. Petco, for example, offers more than ninety dog beds to choose from. They range from the austere fleece donut bed (available in coral, eggshell, rose, and teal) to more elaborate settees like the Cleopatra Chaise in zebra and leopard print, the bamboo spindle bed, and the heated Therabed with eggshell memory foam. It's a wonder poor Polly could sleep at all. As for recreation, she had to content herself with daily saunters and silly pet tricks. Her descendants, on the other hand, have binkies and floppy disks, laser pointer games and motion-activated cosmic rainbow balls (dental rope not included). If they tire of these toys, one of the thousands of pet daycare centers across the country will happily pick up your bored basenjis or basset hounds and take them to dog camp, where they will enjoy social hour, recess, and snacks while you watch it all on a live video stream.

These trends in pet ownership represent a behavioral change in humans that even the dog-loving Darwin couldn't have fully predicted. True, we love our dogs just like the Victorians did. But somewhere along the line, we changed the way we demonstrate this love into nothing short of an entire consumer culture evolution. Consider this: on average, Americans now spend almost $41 billion annually on their pets. Dogs enjoy the lion's share of this output. According to the National Pet Owners Survey — a leading indicator of domestic animal spending — the average dog owner shells out $1,425 each year for his or her dog, including more than $100 for treats and toys. Each of us spends about another $250 on dog food. Do we question this expense? Not really. My dog, Ari, has a custom-made cedar doghouse, complete with shingles and trim. She hasn't spent a single moment inside it, since she much prefers our upholstered sofa. I regularly bake her biscuits made from the sort of organic ingredients generally reserved for use by celebrity chefs. Am I excessive? Maybe. But I am also not alone. I'm probably not even all that unusual or extreme in my doting.

People like me are good news for domestic canines.

Without a doubt, the latest trends in dog owner behavior have proven an evolutionary jackpot, at least in terms of dog population numbers. In spite of the fact that they are a relatively new species, four hundred million domestic dogs now occupy the planet — far outpacing the four hundred thousand wolves and even the four million coyotes thought to exist in the wild. And why not? Approximately seventy-five million pet dogs reside in the United States alone, and we're spending more than $22 billion making sure they're fat and sassy.

These figures make a lot of sense to people who study the success of canine populations. For every calorie a dog doesn't have to spend searching for food, that dog can devote one more bit of energy to enhancing sexual prowess and providing for a new litter of pups. And each time one domesticated dog reproduces, he or she passes on a genetic docility and willingness to ply human civilization. Pups frightened of humans tend to peel off from the existing population, taking their wary genes along with them. And, because of human responses to neoteny, we tend to reward those dogs who seem the most adorable in their infantile appearance and behavior. We encourage them to breed; we give them treats and opulent beds; we allow them to be adopted by people like Paris Hilton. As a result, there are more Chihuahuas on the planet than there are wolves. In the past ten years alone, Americans have registered more than 365,000 Chihuahuas with the American Kennel Club. That, of course, doesn't include nonregistered members of the breed or the hundreds of thousands of little dogs living in other countries. Just as staggering is the fact that Chihuahuas are ranked eleventh in terms of numbers of dogs registered with the AKC each year — well behind Shih Tzus, dachshunds, and retrievers.

But in spite of the obvious differences between a starlet's pocket companion and a timber wolf, scientists still believe that the basic blueprint for both animals has remained surprisingly similar over the past several hundred years. When it comes to wolves and domestic dogs, any genetic difference is best considered in terms of degree — and it is a very small degree. Ed Bangs, the wolf recovery coordinator for the U.S. Fish and Wildlife Service, explains the similarity this way: "Basically if you drop your beagle in a blender and look at the DNA it's pretty indistinguishable from a wild wolf." Such an assertion begs two questions for me. First, how closely related are wolves and beagles? Second, and perhaps more important, what kind of ghoulish cocktails are served at USFWS parties? I haven't yet found an answer to that second question. But I do know that DNA analysis of the aforementioned species reveals that wolves and domestic dogs share a whopping 99.8 percent of their DNA. According to the ethological scholar Robert K. Wayne, the next closest relative to the wolf is the coyote, which shares only 96 percent of its DNA with the wolf.

For well over a decade, this chromosomal link was enough to persuade scientists that Darwin was wrong: domestic dogs must have come from wolves, and only wolves. However, more recent mitochondrial analysis suggests that Darwin might have been on to something. Stanley Coren's recent book *Why Does My Dog Act That Way?* shows that although canine genome projects continue to support the hypothesis that the first domestic dog was a direct descendant of a wolf, additional evidence indicates that, over time, these early dogs probably also mated with dingoes, coyotes, jackals, and certain breeds of fox. Not exactly the direct descent Darwin was looking for, but closer than we once thought.

We might, then, be best served in viewing dogs and multiple wild canids as something between siblings and kissing cousins: close enough to be a part of the same genus and even interbreed, but worlds apart when it comes to a few key attributes — particularly those attributes that come to light in the natural world. This is the real power of genetic selection and species origination. That tiny fractional difference between dogs and their wild kin is all it takes to mold an eighty-pound timber wolf into any number of AKC toy breeds — including a wirehaired terrier like Polly.

Getting a wolf into the shape of a toy breed is where we demonstrate the real force of our Darwinian inheritance. Thanks to those human-induced behavioral changes that include high-protein diets and state-of-the-art veterinary care, dogs are surpassing their wild progenitors in more than just population numbers. The average life expectancy of a wolf is about seven years. Compare this to Darwin's beloved pointers (fourteen years) or the Jack Russell terrier (sixteen years). In just about every category, domestic dogs trump wolves when it comes to survival and life span. They also beat wolves and even chimpanzees when it comes to interpreting human behavior and interacting with our species. Again, through selection, dogs and people have created an interspecies bond second to none.

We've also shown the extent, both legitimate and ludicrous, of genetic selection. More than any other single species, dogs show tremendous range in physical attributes. An average Newfoundland weighs in at approximately 150 pounds; a Yorkshire terrier rarely exceeds 5. The bloodhound possesses twice as much skin as it needs, and its snout is almost as long as the rest of its head. The Pekingese's face contains far more cat than dog, what with its petite ears and very flat countenance, and you have to look awfully hard to see its taut skin under all that fur. Its geographic cousin, the Chinese crested dog, is bald except for enormous patches of hair on its equally enormous ears. Yet all of these dog breeds (and the hundreds of others) are able to mate successfully.

We humans are almost completely responsible for this variance within *Canis familiaris*. But that's not to say we've really helped all that much with dog evolution. To the contrary, as much as we would like to believe we are in a mutually rewarding relationship or even one that benefits the canine species, many scholars speculate that we actually do a fair amount of harm. The Coppingers write that whether through neglect and abuse or through the controlled reproduction of breeds, we not only compromise the evolutionary development of canines, we also create situations in which they can be hurt or even killed. For the most part, we humans don't mean to do so — we just tend not to see things from a dog's point of view.

Our continued interest in designer dogs, for instance, is creating more and more aesthetically appealing but physiologically problematic breeds. Darwin referred to these breeds as "monsters," in the sense that they were gross, Frankensteinian distortions of the evolutionary process. What struck Darwin as most remarkable was their ability to reveal that their selection had been made not on behalf of evolutionary development but, as Darwin puts it, for "man's use or fancy." I doubt he'd be pleased with how right we've proven him over the past century and a half. The contemporary bulldog, for instance, has a difficult time merely surviving as a breed. Females often have to give birth by cesarean section, and they all tend to have respiratory and joint problems. Even so, we continue to make bulldogs bigger and more physiologically problematic each year. Meanwhile, other dogs, like pugs and Boston terriers, have been so bred for their infantile appearance that their skulls can barely contain the eyeballs. Those dogs who manage to keep their eyes in their sockets run the risk of lacerations and abrasions to the eye, since they protrude to nearly the same degree as their noses.

None of this bodes well for dogs inside or outside the domestic realm. And the species has come to rely directly on humanity for its very survival. We embrace this dependency, and go out of our way to foster it. Meanwhile, natural selection necessitates that wild canids stay well out of view, keeping their numbers sparse and their genetics under lock and key, as it were.

There are exceptions within both species, of course. But these, too, are of our making.

In Chicago this past year, three different coyotes have been found wandering the downtown streets. And recently one entered a Quiznos sub shop in the city's busy shopping district. Remarkably, no one remembers him entering the store, but they certainly noticed when he hopped into the refrigerated drink case — presumably to cool an injury on his back leg. Millions of TV viewers watched as the coyote was captured, then taken to a wildlife rehabilitation center, where he was named Adrian. They sent text messages of support and offers to adopt the juvenile coyote. The next day, those same viewers fawned when the sub shop's manager brought Adrian a meat lover's sandwich.

Meanwhile, even the most bred of all show dogs are proving that you can't select out all that is wild in a dog. The show whippet Bohem C'est la Vie, or Vivi, famously escaped her crate at New York's JFK Airport in February 2006. In the days that followed, several airport employees spied her moving across the airport's five thousand acres, largely grass and swamp, but they were unable to catch her — even after tailing her in airport vehicles at speeds of thirty miles an hour. And in spite of her breed's "monstrous" weaknesses (like sensitivity to cold and sun, or a famously temperamental digestion), Vivi has remained on the loose ever since. In the year after her escape, animal rescue organizations received hundreds of calls from people who had spotted her in alleys or parks. The last such sighting was — fittingly — in a Queens cemetery, near the grave of Harry Houdini.

Animal behaviorists are divided on what has become of Vivi. Some think she has died or been captured, others maintain she has become feral and is living off the fat of the land. If that's true, it's probably because she has managed to find a career scavenging human-generated trash — further proof that contemporary dog survival depends on human tinkering. Somewhere in their genetic coding, all dogs seem to know this. They also seem to intuit, on a biological level, the truth in Darwin's observations about speciation and our ability to create animals that don't always resemble their genetic progenitors.

As for humans, we're more conflicted than ever.

Take our increased obsession with dog classification. Currently the AKC recognizes more than 150 official breeds, and it's preparing another six for eventual inclusion. The club is also becoming far more fastidious about what constitutes a breed standard. Once upon a time, Darwin's Polly would have been classified as a Jack Russell terrier without any debate. That was before purists worried that the colloquial use of the category to describe any scrappy little terrier was diluting the breed standard. So recently the AKC created the more rigid designation of the Parson Russell terrier, to distinguish the highbrow Pollys of the world from any shaggy interloper trying to pose as pure. In so doing, the club took away John Russell's jaunty nickname and replaced it with his formal title, emphasizing Russell's occupation: parson priest. This is perhaps ironic given the perceived discord between Russell's theology and the theory behind his biggest hobby.

Meanwhile, those individuals fed up with the eugenics of the AKC have broken away and formed their own organization, the American Canine Hybrid Club, or ACHC. Make no mistake, however: this is not an organization for lovers of mixed breeds and mutts. Members of the ACHC are very specific in their aims: to explore the creation of deliberate hybrids and the scope of evolutionary selection. The ACHC now recognizes more than four hundred new hybrid breeds, with names like the giant schnoodle, pogle, chiweenie, pom-a-poo, taco terrier, cock-a-chon, schneagle, and, my personal favorite, the rat-a-dorkie.

Not content with this amalgamation, a woman in California named Dawn Houston is now marketing the "puppykat." Houston told a reporter for the *Californian* that, after spying two stray cats with dog-like tendencies, she engaged them in a *Hustler*esque breeding orgy until she derived standard litters of creatures with downturned ears, short tails, and a willingness to come when called. Houston has had tremendous success in marketing the so-called exotic breed — new owners are thrilled at how much like dogs their strange little cats behave, and they're thrilled by the amiability and loyalty of their misshapen new friends — perhaps proving once and for all that evolution and the human desire for companionship don't always square, at least as far as the advancement of a species is concerned.

But would Darwin agree?

When writing *The Origin of Species,* he chose to include an oft-overlooked subtitle: *The Preservation of Favoured Races in the Struggle for Life.* From Polly the Parson terrier to the idea behind pampered puppykats, no race has proven itself more favored than the contemporary dog, in all its cultural permutations. What began as Victorian dog fancy has evolved into something far more zealous on the part of *Homo sapiens sapiens.* We don't just fancy dogs; we exalt them. And because they acknowledge our affections so fetchingly, we increase our overtures tenfold. Our species may sometimes be misguided in how we demonstrate this favoritism, but that preference is commanding all the same. In our journey through science and genetic manipulation, what we know — and how we live — has become utterly intertwined with *Canis lupus familiaris.* Along the way, we've proven just how far selection can change the behavior of humans and animals alike. These days (and with all apologies to the writers at *Bark* magazine who coined the original phrase), dogs aren't just our copilots. When it comes to consumer spending and human lifestyle, sometimes dogs actually appear to be flying the plane. There's an important evolutionary lesson to be learned, particularly when it comes to understanding not only how we can effect change in a species, but also how that change can alter us.

Furthermore, we can learn far more than adaptive theory from our continued association with dogs. More than just companions and assistants, dogs are uniquely suited to translate the world for us. As ecological generalists, canines succeed in just about every biome: from the trash heaps of Tijuana to the streets of Tokyo, dogs know not only how to exist, but also how to thrive. They can take both the refuse of human civilization and its most consumer-based goods and find a way to make it benefit them: carrot tops and half-eaten sandwiches, deep-tissue massage and oatmeal-based conditioner, all work to advance the canine species. Meanwhile, these same dogs maintain a particular — and highly liminal — place in the environment, straddling the wild and the domestic as they continue to help humans sort out what it means for a species to descend.

GREGORY ORR

Return to Hayneville

FROM *The Virginia Quarterly Review*

I WAS BORN and raised in rural upstate New York, but who I am began with a younger brother's death in a hunting accident when I was twelve and he was eight. I held the gun that killed him. But if my life began at twelve with my brother's sudden, violent death, then my end, determined by the trajectory of that harsh beginning, could easily have taken place a scant six years later, when, in June 1965, I was kidnapped at gunpoint by vigilantes near the small town of Hayneville, Alabama.

When I was sixteen, in my senior year of high school, I became involved in the civil rights movement partly because I hoped I could lose myself in that worthwhile work. I became a member of CORE (Congress of Racial Equality) and canvassed door-to-door in poorer neighborhoods in the nearby city of Kingston. I traveled down to Atlantic City with a carload of CORE members to picket the Democratic National Convention in August 1964. Earlier that summer, the Mississippi Freedom Democratic Party — another civil rights group — had chosen a slate of racially integrated delegates to challenge Mississippi's all-white official Democratic Party delegates for seats at the convention. The goal was to put Lyndon Johnson and the whole liberal wing of the party on the spot — testing their commitment to change. I was one of about twenty or so people parading in a small circle on the dilapidated boardwalk outside the convention hall. We carried signs urging on the drama inside: SUPPORT THE FREEDOM DELEGATION and ONE MAN, ONE VOTE. I felt confused and thrilled and purposeful all at the same time.

Three marchers carried poles, each bearing a huge charcoal portrait of a different young man. Their larger-than-life faces gazed down at us as we walked our repetitious circle. They were renditions of Andrew Goodman, James Chaney, and Michael Schwerner, SNCC (Student Nonviolent Coordinating Committee) volunteers who had been missing for months, whose bodies had only recently been discovered. They had last been seen alive on June 21, driving away from the Neshoba County sheriff's office in Philadelphia, Mississippi. When an informer led investigators to the spot where their tortured bodies had been bulldozed into a clay dam, the mystery of their whereabouts ended abruptly and they began a second life — the life of martyrs to a cause. Those three faces mesmerized us as we circled the boardwalk, singing and trying to ignore the heckling from bystanders. The artist who had drawn them had resolved their faces into a few bold lines that gave them a subtle dignity. They seemed at peace, all their uncertainties and inner complexities over. I longed to be like them, to transcend my confusions and the agonies of my past and be taken up into some noble simplicity beyond change. I longed to sacrifice myself and escape myself — to become a martyr for the movement. If it took death to gain access to the grandeur of meaning, so be it. And thus are young soldiers born.

I was too young, only seventeen, to go to Mississippi that summer, but a year later I was on my way. I drove south, alone, in a '56 Ford my father had bought me for the trip. And so it commenced — my instruction in the grim distance between the myth of the martyr and the intimate reality of violence.

Cut to November 2006 — more than forty years have passed since my late-adolescent misadventures in the Deep South. I'm a poet and a professor — that's how I've spent my life. One of the happier perquisites of my profession is that I'm sometimes asked to read my poems at various colleges and universities. One such invitation has come my way: a former student of mine, a poet named Chris, is teaching at Auburn University and has invited me down. I'm reading that same week in Atlanta, and as I look over my Rand McNally, I see that I can not only drive from Atlanta to Auburn, but proceed an hour or so farther and drive straight through time and into my own past. I decide to go back to Hayneville, the tiny town that has been so long lodged like a sliver in my memory.

Chris says he'll take the trip with me, and he brings Brian, a former student of his own. I'm glad of the company. Three poets from three generations: I'll turn sixty within the year, Chris is in his early forties, Brian in his mid-twenties. As we leave town in my rented, economy-size Hyundai, pulling onto the interstate in the late-afternoon drizzle, Brian asks where we're headed. For several days, I've felt a quiet tension about this trip, and suddenly it seems I can release some of the tension by telling Brian and Chris the story of that long-ago summer. At first, I try to talk about what happened to me in Hayneville itself, but I quickly see that I'll have to start further back in order to make a coherent story of it.

As we drive down the highway toward Montgomery, I feel like one of those pilgrims in Chaucer, challenged by my travel companions to entertain them on the journey. Brian's in the back seat, and as I begin my story, I occasionally turn my head slightly as if acknowledging I'm aware of him as an audience, but soon I'll become so caught up in the narrative that I'll lose all sense of my companions and of time and distance passing. I'll drive steadily toward Hayneville, as though the story and the highway were a single, fused flowing.

It was late May 1965. After brief training, another volunteer, a man from Pittsburgh named Steve, and I were assigned to work in Bolivar County, Mississippi — the Delta region, where COFO (Council of Federated Organizations) was trying to gain momentum for a strike of field workers. The going wage was $4 a day — dawn to dusk, hoeing the cotton by hand, everyone from seven-year-old kids to octogenarians. We'd been in Bolivar only a week or so, helping out at the office. Suddenly there was a summons from headquarters: everyone who could be mustered and spared from their local work — any new volunteers and all the local residents who could be persuaded — should report to the state capital in Jackson. The governor of Mississippi had called a secret session of the legislature, and the movement was organizing a mass demonstration to draw national attention to what it suspected was serious political skullduggery.

At ten in the morning on June 14, about five hundred of us — men, women, teenagers, old folks — assembled in Jackson. We walked two abreast down the sidewalk toward the capitol. Our leaders told us we'd be stopped by the police and warned we could not parade without a permit. At that point, we would have to choose to be arrested or to disperse. We were urged to let ourselves be arrested — the plan was to fill the jail to overflowing and apply the steady pressure of media and economics (they'll have to feed and house us at city expense). The powers that be had learned to present a sanitized image to the media, so our arrest was very polite. Journalists and photographers there watched each of us being ushered onto a truck by two city policemen, who held us by both arms, firmly but calmly. The trucks themselves were large, enclosed vehicles, the kind you'd use to transport chairs for a rally or municipal lawnmowers. They packed about thirty of us inside, then closed the doors. And we were off — each truck with its own motorcycle escort gliding through red lights, heading, we presumed, toward the city jail. But the actual destination was our first big surprise. We activists may have had a plan to demonstrate, but the State of Mississippi and the City of Jackson had their own plan. We were taken to the county fairgrounds — twenty or so fenced acres of clear-cut land set with half a dozen long, low, tin-roofed barns. Another thing we didn't know: when each truck entered the fairgrounds, the gate swung shut behind it, and police turned back anyone else who tried to enter.

The truck I was on stopped, backed up, then came to a final halt. When the doors opened and our eyes adjusted to the flood of light, we saw that we weren't at the jail at all but in a narrow alley between two barns. A score of uniformed officers were gathered there, wearing the uniforms of motorcycle cops — tall leather boots, mirrored sunglasses, and blue helmets with the black earflaps pulled down. Each tanned face was almost indistinguishable under its partial disguise — only the nose and mouth showing — some already grinning at the joke of our surprise and what was in store for us. Each of them had his nightstick out, some tapping their clubs rhythmically in the palms of their hands, others just standing there expectantly with the stick held at each end. I didn't notice until I was up close, and even then, in my confusion, didn't comprehend, that the lower half of each officer's silver badge, where the identifying number should have been displayed, was neatly covered with black tape. An officer ordered us to climb down, and when some of us didn't, two officers climbed up and pushed us to the edge where others pulled us down. And it began. They swung their clubs right and left, randomly but thoroughly, for about ten minutes. It made no difference what you did, whether you screamed or were silent — you were struck again and again and, if you fell to the ground, kicked. It hurts to be beaten over the head or back or shoulders with a wooden club. It's also terrifying. Then an order came and the clubbing stopped. We were told to get up. One kid couldn't and was dragged away somewhere, his leg too damaged to stand on.

We filed through a door into one of the barns. Inside, there was a calm that felt surreal after the violence outside. In the middle of the empty concrete floor, five card tables had been set up in a row, each with a typewriter and a city policeman seated in a folding chair. At the far end of the barn, half hidden in shadow, was a milling cluster of frightened women and girls who, their initial beating and processing over, had been told to assemble there. Our dazed group lined up, and each of us in turn was formally processed and charged. The women from our truck were sent to join the other women at the far end of the barn. I was told to go out one of the side doors to the next barn, where the men were being confined. Just as I was about to go through the door, an officer told me to take my straw hat off and carry it in my hands. I emerged into the outdoors and the bright sunlight and saw them — two lines of about fifteen highway patrolmen on either side. I was ordered to walk, not run, between them. Again I was beaten with nightsticks, but this time more thoroughly, as I was the only target. When I covered my head with raised arms to ward off the first blow from the officer on my right, I was jabbed in the ribs with a club from the other side. Instinctively, I pivoted in that direction, only to be left vulnerable in the other. I heard blows and felt sharp pokes or slaps fall flat and hard across my ribs and back from both directions. Whether they were simultaneous or alternating, it made no difference; my defense was hopeless. By the time I neared the end of this gantlet, I was cringing from feinted blows, the humiliation of my fear and their laughter far worse than the physical pain.

Inside the other barn, men and boys were assembled in a dense clump surrounded by a loose ring of officers. Later that afternoon we would go through another ritually structured set of beatings. When anyone tried to sit down or move out to the edge of the impacted group to get some air, two or three officers dashed across

the small, intervening space and beat him with clubs. This tech-
nique was designed to make us prisoners panic and fight one another to get to the safer center of the mass. But it didn't work. We
tried to protect ourselves as best we could and keep the most vulnerable, especially the children, safe in the middle. A bearded
young man in our group was noticeably defiant, and at a certain
point an officer ran in and deftly struck him with a slicing motion
of the blunt end of his nightstick in such a way that the taut skin of
his forehead split and blood streamed down over the whole of his
face. To see an individual human face suddenly turned into a mask
of blood is to witness the eradication of the personal, and, if you're
standing nearby as I was, to be sickened and unnerved.

The hours went by as more prisoners were processed and our
group continued to grow — there were more than 150 men and
boys in the barn. Evening fell. We were ordered to sit in rows on
the concrete floor, three feet apart, three feet between the rows.
We didn't know it, but we were waiting for mattresses to be delivered. We were told to sit bolt upright and not move; officers walked
up and down the rows. If you leaned a hand down to rest or shifted
your weight, a shouting patrolman rushed up with his club raised.

A black kid of maybe ten or twelve sat next to me. We'd been
there for an hour and things were pretty quiet when a state patrolman stopped in front of the boy. He looked him over for a minute,
then ordered him to take off the pin he was wearing — one of
those movement buttons that said FREEDOM NOW or ONE MAN,
ONE VOTE. No safety clasp, just an open pin. The guard told the
kid to pull the pin off his shirt. He did. "Put it in your mouth," the
guard said. I turned my head to the right and saw the boy place it
in his mouth. "Swallow it," the guard said, his voice menacing, but
not loud. If the kid tried to swallow it, the pin would choke him or
pierce his throat and lodge there until he bled to death in agony.

Watching the scene, I felt murderous rage fill my whole being,
geysering up in the single second it took to see what seemed about
to happen. I became nothing but the impulse to scramble to my
feet, grab the guard's pistol before he knew what was happening,
and shoot him as many times as possible. Nothing but that intense
impulse and a very small voice inside me that said: "You don't
stand a chance. It would take longer than you imagine — long
enough for him to turn on you, for his buddies to rush up and

grab you. And then what? You would be their sudden and absolute target."

How long did that moment last? How long did the guard loom over the boy with his threats? How long did the boy sit there with the pin in his mouth, tasting its metallic bitterness but refusing to swallow, or unable to swallow? It could have been five minutes; it could have been less. The guard repeated his command several times, along with profanities. And then other officers were there, urging him to give it up, persuading him to move on, to move away.

The mattresses finally arrived, and each of us dragged one off to his place in a row. We were officially segregated according to the laws of the sovereign state of Mississippi — a vigilantly patrolled lane separated two imaginary cellblocks, one for blacks and one for whites. We lay down to sleep. The pounding of nightsticks on the concrete floor woke us at dawn, and we realized the highway patrolmen who had abused us with such relish and impunity the previous day were nowhere in sight. They'd been replaced by Fish and Game wardens, who looked altogether more rustic and thoughtful (some had mustaches) and made no effort to conceal their badge numbers and even wore nametags. Later that morning, a plainclothes officer entered our barn and announced that the FBI had arrived and that if anyone had complaints about their treatment, they should step forward to be interviewed. I did so and was ushered out into the same alley where we'd first been greeted and beaten. The narrow lane had been rigged at one end with an awning for shade. Under the awning, four FBI agents sat at small desks. When my turn came, I told my narrative about the beatings, but how could I identify the perpetrators? The agent asked if I could specify hair or eye color or badge number. I couldn't. Could I point out now, in person, any of the officers who had beaten me? They weren't there, of course; they'd left in the middle of the night. The agent recorded my story of the previous day's beatings and violence and thanked me for my time. If they had actually wanted to protect us, the FBI could easily have arrived anytime the preceding day. Many in the movement already knew what was inconceivable to me at the time — that events like this were stage-managed and that the FBI wasn't a friend or even a neutral ally of the civil rights movement.

For the next ten days, we lay each morning on our mattresses until breakfast — grits and a molasses syrup and powdered milk so watered down I could see all the way to the bottom of the fifty-gallon pot that held it. After breakfast, we rolled up our mattresses and either sat all day on the concrete floor or paced the imaginary confines of our collective cell. Twice a day, we were lined up for the bathroom — it was then or never as we stood pressed up against one another, waiting for our brief turn in one of the five stinking stalls. No showers, no chance to wash at all, the same reeking clothes day after day. Hot as hell once the sun heated the tin roof, but chill at night when we huddled, blanketless, in the dark on our bare mattresses. The mosquito fogger sprayed around the outside of the barn each evening, sending its toxic cloud in under the closed doors to set us all coughing. Boredom, stench, heat.

Word came from outside: we could, at any time, be released by posting a $50 bond that the movement would provide, but the plan called for as many as possible to stay inside for as long as we could. There was hope that we would seriously inconvenience the state by staying, that another demonstration in support of us might take place — there was even talk of Martin Luther King Jr. himself showing up for it. Rumors and hope, and a request to persevere. Most of us stayed, though some of the youngest and oldest chose to leave. The violence mostly gone; if it occurred, it was sporadic and spontaneous and ended quickly without major consequence. Exhausted by the lack of substantial food, worn down by boredom and discomfort, I gradually lost heart. I had dreamed of meaningful work and even heroic martyrdom, but here I was merely cannon fodder. I held a place, I counted, but only as an integer in the calculus of a complex political game playing out in rooms far above me. And close up, as close as the arc of a swung billy club, I had discovered that for every martyr whose life was resolved into a meaningful death, there were hundreds of others who were merely beaten, terrorized, humiliated. As I sank into depression and brooded in the stifling heat of that jail-barn, I was learning that I wanted to live.

On the tenth day there, my name was called and I was led outside and taken to a pay phone attached to a post near our barn. Picking up the receiver, I heard the voice of my father's lawyer, who was calling from upstate New York. We'd met only once; I hardly knew him. He began by saying he couldn't stand me or any of the causes I believed in, but my father was his dear friend and was frantic with worry. My fine had been paid. I was to leave now and drive back north immediately if I cared a damn about my family. End of story. His tongue-lashing eliminated the last of my resolve. The officer standing beside me took me in a patrol car to where I'd left the Ford ten days ago, as if the whole thing had been prearranged.

I should have called the COFO office and told them I was leaving, heading north that very day, but I was ashamed. I was deserting — a frightened and confused teenager. The map told me my quickest route north was by state roads from Jackson to Selma, Alabama, and then on to Montgomery, where the interstate began. When I passed through Selma it was early evening and I was starved (we'd been fed nothing but vegetables and grits for ten days), but I was too afraid to stop for dinner.

It was dusk on U.S. 80, past Selma and within fifteen miles of Montgomery, when I heard a siren. A white car pulled up close behind me, flashing its lights. I thought it was a police car and pulled over, but the two men who jumped out, one tall and rather thin, the other shorter and stout, wore no uniforms. They did each wear holsters, and as they approached, one on each side of my car, they drew their pistols. I rolled up my windows and locked my doors. Rap of a pistol barrel on the window two inches from my head: "Get out, you son of a bitch, or I'll blow your head off."

I got out and stood on the road's shoulder, beside my car. They prodded me with their guns and told me they were going to kill me. They searched my car and found SNCC pamphlets in the trunk. They were sure I was an agitator rumored to be coming to their town — my New York license plates had been a strong clue that the pamphlets confirmed. The men made two promises about my immediate future. The first was that they would kill me and dump my body in the swamp. The second, made a few moments later, was that they were going to take me to a jail where I would rot. With those two contradictory threats left floating in the air, they took my wallet and went back to their vehicle, ordering me to follow them in my own car. They pulled onto the highway and zoomed off. I started my car and followed them. We hadn't driven more than a mile when they signaled and turned off to the right, onto a smaller road. I hesitated, uncertain what to do, then made the turn and followed.

*

I pause in this story I'm telling Chris and Brian when I realize we've reached the green sign marking the turnoff for Hayneville. I'd been so caught up in telling it that I hardly noticed we'd passed through Montgomery and were speeding down Route 80 toward Selma. Suddenly I realize the old story and my present journey are eerily coinciding at this forlorn intersection. It's as if my ghost Ford from forty years ago is approaching the turnoff from the west, coming from Selma, at the same moment that my shiny white rental reaches that same turn from the direction of Montgomery. The terrified boy in the ghost Ford drives right into us, and for a moment we and the story are one and the same. Now I'm driving slowly down that back road toward Hayneville, telling Chris and Brian what it felt like the first time I took this road, alone, following the car driven by my would-be killers.

Their car was newer than mine and faster. It sped up. A voice in my head started screaming: "What are you doing? You are obligingly speeding to your own death — driving to your own grave! Turn around and make a run for it!" But how could I? They had my wallet with my license and all my money. It was pitch-dark now. The road was so narrow there was no place to turn around; there were swamps on either side. If I tried to make a getaway, their car could easily overtake mine, and they would surely shoot me. This hysterical dialogue raged in my head for the ten long minutes of that ride, and then we emerged out of the dark into Hayneville. We passed the courthouse, pulled into a narrow street, and stopped in back of a small jail.

Even as I describe that terrifying drive, I see that the wooded swamps are gone. (Or were they imagined in the dark so long ago?) It's mostly fields and pasture, with a pond here and there gleaming like oil in the deepening gloom. And now we're arriving in the town itself. Again, as with the first time I was here, it's almost completely dark under the overarching trees, only a glimpse of a gray sky from which all trace of light is gone. I recognize things: there is the courthouse — no wonder it stood out — white and two stories high on its tree-filled lawn in a town of twenty or so tiny houses and bungalows. And there is something completely new in town, the only new thing as far as I can see: a BP convenience store, where I stop for gas. The station is shiny and all lit up, its blue-green signs glowing intensely in the dark like those roadside stores in Edward Hopper paintings, gleaming forlornly against the primeval dark of rural Anywhere, America. I'm trembling with a kind of giddy excitement as I pump the gas. Even here I can see changes — the man behind the counter in the station, whom I take to be the owner, is black, and so are most of his customers. Back then, whites owned everything. As I pull my car out of the station across from the courthouse, I see that the sheriff's car, just now parking beside the small police bungalow behind the courthouse, is driven by a black officer.

When we got to the jail forty years ago, I felt relieved. At least the terrifying drive was over. But my torment was only entering another phase. I'd be held there in solitary confinement, without charges, for eight days. I was kept on the second floor the entire time, separate from all other prisoners and personnel, seeing and talking to no one except the silent trusty who brought me food twice a day and took away my empty tray. Why was I so isolated from the rest of the prisoners? It was possible they didn't want people to know where I was, as they waited to find out if anyone was aware that I was "missing." Ever since the murders of Goodman, Schwerner, and Chaney, volunteers were under strict orders to check in with headquarters before traveling any distance, to record their destination and expected arrival time, so that if anything went wrong an alert could be sent out for an immediate search. I hadn't called, so no one knew I was in Hayneville's jail.

Four days into my incarceration, my father's lawyer called the DA in Jackson, Mississippi, to ask if he knew why I hadn't arrived home. The DA didn't know; they'd let me go. Then he tried the state attorney general's office in Montgomery, which was run at the time by Richmond Flowers, a racial moderate. His office made inquiries and learned I was being held in Hayneville, but they couldn't offer any help. They told Dad's lawyer that Lowndes County resisted all outside interference, even from Alabama state authorities. On my fifth day there, my father's lawyer managed to call the jail and was told (by the sheriff himself, slyly posing as a deputy) that indeed a young man named Greg Orr was there and was at that moment playing checkers with the sheriff.

Of course this was a lie. I had no knowledge of the call, no sense that anyone in the world knew where I was. Each day I spent in that cell was an eternity. I was unmoored from structures except food and the alternation of day and night. I didn't know when my spell in solitary would end. If someone had said to me, "You'll be kept alone in a small cell with no one to speak to for eight days," I could have tried to organize the ordeal in my mind — I could have, for starters, kept track of the days and known that each one passing brought me closer to the end. But there was no known end point, and so no measurement — it was wholly arbitrary and made me more aware of my own powerlessness. Already depressed and disoriented by the ten days in "jail" in Jackson, I was even more frightened in Hayneville. I had a better sense of how dangerous my situation was, and my imagination took over from there.

In the middle of my eighth day the sheriff came to my cell, unlocked it, and told me I was free to go. That was it: no apology, no formal charges, no anything. I was taken to my car, told to get out of town. I was set free as abruptly and mysteriously as I had been captured and incarcerated. I got in my car and drove. I drove and drove. I have one memory of stopping in some rest area in South Carolina in the middle of the night and trying to wash and shave, but my hands were shaking too much to control the razor. I slept whenever I couldn't drive any longer, pulling into parking lots and climbing into the back seat. By the time I reached New Jersey, I was hallucinating huge rats running across the highway in front of my headlights. And then I was home, back in the Hudson River valley town I'd left only a month or so earlier.

I spent July in my hometown, but in early August I took a job in New York with a small film company, synchronizing sound and picture. On my way home from work one August day, I bought a *New York Times* to read on the subway. When I looked at the front page, I saw a story about a murder that had just taken place in Hayneville. I turned to the inner page to finish the article and was stunned to see a photograph of one of the men who had kidnapped me on the highway. The news article related that he had shotgunned Jonathan Daniels, an Episcopal seminary student and civil rights volunteer, in broad daylight on the courthouse lawn, in front of half a dozen witnesses. From what I could tell, the victim and the others with him might have been the "outside agitators" whom I had been mistaken for. According to the newspaper, they, like me, had been arbitrarily arrested and held without charges for days in the jail and then suddenly released. But unlike me, they had no car. They spent several hours desperately trying to find someone to drive them to Montgomery, while the murderer, a friend of the sheriff's and a "special unpaid deputy," became more and more agitated. He found the released organizers near the courthouse and aimed his shotgun at a young black woman, Ruby Sales. The seminary student pushed her aside and stood in front just as the gun went off.

Though the sheriff's friend was charged with murder, the verdict, given by a local, all-white jury in that very courthouse, was not guilty on the basis of self-defense. The same courthouse later saw the trial of the killers of Viola Liuzzo, the Detroit housewife who, three months before my arrival in town, had participated in the Selma-to-Montgomery march. On the evening of March 25, she was killed by gunfire while ferrying marchers in her car on Route 80. Her slayers, quickly apprehended, were also found not guilty by another all-white Hayneville jury, even though eyewitness prosecution testimony was given by one of the four Klansmen (a paid FBI informer) present that night in the murder car.

My situation in Hayneville resembled the seminary student's: arbitrary arrest, jail time without arraignment or trial, and then sudden release. But I had a car, and timing mattered: the *New York Times* article stressed that the killer had been upset about the passage of the Voting Rights Act — as if part of his motivation was a kind of crazed act of political protest. When I was apprehended and jailed, the status quo in Hayneville seemed secure — if my presence there was a sign of change, it was the sort of change the town felt it could easily contain and control.

Two others died there: a murder in March, another in August. And in between, in late June, my own narrow escape, as I slipped through the same violent landscape. "Slipped through" makes me sound like a fish that found a hole in the net, but surely I was trapped in it, surely it was luck that pulled me from its entanglements and casually tossed me back into the sea.

And here I am again, forty-one years later, approaching the jail, that brick edifice in which all my emotions and memories of Hayneville are concentrated. Not the memory or idea of jail, but this dingy incarnation of incarceration — a building full of little cages where people are captive. I've been monologuing until now, spewing out nonstop the whole story that brought me here, but as we travel the last few blocks, I go silent with anticipation. Chris and Brian are also quiet but excited. Now that we're in the town itself, certain key nouns connect to real things. There is the courthouse pretty much as I described it. And here, down this little lane a half block past the courthouse, is the jail itself, that brick, L-shaped building I've been talking about. But how different it is from what I remembered and described! It's an empty husk. Boarded up — from the looks of it, abandoned a number of years ago. Deserted, dilapidated, the mortar rotted out between the grimy bricks. The only thing not in utter disrepair is a small exercise yard attached to the back, behind a chain-link fence topped with razor wire.

When I stop in the cinder parking lot and hop out of the car I feel like a kid who has arrived at a playground. I'm surprised by my responses. Here, at a place that was a locus of some of the most intense misery I've ever known, I'm feeling curiously happy. Chris and Brian have also climbed out. I can see they're glad, too, pleased to have found some real, palpable thing at the end of a tunnel of words burrowing from the distant past. Chris has a camera and begins to take pictures, though it's night now and there's no way of knowing if anything will register. The doors to the building are locked, but Brian, exploring the fence's gate, finds it's open, and we're able to enter the yard. We climb some rusty steps to a second-floor landing; from there I can point to the window that was across the corridor from my cell and that I peered out of after shinnying up my cell door's bars and craning my neck. That giddiness I felt when I first set my feet on the parking lot has been growing more intense. I'm laughing now, and when I'm not laughing, I'm unable to stop grinning. Earlier, in the car, telling the stories of my long-ago misadventures, the words had zipped directly from my brain's private memory to my tongue in a kind of nonstop narrative that mostly bypassed my emotions. Now my brain has stopped functioning almost entirely, and I'm taken over by this odd laughter that's bubbling up from some wordless source far down in my body — some deep, cellular place.

Brian and Chris poke around the weed-grown yard, looking for anything interesting, some rusty artifact to point to or pick up and ponder. I'm ordinarily a person who likes souvenirs — a shell from a beach, a rock from a memorable walk in the woods — but I have no wish to take anything physical from this place. Even a pebble would weigh me down, and the truth is I feel weightless right now, as if I'm a happy spirit moving through a scene of desolation.

My beginning was a rifle shot and someone innocent suddenly dead. My end might well have been something eerily similar: perhaps a pistol shot, my own death in this tiny town so far from my home — a beginning and end so close to each other as to render the life cryptic and tragic by way of its brevity. Only, Hayneville *wasn't* my end. It was a place where my life could have ended but didn't, and now, almost half a century later, I stand beside that closed-down, dilapidated jail, laughing. But laughing at what, at whom? Not at the confused and earnest kid I was all those years ago, the one who blundered through and escaped thanks to blind luck. What is this laughter that's fountaining up through me?

As we're leaving and I pause in the cindery parking lot with one hand on my car-door handle, taking a last look at the old jail, a single word comes to me: *joy*. It's joy I'm feeling — joy is at the heart of this peculiar laughter. Joy is my body's primal response to the enormity of the gift it has been given — a whole life! A whole life was there waiting for me the day I left this town. A life full of joys I couldn't imagine back then: a long, deeply satisfying marriage to a woman I love, two wonderful daughters, forty years of writing poems and teaching the craft of poetry. Laughing to think that the kid I was had gone south seeking the dark blessing of death in a noble cause, but had instead been given the far more complex blessing of life, given his whole existence and all the future struggle to sort it out and make it significant — to himself and, if he was lucky as a writer, to others also. Laughing at how my life went on past this town and blossomed into its possibilities, one of which (shining in the dark) was love.

CYNTHIA OZICK

Ghost Writers

FROM *PEN America*

WRITERS ARE HIDDEN BEINGS; you have never actually met one. If you should ever believe you are seeing a writer, or having an argument with a writer, or going to lunch with a writer, or listening to a talk by a writer, then you can be sure it is all a mistake.

Henry James long ago made this clear. In a story called "The Private Life," a writer burdened by one of those peculiar Jamesian names, one Clare Vawdrey, rhyming perhaps not accidentally with "tawdry," is visible everywhere in every conceivable social situation. He is always available for a conversation or a stroll, always accessible, always pleasantly anecdotal, never remote or preoccupied. He has a light-minded bourgeois affability: "He talks, he circulates," James's narrator informs us, "he's awfully popular, he flirts with you." Yet his work is the very opposite of his visible character; his work is steeped in unalloyed greatness. One evening, while Vawdrey is loitering outdoors on a terrace, exchanging banalities with a companion, the narrator steals into Vawdrey's room — only to discover him seated at his writing table in the dark, feverishly driving his pen. Since it is physically impossible for a material body to be in two places at the same time, the narrator concludes that the social Vawdrey is a phantom, while the writer working in the dark is the real Vawdrey. "One is the genius," he explains, "the other's the bourgeois, and it's only the bourgeois whom we personally know."

And lest we dismiss this as merely another one of James's ghost stories, or simply as a comical parable, we had better recall that celebrated Jamesian credo, a declaration of private panic mixed with prayerful intuition, which so many writers secretly keep tacked over their desks: "We work in the dark — we do what we can — we give what we have. Our doubt is our passion, and our passion is our task." The statement ends memorably, "The rest is the madness of art."

The madness of art? Maybe so. But more likely it is the logic of invisibility. James has it backwards. It's not the social personality who is the ghost; it is the writer with shoulders bent over paper, the hazy simulacrum whom we will never personally know, the wraith who hides out in the dark while her palpable effigy walks abroad, talking and circulating and sometimes even flirting. Sightings of these ghost writers are rare and few and unreliable, but there is extant a small accumulation of paranormal glimpses that can guide us, at least a little, to a proper taxonomy. For instance: this blustering, arrogant, self-assured, muscularly disdainful writer who belittles and brushes you aside, what is he, really? When illicitly spotted facing the lonely glow of his computer screen, he is no more than a helpless milquetoast paralyzed by the prospect of having to begin a new sentence. And that apologetically obsequious, self-effacing, breathlessly diffident and deprecatory creature turns out, when in the trance-like grip of nocturnal ardor, to be a fiery furnace of unopposable authority and galloping certainty.

Writers are what they genuinely are only when they are at work in the silent and instinctual cell of ghostly solitude and never when they are out industriously chatting on the terrace.

What is the true meaning of "the madness of art"? Imposture, impersonation, fakery, make-believe — but not the imposture, impersonation, fakery, or transporting make-believe of inventive storytelling. No; rather, art turns mad in pursuit of the false face of wishful distraction. The fraudulent writer is the visible one, the crowd-seeker, the crowd-speaker, the one who will go out to dinner with you with a motive in mind, or will stand and talk at you, or will discuss mutual writing habits with you, or will gossip with you about other novelists and their enviable good luck or their gratifying bad luck. The fraudulent writer is like Bellow's Henderson: I want, I want, I want.

If all this is so — and it is so — then how might a young would-be writer aspire to join the company of the passionately ghostly invisibles? Or, to put it another way: though all writers are now and again unavoidably compelled to become visible, how to maintain a coveted clandestine authentic invisibility? Don't all young would-be writers look to the precincts of visibility, where heated phalanxes of worn old writers march back and forth, fanning their brows with their favorable reviews? Isn't that how it's done, via models and mentors and the wise counsel of seasoned editors? "I beg you," says Rilke, addressing one such young writer, "I beg you to give all that up. You are looking outwards, and of all things that is what you must now not do. Nobody can advise you and help you, nobody. There is only one single means. Go inside yourself. Discover the motive that bids you to write; examine whether it sends its roots down to the deepest places in your heart, confess to yourself whether you would have to die if writing were denied you. This before all: ask yourself in the quietest hour of the night: must I write? Dig down into yourself for a deep answer. And if this should be in the affirmative, if you may meet this solemn question with a strong and simple 'I must,' then build your life according to this necessity."

Thus the poet Rilke, imploring the untried young to surrender all worldly reward, including the spur, and sometimes the romantic delusion, of fame, in order to succumb to a career in ectoplasm. Note that he speaks of "the quietest hour of the night," which is also the darkest, where we do what we can and give what we have. The madness of art — and again I willingly contradict Henry James — is not in the art, but in the madding and maddening crowd, where all manner of visibilities elbow one another, while the ghosts at their writing tables sit alone, and write, and write, and write, as if the necessary transparency of their souls depended upon it.

And here for a moment I will give up the ghost, materialize into visibility, and tell a long-ago autobiographical tale. Like tricky though hapless Jacob in the Bible, I first wooed Leah while desiring Rachel. The wooing of Leah took seven years, the wooing of Rachel another seven years. Leah was my first first novel. Far too ambitious, it was abandoned after 300,000 words. Rachel was my second first novel, even more afflicted by ambition, and was completed at more than 800 pages. Ah, the wages of frenzied gluttony! Fourteen years had flown away. And then I submitted the second first novel to an editor in a publishing house. Back came the manuscript in the mail, with one hundred pages all marked up in red pencil, and a note. The note said, "If you do everything my red pencil suggests, and of course there will be more in this vein, we will accept your novel for publication. But if you decline to follow my red pencil's indispensable advice, then we will decline to publish." Fourteen years gone! Outrun by the cohort of my generation, I lusted for print as Jacob had panted after Rachel. To the editor I wrote: "Seven years have I labored for those words, and yet another seven years; so I say unto you, Nay, not one jot or tittle will I alter or undo." To which the blessed editor replied, "O.K., we'll take it anyway." He died suddenly and young, at forty-two, and by then I had praised him a thousand times over. And a thousand times over he admonished me, "You think I'm a great editor because I never edited you."

And that is how one diffident, obsequious, self-effacing writer became ferociously invisible, at home among the ghosts.

The God of the Desert

FROM *Harper's Magazine*

ON THE FLIGHT FROM London I sit opposite a rumble seat where the stewardess places herself during takeoff. The stewardess is an Asian woman with a faraway look. I ask how often she makes this flight. Once or twice a month. Does she enjoy Israel? Not much. She stays in a hotel in Tel Aviv. She goes to the beach. She flies back. What about Jerusalem? She has not been there. What is in Jerusalem?

The illustrated guidebook shows a medieval map of the world. The map is round. The sun has a beard of fire. All the rivers of the world spew from the mouth of the moon. At the center of the world is Jerusalem.

Just inside the main doors of the Church of the Holy Sepulcher, tourists seem unsure how to respond to a rectangular slab of marble resting upon the floor. Lamps and censers and trinkets hang suspended above the stone. We watch as an old woman approaches. With some effort, she gets down on her knees. I flip through my book: *This marble represents the Stone of Unction where Jesus's body was anointed. This is not original; this stone dates from 1810.* The old woman bends forward to kiss the pale stone.

I have come to the Holy Land because the God of the Jews, the God of the Christians, the God of the Muslims — a common God — revealed Himself in the desert. My curiosity about an ecology that joins three desert religions dates from September 11, 2001, from prayers enunciated in the sky over America on that day.

Most occidental Christians are unmindful of the orientalism of Christianity. Over two millennia, the locus of Christianity shifted westward — to Antioch, to Rome, to Geneva, to the pale foreheads of Thomistic philosophers, to Renaissance paintings, to glitter among the frosts of English Christmas cards. Islam, too, in the middle centuries, swept into Europe with the Ottoman carpet, but then receded. Only to reflux. Amsterdam, Paris are becoming Islamic cities.

After centuries of Diaspora, after the calamity of the Holocaust in Europe, Jews turned once more toward the desert. Zionists did not romanticize the desolate landscape. Rather, they defined nationhood as an act of planting. The impulse of the kibbutz movement remains the boast of urban Israel: to make the desert bloom.

The theme of Jerusalem is division. Friday. Saturday. Sunday. The city has been conquered, destroyed, rebuilt, garrisoned, halved, quartered, martyred, and exalted — always the object of spiritual desire, always the prize, always the corrupt model of the eventual city of God. Recently, the government of Ariel Sharon constructed a wall that separates Jerusalem from the desert, Jerusalem from Bethlehem, Easter from Christmas.

Jerusalem was the spiritual center of the Judean wilderness. It was Jerusalem the desert thought about. It was Jerusalem the prophets addressed. Jerusalem was where Solomon built a temple for the Lord and where God promised to dwell with His people. Jerusalem was where Jesus died and was resurrected. It was from Jerusalem Muhammad ascended to heaven during his night journey.

My first impression of the city is my own loneliness: oil stains on the road, rubble from broken traffic barriers, exhaust from buses, the drift of cellophane bags. At the Damascus Gate an old woman sits on the pavement sorting grape leaves into piles — some kind of leaves. It is hot. Already it is hot. Late spring. It is early morning. There is a stench of uncollected garbage, and the cats, light and limp as empty purses, slink along the blackened stone walls. Shopkeepers are unrolling their shops.

I turn into the courtyard of the Church of the Holy Sepulcher, the site of Christ's burial and resurrection. A few paces away, within the church, is Golgotha, where Jesus was crucified. Golgotha, the Place of the Skull, is also, according to Jerusalem tradition, the grave of Adam. Jerusalem is as condensed, as self-referential, as Rubik's Cube.

I wait in line to enter the Sepulcher, a freestanding chapel in the rotunda of the basilica. A mountain was chipped away from the burial cave, leaving the cave. Later the cave was destroyed. What remains is the interior of the cave, which is nothing. The line advances slowly until, after two thousand years, it is my turn. I must lower my shoulders and bend my head; I must almost crawl to pass under the low opening.

I am inside the idea of the tomb of Christ.

I return many times to the Church of the Holy Sepulcher and form in my mind an accommodation to its clamorous hush, to the musk of male asceticism — indeed, I form a love for it that was not my first feeling, though my first impression remains my last: emptiness.

I wait for Haim Berger in the lobby of a hotel in Ein Bokek, one among an oasis of resorts near the Dead Sea. The lobby is a desert of sand-colored marble. The lobby's temperature is oppressively beige — it would be impossible to cool this useless atrium. My cell phone rings. It is Maya, the director of the agency attached to my hotel in Jerusalem. Haim will be late one hour. Look for him at ten o'clock.

I watch a parade of elderly men and women crossing the lobby in bathing suits to catch a shuttle to the sulfur baths. They are so unselfconscious about their bodies, they seem to walk in paradise.

I believe I am waiting for someone in shorts and boots and aviator glasses, driving a Jeep. A Volkswagen pulls up and parks haphazardly. A man bolts from the car. He is willowy of figure, dressed all in white; sandals; dark curly hair. He disappears into the hotel; reemerges. We wait side by side.

I cannot go to the desert alone. I am unfit for it. The desert requires a Jeep. It requires a hat and sunglasses and plastic liters of warm water it is no pleasure to drink. It requires a guide. It requires a cell phone.

Just now the man dressed in white begins patting his pockets, searching for his chiming cell. "*Keyn . . . Shalom, Maya,*" I hear him say. Then, turning toward me, "Ah."

Haim Berger is full of apology. He has taken his wife to an emergency room. Yes, everything is all right. Just a precaution. There is an Evian bottle for me in the car. We will switch to the Jeep later.

Within ten minutes, I am standing with Haim on the side of a highway. We look out over a plain, over what once was Sodom and Gomorrah. Haim asks if I know the story. Of course I know the story. Which nevertheless does not stop him from telling it. We might be standing near where Abraham stood when "Abraham saw dense smoke over the land, rising like fumes from a furnace."

I ask Haim if he is religious. He is not.

All three desert religions claim Abraham as father. A recurrent question in my mind concerns the desert: Did Abraham happen on God, or did God happen on Abraham? The same question: Which is the desert, or whom? I came upon a passage in 2 Maccabees. The passage pertains to the holiness of Jerusalem: *The Lord, however, had not chosen the people for the sake of the Place, but the Place for the sake of the people.* So God happened on Abraham. Abraham is the desert.

An old man sits at the door of his tent in the heat of the day.

Between that sentence and this — within the drum of the hare's heart, within the dilation of the lizard's eye, God enters His creation. The old man, who is Abraham, sits at the door of his tent and becomes aware of three strangers standing nearby. They arrive without the preamble of distance. The nominative grammar of Genesis surpasses itself to reveal that one of these travelers is God, or perhaps all three are God, like a song in three octaves. Abraham invites the Three to rest and to refresh themselves. In return, God promises that in a year's time Abraham's wife, who is long past childbearing, will hold in her arms a son.

Abraham's wife, Sarah, in the recesses of the tent, snorts upon hearing the prognostication; says, not quite to herself: *Oh, sure!*

God immediately turns to Abraham: *Why does Sarah laugh? Is anything too marvelous for God?*

Sarah says: *I am not laughing.*

God says: *Yes you are.*

In 1947 a Bedouin goatherd lost a goat and climbed the side of a mountain to look for it. The boy entered a cave — today the cave is known worldwide among archaeologists as Cave Number One. What the boy found in the cave — probably stumbled upon in the dark — were broken clay jars that contained five sheepskin scrolls. Four of the scrolls were written in Hebrew, one in Aramaic. More scrolls were subsequently found by other Bedouin and by scholars in caves nearby. The discovered scrolls, including a complete copy of the book of Isaiah, are the oldest known manuscript copies of books of the Bible.

The scrolls date to the second century B.C. Scholars believe the Jewish sect of Essenes, of the proto-monastic community of Qumran, hid the texts we now know as the Dead Sea Scrolls.

No one remembers whether the goatherd found his goat.

Haim is not religious, but he offers to tell me a curious story: Last year he took a group of students into a mountainous part of the desert. He had been there many times. He had previously discovered markings on rocks that seemed to indicate religious observance; he believes the markings are ancient.

On the particular day he describes — it was the winter solstice — as the group approached a mountain, they saw what appeared to be a semicircle of flame emanating from the rock face, rather like the flame from a hoop in the circus. Haim knew it was a trick of the light, or perhaps gases escaping from a fissure in the rock. He walked before the mountain in an arc to observe the phenomenon from every angle. He repeats: He was not alone. They all saw it. He has photographs. He will show me the photographs.

Haim's love for the desert dates from his military service. His Jeep broke down. He cursed the engine. He slammed the hood. He took a memorable regard of the distance. Since that day, he has become intimate with the distance; he has come to see the desert as a comprehensible ecosystem that can be protective of humans.

Haim has tied a white kerchief over his hair.

Haim says: Bedouin know a lot. Bedouin have lived in the desert thousands of years. Haim says: If you are ever stranded in the desert — *Are you listening to me? This may save your life!* — in the early morning, you must look to see in which direction the birds are flying. They will lead you to water.

Haim stops to speak with admiration of a bush with dry, gray-green leaves. "These leaves are edible." (Now I must sample them.) "They are salty, like potato chips." (They are salty.)

Of another bush: "These have water. If you crush them, you will get water. These could save your life." He crushes a fistful of leaves and tears spill from his hand.

*

The child of Abraham and Sarah is named Isaac, which means "he laughs." Sarah proclaims an earthy magnificat: *God has made laughter for me, and all who hear of it will laugh for me.* From the loins of these two deserts — Abraham, Sarah — God yanks a wet, an iridescent caul — a people as numerous as the stars. From the line of Sarah, royal David. From King David's line will come Jesus.

One's sense of elision begins with the map. Many tourist maps include the perimeter of the city at the time of Herod's Temple, the time of Christ. *This once was. Built over the site. All that remains. This site resembles. This is not the room of the Last Supper; this is a Crusader structure built over the room, later converted to a mosque — note the mihrab, the niche in the wall.*

The empty room is white, not white, golden. *Is the air really golden?* As a child in Omaha, my friend Ahuva was ravished by the thought — told to her by an old man in a black hat — that the light of Jerusalem is golden. An ultra-Orthodox boy wanders into the room (a few paces from this room is the tomb of King David, the anteroom to which is dense with the smell of men at prayer; upstairs is a minaret). The boy is eating something, some kind of bun. He appears transfixed by a small group of evangelical Christian pilgrims who have begun to sing a song, what in America we would call an old song.

I am kneeling in the early morning at St. Anne's, a Romanesque church built in the twelfth century. The original church was damaged by the Persians; restored in the time of Charlemagne; destroyed, probably by the caliph Hakim, in 1010. The present church was built by the Crusaders. Sultan Salah-ed-Din captured the city in 1192 and converted the church to a madrasa. The Ottoman Turks neglected the structure; it fell to ruin. The Turks offered the church to France. The French order of White Fathers now administers St. Anne's. Desert sun pours through a window over the altar.

Not only is the light golden, Ahuva, but I must mention a specific grace. Each afternoon around four o'clock, without fail, the most delightful breeze comes upon Jerusalem, I suppose from the Mediterranean, miles away. It begins at the tops of the tallest trees, the date-palm trees; shakes them like feather dusters; rides under the bellies of the lazy red hawks; snaps the flags on the consulate roofs; lifts the curtains of the tall windows of my room at the hotel — sheer curtains embroidered with an arabesque design — lifts

them until they are suspended perpendicularly in midair like the veil of a
bride tormented by a playful page, who then lets them fall. And then lifts.
And then again.

I walk around the wall of the city to the Mount of Olives, to a
Christian sensibility the most evocative remnant of Jerusalem, for it
matches — even including the garbage — one's imagination of
Christ's regard for the city he approached from Bethany, which
was from the desert. The desert begins immediately to the east of
Jerusalem.

All the empty spaces of the holy city — all courts, tabernacles,
tombs, and reliquaries — are resemblances and references to the
emptiness of the desert. All the silences of women and men who
proclaim the desert God are references and resemblances to this
— to the holy city, to the hope of a holy city. Jerusalem is the Bride
of the Desert.

The desert prowls like a lion. I am fatigued from the heat, and I
look about for some shade and a bottle of water. Having procured
both at an outdoor stand (from a young man whose father kneels
in prayer), I grow curious about an entrance I can see from the
courtyard where I rest. Perhaps it is a chapel. An old man is sitting
on the steps near the entrance. I approach him. What is this place?

The tomb of Mary, he answers.

Inside the door I perceive there are steps from wall to wall, leading downward. I can discern only the flickering of red lamps below,
as if at the bottom of a well. When I reach the level of the tomb, an
Orthodox priest throws a switch and the tomb is illuminated. It is a
shelf of rock. The legend of the Dormition of Mary and the Catholic doctrine of the Assumption — neither of which I understand
very well — lead me to wonder if this is a spurious site. I decide I
will accept all sites in this junk room of faith as true sites. I kneel.

A couple of years ago the bone box of James, the brother of Jesus, was raised from the shady world of the antiquities market. I believe the box has been discredited (dust not of the proper age
within the incising of the letters). Authenticity is not my point. The
stone box is my point. For it creates emptiness. Jerusalem is just
such a box — within its anachronistic walls — a city of ossuaries,
buried, reburied, hallowed, smashed, reconstructed, then called
spurious or probable in guidebooks.

I have brought five guidebooks to Jerusalem, my Pentateuch:

The Archaeological. The Historical. The Illustrated. The Practical. The Self-Absorbed. Each afternoon, when I return to my hotel, I convene a colloquy among them — the chatter of guidebooks. I read one and then another.

The closed nature of the city frustrates my interest. My mind is oppressed by the inaccessibility of the hive of empty chambers, empty churches, empty tombs. The city that exists is superimposed in some meaty way over the bone city I long to enter. The streets are choked and impassible with life; the air stifling, the merchandise appalling. I feel feverish, but I think it is only the heat. I make the rounds of all the gates to the Temple Mount until at last I find the entrance that Israeli security will let me through — the passageway for infidels.

The sun is blazing on the courtyard. Even the faithful have gone away. Elsewhere the city is vertiginously sunken — resentments and miracles parfaited. Here there is a horizontal prospect.

The Al-Aqsa Mosque and the Dome of the Rock have been closed to non-Muslims since my last visit. I stand outside the shrine and try to reconstruct the interior from memory — the pillars, tiles, meadows of carpet. The vast Muslim space is what I remember. Islamic architecture attempts the sublime feat of emptiness. It is the sense of emptiness enclosed that is marvelous. The dome is the sky that is made. The sky is nothing — the real sky — and beggars have more of it than others.

Muslims own Jerusalem sky. This gold-leafed dome identifies Jerusalem on any postcard. The conspicuous jewel. Jews own the ground. The enshrined rock was likely the foundation for the Holy of Holies of Solomon's Temple, the room that enclosed the Ark of the Covenant. The rock is also the traditional site of the near-sacrifice of Isaac by Abraham. God commanded Moses to commission Bezalel the artisan to make the Ark. The book of Exodus describes two golden cherubim whose wings were to form above the Ark a Seat of Mercy — a space reserved for the presence of the Lord. The architecture for the presence of God has been conceptualized ever after as emptiness.

The paradox of monotheism is that the desert God, refuting all other gods, demands acknowledgment within emptiness. The paradox of monotheism is that there is no paradox — only unfathomable singularity.

May I explain to you some features of the shrine?

A man has approached as I stand gazing toward the dome. He looks to be in his sixties; he is neatly dressed in a worn suit. The formality of syntax extends to his demeanor. Obviously he is one of the hundreds of men, conversant in three faiths, who haunt the shrines of Jerusalem, hoping to earn something as informal guides.

No thank you.

This is the Dome of the Rock, he continues.

No thank you.

Why are you so afraid to speak to a guide? (The perfected, implicating question.)

I am not afraid. I don't have much time.

He lowers his eyes. *Perhaps another time.* He withdraws.

My diffidence is purely reflexive. One cannot pause for a moment on one's path through any of the crowded streets or souks without a young man — the son, the nephew, the son-in-law of some shopkeeper — asking, often with the courtliness of a prince, often with the stridency of a suitor: *May I show you my shop?*

Emptiness clings to these young men as well — the mermen of green-lit grottoes piled with cheap treasure — men with nothing to do but fiddle with their cell phones or yawn in their unconscious beauty and only occasionally swim up to someone caught in the unending tide of humanity that passes before them.

May I show you my shop?

No thank you.

Behind the wall of my hotel in East Jerusalem are a gasoline station and a small mosque. The tower of the mosque — it is barely a tower — is outfitted with tubes of green neon. Five times in twenty-four hours the tubes of neon flicker and sizzle; the muezzin begins his cry. Our crier has the voice of an old man, a voice that gnaws on its beard. I ask everyone I meet if the voice is recorded or live. Some say recorded and some say real.

I believe God is great. I believe God is greatest.

The God of the Jews penetrated time. The Christian and the Muslim celebrated that fact ever after with noise. In the medieval town, Christian bells sounded the hours. Bells called the dawn and the noon and the coming night.

In the secular West, church bells have been stilled by discretion and by or-

dinance. In my neighborhood of San Francisco the announcement of dawn comes from the groaning belly of a garbage truck.

No one at the hotel seems to pay the voice any mind. The waiters serve. Cocktails are shaken and poured. People in the courtyard and in the restaurant continue their conversations. The proprietress of the place turns a page of the book she is reading.

At four o'clock in the morning, the swimming pool is black. The hotel is asleep and dreaming. The neon ignites. The old man picks up his microphone to rend our dream asunder.

It is better to pray than to sleep.

The voice is not hectoring; it is simply oblivious. It is not like one's father, up early and dressing in the dark; it is like a selfish old man who can't sleep. The voice takes its permission from the desert — from the distance — but it is the modern city it wakes with enforced intimacy.

The old man's chant follows a tune; it is always the same tune, like a path worn through a carpet. And each day the old man becomes confused by the ornamental line — his voice is not agile enough to assay it. His voice turns ruminative, then puzzled. Finally, a nasal moan:

Muhammad is the prophet of Allah.

River Jordan water runs between my toes — a breathtakingly comfortable sensation. I have taken a bus tour of Galilee; the bus has stopped at the Yardenit baptism site, which resembles a state picnic grounds. I watch a procession of Protestant pilgrims in rented white smocks descend some steps into the comfortable brown water.

Protestantism is the least oriental of the desert faiths. Protestants own little real estate within the walls of Jerusalem. They own nothing of ancient squabbles between the Holy Roman Empire, the Byzantine Empire, the Ottoman Empire. Protestants are free to memorialize sacred events without any compulsion to stand guard over mythic ground.

For example, the traditionally venerated site of Christ's baptism is near Jericho. After the Six Day War in 1967, that location was declared off-limits to tourists. And so this place — Yardenit — of no historical or religious significance was developed as a place to which Christians might go for baptism ceremonies. The faith of evangelical pilgrims at Yardenit overrides the commercialism that attaches to the enterprise (*Your Baptism videotaped by a professional*).

One bank or the other, it is the same river, and pilgrims at Yardenit step confidently into the Bible.

Distance enters Abraham's seed with God's intimacy. A birth precedes the birth of Isaac. There is domestic strife of God's manufacture. For God also arranges that Sarah's Egyptian servant, Hagar, will bear Abraham a son. That son is Ishmael; the name means "he listens." Sarah soon demands that Abraham send Hagar and her son away. *I cannot abide that woman. She mocks me.*

So Hagar and Ishmael are cast into the desert of Beersheba as Abraham and Sarah and the camels and tents and servants and flocks flow slowly away from them like a receding lake of dust.

Abruptly Haim tells me to stop. Listen! The desert has a silence like no other, he says. Do you hear a ringing in your ear? It is the bell of existence.

Not far from here, in Gaza, missiles are pitched through a blue sky. People who will be identified in news reports this evening as terrorists will shortly be killed, or the innocent will be killed, people who even now are stirring pots with favored spoons or folding the last page of the morning paper to line the bird's cage.

I hear. What do I hear? I hear a truck shifting gears on a highway, miles away.

God hears the cry of Ishmael. God finds Hagar in the desert and rescues her dying child by tapping a spring of water — a green silk scarf pulled from a snake hole. God promises Hagar that Ishmael, too, will be a nation. From Ishmael's line will come the Arab tribes, and from the Arab tribes the prophet Muhammad.

Mahdi, my Palestinian guide, pulls off the main road so I can see the Monastery of the Temptation in the distance. (Mahdi has been telling me about the years he lived in Riverside, California.) The monastery was built on the mountain where Christ was tempted by Satan to consider the Kingdoms of the World. And here are we, tourists from the Kingdoms of the World, two thousand years later, regarding the mountain.

A figure approaches from the distance, surrounded by a nimbus of moisture. The figure is a Bedouin man on foot. A young man but not a boy, as I first thought. He is very handsome, very thin, very small, very dusty, utterly humorless. He extends, with his two hands, a skein of perhaps twenty-five bead necklaces. He speaks English — a few words like beads. *Camel,* he says. *For your wife, your girlfriend.*

This is camel, he says again, fingering some elongated beads. I ask him who made the necklaces. His mother.

There is no sentimentality to this encounter. Sentimentality is an expenditure of moisture. The Bedouin's beseeching eyes are dry; they are the practice of centuries. He sits down a short distance away from us while we contemplate the monastery. He looks into the distance, and as he does so, he becomes the desert.

Moses, Jesus, Muhammad — each ran afoul of cities: Moses of the court of Egypt, Jesus of Jerusalem, Muhammad of Mecca. The desert hid them, came to represent a period of trial before they emerged as vessels of revelation. Did they, any of them, experience the desert as habitable — I mean in the manner of Haim, in the manner of the Bedouin?

After he fled Egypt, Moses took a wife; he took the nomadic life of his wife's people as a disguise. Moses led his father-in-law's flock across the desert to Mount Horeb, where God waited for him.

As a boy, Muhammad crossed the desert in Meccan caravans with his uncle, Abu Talib. Muhammad acquired the language of the Bedouin and Bedouin ways. As a middle-aged man, Muhammad was accustomed to retire with his family to a cave in the desert to meditate. During one such retreat Muhammad was addressed by God.

The Jews became a people by the will of God, for He drove them through the desert for forty years. God fed the people Israel with manna. Ravens fed Elijah during his forty days in the desert. After his ordeal of forty days, Jesus accepted the ministrations of angels. Such supernatural nourishments of the body suggest a reliance on God rather than an embrace of the desert.

In *The Desert Fathers,* Helen Waddell writes that the early Christian monks of the desert gave a single intellectual concept to Europe — eternity. The desert monks saw the life of the body as "most brief and poor." But the life of the spirit lies beyond the light of day. The light of day conceals "a starlit darkness into which a man steps and becomes suddenly aware of a whole universe, except that part of it which is beneath his feet."

There are people in every age who come early or late to a sense of the futility of the world. Some people, such as the monks of the desert, flee the entanglements of the world to rush toward eternity. But even for those who remain in the world, the approach of eternity is implacable. *The glacier knocks in the cupboard, / The desert sighs in the bed* was W. H. Auden's mock-prophetic forecast. He meant the desert is incipient in the human condition. Time melts away from us. Even in luxuriant weather, even in luxuriant wealth, even in luxuriant youth, we know our bodies will fail, our buildings will fall to ruin.

If the desert beckons the solitary, it also, inevitably, gives birth to the tribe. The ecology of the desert requires that humans form communities for mutual protection from extreme weathers, from bandits, from rival chieftains. Warfare among Arab tribes impinged often upon the life of the prophet Muhammad. In response to the tyranny of kinship, Muhammad preached a spiritual brotherhood — discipleship under Allah — that was as binding as blood, as expansive as sky.

The Christian monastic movement in the Judean wilderness reached its peak in the sixth century, by which time there were so many monks, so many monasteries in the desert (as many as eight hundred monks in some of the larger communities), it became a commonplace of monastic chronicles, a monkish conceit, to describe the desert as a city.

I am driving with Mahdi through Bethlehem, then several Bedouin settlements to the east, leading into the desert. The road narrows, climbs, eventually runs out at the gates of Mar Saba, a Greek Orthodox monastery.

A monk opens the gate. Mahdi asks in Arabic if we may see the monastery. The monk asks where we are from. The monk then takes up a metal bar, which he clangs within a cast-iron triangle.

Waiting in the courtyard below is another monk. He greets us in English. Obviously four bangs, or however many, on the contraption upstairs summons English. The monk's accent is American. He, too, asks where I am from. He is from St. Louis.

We are first shown the main church. The church is dark, complexly vaulted, vividly painted. We are told something of the life of

St. Saba, or Sabas, the founder of the monastery. Saba died in 532. "He is here," the monk then says, ushering us to a glass case in a dark alcove, where the saint lies in repose. "The remains are uncorrupted."

The monk carries a pocket flashlight that he shines on the corpse of the saint. The thin beam of light travels up and down the body; the movement of the light suggests sanctification by censing. The figure is small, leathern, clothed in vestments. This showing takes place slowly, silently, as someone would show you something of great importance in a dream.

We ask about another case, the one filled with skulls. They are the skulls of monks killed by Persians in 614. One has the impression the young monk considers himself to be brother to these skulls, that they remain a part of the community of Mar Saba, though no longer in the flesh. One has the impression grievance endures.

The monk next leads us to the visitors' parlor. No women are allowed in the monastery. In this room the masculine sensibility of the place has unconsciously re-created a mother's kitchen. The monk disappears into a galley; he returns with a repast that might have been dreamed up by ravens: tall glasses of lemonade, small glasses of ouzo, a plate of chocolates. The lemonade is very cool, and we ask how this can be without electricity. Butane, the monk answers. For cooking and refrigeration.

The monk's patience is for the time when we will leave. Until this: "What has brought you to the Holy Land?"

I have come to write about the desert religions, I reply. I am interested in the fact that three great monotheistic religions were experienced within this ecology.

"Desert religions, desert religions," the monk repeats.

Then he says: "You must be very careful when you use such an expression. It seems to equate these religions."

I do mean to imply a common link through the desert.

"Islam is a perversion," he says.

A few minutes later, the monk once more escorts us through the courtyard and to the stone steps. He shakes my hand and says what I remember as conciliatory, though it may not have been: "The desert creates warriors."

*

Haim makes his living conducting tours of the desert. He is, as
well, a student and an instructor at Ben-Gurion University of the
Negev, where we stop briefly to exchange vehicles.

Haim invites me into his house; he must get some things. Haim's
wife is also a graduate student at the university. There are some
pleasant drawings of dancers on the walls. The curtains are closed
against the desert. Mrs. Berger returns while I am waiting. She is attractive, blond, pregnant, calm. "You turned on the air conditioning," she says to Haim — not accusatorily but as a statement of (I
assume unusual) fact. "I have to gather some things," he replies. I
ask if I may see the photograph of the mountain.

"Ah, Haim's mountain." Mrs. Berger conveys affection, indul-
gence.

Haim goes to his computer, pulls up the images: the mountain
from a distance. Closer. Closer. The suggestion of a rectangular
shape, I hesitate to say the shape of tablets; nevertheless that is how
it appears. It is difficult to ascertain the scale. Yes, I can see —
along the top and side of the rectangular shape there are what appear to be flames.

Haim carries several filled grocery bags out to the Jeep. We leave
Mrs. Berger standing in the dark kitchen. *Goodbye.*

Stephen Pfann looks to be in his forties. His hair is white; he wears
a beard. He has large, pale eyes of the sort one sees in Victorian
photographs. It is because of his resemblance, in my imagination,
to a Victorian photograph that I attribute to him the broad spirit of
Victorian inquiry. Stephen's discourse has a dense thread count,
weaving archaeology, geology, history, theology, botany, biology.
Stephen's teenage children seem adept at reining him in when he
is kiting too high. Stephen and his wife, Claire, administer the University of the Holy Land, a postgraduate biblical institute in Jerusalem. Stephen says he would be willing to take me to Qumran. He
suggests an early-morning expedition and promises, as well, an
Essene liturgy at sunrise.

My imagination runs away: prayers within a cave. Clay lamps,
shadows. Some esotericism in the liturgy and a sun like the sound
of a gong.

On the appointed morning, Stephen picks me up at my hotel.
As it is already bone-light, I presume we have missed the sunrise.
But in fact we are reciting psalms on a level plain beneath Cave

Number One as the sun comes up over Arabia, over Jordan, over the Dead Sea. The light is diffuse, though golden enough. The texts remark the immensity of creation. (I am thinking about a movie I saw. An old man — Omar Sharif — whispers as he dies: "I join the immensity.")

We have been joined here by several others, two Pfann children, a forensic pathologist connected with the University of the Holy Land.

Stephen mentions "the umbilicus," by which term he means the concentration of God's intention on this landscape. Underfoot is a large anthill — a megalopolis — then a satellite colony, then another, then another, the pattern extending across the desert floor.

The old woman leans forward to kiss the pale stone.

We begin our climb to Cave Number One. The air has warmed. Pfann, in his stride, points at minute flora; his daughter nods and photographs them. Pfann and his children are as nimble as goats. "Is everyone all right?" Pfann calls backward.

I am not all right. I am relegated at times to using both hands and feet. The good-natured pathologist climbing ahead of me is watchful and discreet with his helping hand, all the while recounting the religious conversion that brought him to the Holy Land.

The cave is not cool, by the way. A smell of bat dung. I hear Stephen saying something about the rapidity of the transfer of heat molecules from one substance to another. (The dryness of the cave preserved the scrolls.) I am perspiring. I am making toe marks in the dust.

Hundreds of thousands of years ago, water receded from this cave. Two thousand years ago, an Essene — probably an Essene — filled a basket with grating clay jars and climbed to this cave to hide the holy scrolls against some intimation of destruction. Sixty years ago, a Bedouin goatherd, muttering goat curses — an old man now if he lives — came upon five clay vats spilling revelation.

The community of Qumran was destroyed by Roman legions in 68 A.D.

The desert resembles dogma: it is dry, it is immovable. Truth does not change. Is there something in the revelation of God that retains — because it has passed through — properties of desert or maleness or Semitic tongue? Does the desert, in short, make warriors? That is the question I bring to the desert from the twenty-first century.

The Semitic God is God who enters history. Humans examine every event that pertains to us for meaning. The motive of God who has penetrated time tempts us to imperfect conjecture. When armies are victorious, when armies are trodden in the dust, when crops fail, when volcanoes erupt, when seas drink multitudes, it must mean God intends it so. What did we do to deserve this? King David psalmed for the vanquishing of his enemies, did he not? There is something in the leveling jealousy of the desert God that summons a possessive response in us. *We are His people* becomes *He is our God.* The blasphemy that attaches to monotheism is the blasphemy of certainty. If God is on our side, we must be right. We are right because we believe in God. We must defend God against the godless. Certitude clears a way for violence. And so the monk's dictum — the desert creates warriors — can represent centuries of holy war and sordid prayer and an umbilicus that whips like a whirlwind.

In Afghanistan's central plateau, there were two mountain-high Buddhas. For centuries, caravans traveling the Silk Route would mark them from miles away. The Bamiyan Buddhas were destroyed by the Taliban in 2001; their faces are now anvils, erasures. An inscription from the Koran was painted beside the alcove of the larger Buddha: *The just replaces the unjust.* Just so do men destroy what belief has built, and they do it in the name of God, the God who revealed Himself in the desert, the desert that cherishes no monuments, wants none. *There is no God but God.*

On July 16, 1945, the first nuclear weapon was tested in the American desert. The ape in our hearts stood still. Wow.

The desert creates warriors, by which construction St. Sabas meant (for it was his construction) that the monk discerns his true nature in the desert — his true nature in relation to God — and the discernment entails learning to confront and to overcome the temptations of human nature. In that sense a warrior.

The desert creates lovers. St. Sabas desired the taste of an apple. The craving was sweeter to him than the thought of God. From that moment Sabas forswore apples. The desire for apples was the taste of God.

*

Desert is the fossil of water. (Haim has been at great pains to point this out — striations in mesas and the caverns water has bored through mountains of salt, and salt is itself a memory of water.) Is dogma a fossil of the living God — the shell of God's passage — but God is otherwise or opposite? Perhaps it is that the Semitic tongues are themselves deserts — dry records of some ancient fluency, of something feminine that has withdrawn. The Semitic tongues descend from Shem, son of Noah, survivor of the Flood. Abraham was of Shem's line. Perhaps the Semitic tongues, inflected in the throat, recall water, are themselves oases.

I have often heard it observed by critics of the desert religions that monotheism would have encouraged in humankind a different relationship to nature if the Abrahamic God had revealed Himself from within a cloak of green. The desert encourages a sense of rebuff and contest with the natural world. Jesus cursed the recalcitrant fig tree right down to firewood.

Consider Las Vegas and Dubai, two modern desert cities constructed upon an intention to distract. Las Vegas casinos banish clocks, admit neither night nor day. Dubai has wagered its financial future on a time zone that lies conveniently between the markets of Asia and Europe. Both cities defy the desert through exertions of fantasy; both cities pour cooled air. Fountains of electric light tumble and splash in reassuring displays of human will. For thousands of years humans have flaunted their will over nature. What we call global warming now leaves many in the world anticipating a nostalgia for ice, for zero. The ecology least threatened by the work of man is desert, the flowing desert.

The desert's uninhabitability convinces Jew and Christian and Muslim that we are meant for another place. Within the deserts of the Bible and the Koran, descriptions of Eden, descriptions of the Promised Land, resemble oases. For Jews, Eden was pre-desert. For Christians and Muslims, paradise — a reconciliation with God — is post-desert.

In the Koran, paradise is likened to *gardens underneath which rivers flow.* For Christians, paradise is an urban idea, a communion, a city of God. The commendation of the body in the ancient rite of Christian burial prays that angels may come to lead the soul of the departed to the gates of the holy city Jerusalem.

I purchase for five shekels a postcard scene of Jerusalem in the snow — black and white — the sky is dark but Jerusalem shines swan, a royal city.

I follow Haim a quarter of a mile to a grove of untrimmed date palms. I have seen their like only in ancient mosaics, the muted colors, the golden dust. In their undressed exuberance these palms resemble fountains. But they are dry; they prick and rattle as we thread our way among them. We could just as easily have walked around, couldn't we? I suspect Haim of concocting an oasis experience. But his glance is upward, into the branches of some taller trees. Haim is hoping for what he calls a lucky day. If it is Haim's lucky day, we will see a leopard. Recently, a leopard entered the town of Beersheba. Haim suspects the creature may be lurking here.

But it is not Haim's lucky day. We continue up an incline, alongside a muddy riverbed. Winged insects bedevil my ears. We walk around a screen of acacia trees, at which Haim steps aside to reveal: a waterfall, a crater filled with green water! There are several Israeli teenagers swimming, screaming with delight as they splash one another. A tall African youth stands poised at the edge of the pool.

This Ethiopian Jew (we later learn) has come to this desert from another. He has come because the Abrahamic faith traveled like particles of desert over mountains and seas, blew under the gates of ancient cities, and caught in the leaves of books. Laughter, as spontaneous as that of his ancestress Sarah, echoes through the canyon as the boy plunges into the stone bowl of water. Displaced water leaps like a javelin.

John the Baptist wrapped himself in camel hide. He wandered the desert and ate the desert — honey and locusts and Haim's gray leaves. John preached hellfire and performed dunking ceremonies in the river Jordan. People came from far and wide to be addressed by the interesting wild man as "Brood of Vipers." When watery Jesus approached flaming John and asked for baptism, John recognized Jesus as greater than he. It was as though the desert bowed to the sea. But in fact their meeting was an inversion of elements. John said: I baptize only with water. The one who comes after me will baptize with Spirit and fire.

*

Desert is, literally, emptiness — its synonyms desolation, wasteland. To travel to the desert "in order to see it," in order to experience it, is paradoxical. The desert remains an absence: the desert is this place I stand multiplied by infinite numbers — not this place particularly. So I come away each night convinced I have been to the holy desert (and have been humiliated by it) and that I have not been to the desert at all.

Just beyond the ravine is a kibbutz, a banana plantation, a university, a nuclear power plant. But, you see, I wouldn't know that. The lonely paths Haim knows are not roads. They are scrapings of the earth. Perhaps they are tracks that Abraham knew, or Jesus. Some boulders have been removed and laid aside. From the air-conditioned van or from the tossing Jeep or through binoculars, I see the desert in every direction. The colors of the desert are white, fawn, tawny gold, rust, rust red, blue. When the ignition is turned off and the Jeep rolls to a stop, I pull the cord that replaces the door handle; the furnace opens; my foot finds the desert floor. But the desert is distance. Nothing touches me.

Many nights, I return to my hotel with the desert on my shoes. There is a burnt, mineral scent in my clothing. The scent is difficult to wash out in the bathroom basin, as is the stain of the desert, an umber stain.

Standing, scrubbing my T-shirt, is the closest I get to the desert. The water turns yellow.

I tell myself I am not looking for God. I am looking for an elision that is nevertheless a contour. The last great emptiness in Jerusalem is the first. What remains to be venerated is the Western Wall, the ancient restraining wall of the destroyed Second Temple.

After the Six Day War, the Israeli government bulldozed an Arab neighborhood to create Western Wall Plaza, an emptiness to facilitate devotion within emptiness — a desert that is also a well.

I stand at the edge of the plaza with Magen Broshi, a distinguished archaeologist. Magen is a man made entirely of Jerusalem. You can't tell him anything. Last night at dinner in the hotel garden, I tried out a few assertions I thought dazzling, only to be met with Magen's peremptory *Of course.*

Piety, ache, jubilation, many, many classes of ardor pass us by. Magen says he is not a believer. I tell Magen about my recent cancer. If I asked him, would he pray for me here, even though he does not believe? *Of course.*

Western Wall Plaza levels sorrow, ecstasy, cancer, belief. Here emptiness rises to proclaim its unlikeness to God, who allows for no comparison. This is His incomparable Temple. It does not resemble. It is all that remains.

No writing! You cannot write here. A woman standing nearby has noticed I carry a notebook. I have a pen in my hand. The woman means on the Sabbath, I think. Or can one never write here? It is the Sabbath.

"He is not writing anything," Magen mutters irritably, waving the woman away.

JANNA MALAMUD SMITH

Shipwrecked

FROM *The American Scholar*

> This being within about a mile from the shore where I was, and the boat seeming to stand upright still, I wished myself on board, that, at least, I might save some necessary things for my use.
> — *Robinson Crusoe*

IN THE DAYS immediately after my mother's death, as its reality slowly overtook my consciousness, I found myself recalling Robinson Crusoe. Not an association I would have anticipated, since the book holds little conscious meaning for me anymore. Yet there it was in my mind's eye — repeatedly, an indistinct image of a stranded, barefoot man, pant legs ripped at midcalf — straining, poling a raft back to his wrecked ship to gather provisions.

Crusoe, desolate and terrified, mercifully wave-tossed onto an island after a storm has sunk his ship, crawls up a tree to sleep the first night. He feels completely unprotected, and some large part of him expects to die before dawn — savaged by a ravenous beast or a hostile human. But when he awakes the next day, sun returned, water calm, he finds that the tide has delivered his lost vessel back from the depths and stranded it within reach. Like the storm-harried Crusoe, I found myself after her death mucking through strange, flickering, opposite states of mind where, at more than a few moments, a seemingly parallel grand confusion of terror and calm, desolation and thin hope, bereftness and bounty all commingled. I felt as rattled as any half-drowned jack-tar, and like Crusoe I understood that my first labor was to salvage.

Remarkable, really, the way the image from the book came to

mind at a grievous time. How it drifted into sight, intact, uninvited, a dense, symbolic representation in the guise of a mental snapshot. A book first read . . . when? Late childhood, early adolescence? Returned years later, in this case to capture some of my complex feelings about myself, my mother, and my circumstance in the aftermath of her death. Praise the quirky mind. Present yourself at the front desk of its repository, request any volume from its stacks, and discover, once again, how the runners deliver up what suits them: "Bring her Defoe." But from where in the gray matter did they retrieve him? Was the figure on the raft constructed in the moment — in response to my emotional state? Was it borrowed from some film? Or did it linger from when, as a child first reading the book, I assembled my own picture?

Remarkable, too, how words read on a page are translated and transformed by all of us into our own archives. How does my Crusoe resemble or not resemble yours, both in profile and in the intimate psychic purpose each may serve? Of course, not everyone who has read Defoe has kept a Crusoe. (I was unaware of mine until lately.) To stay, he had to fit in, find useful work; brace some part of the psyche, the way a piece of cedar — cut, carved, steamed to curve — will rib a boat. The quick description of why I kept my Crusoe summarizes blandly: he takes care of himself in tough circumstances; he is ingenious and resourceful; his story ends well. As an overprotected daughter of a mother I deemed weak, I longed to be more like him. I borrowed a rib. Perhaps a book becomes a classic in proportion to how broadly its characters can be scavenged, how many readers find within it something they experience as desirable or even intimately necessary.

A shipwreck, now rare, but once a tragedy so common that whole schools of landscape painting prospered in detailing its vicissitudes, seems an apt metaphor for maternal death. However much you equivocate, your mother is the vessel you inhabit. And shipboard death by catastrophic storm — plunging all unselectively — holds within it something true about the strange "me and not me" of intimate loss. Several years ago at the Whitney Museum, I spent a good long time watching Bill Viola's video loop of a human figure underwater in darkness very slowly surfacing, and then surfacing again, as if enacting my future quandary. Will I stay under, too? Is her death also mine? No, but perhaps, well, yes, if we speak not just of the past when we were one, nor of the future when I too shall die, but if we try to capture and describe something larger than influence, something genuinely uncanny. I'm not sure how to name it. The voyage, the direction set, the cargo carried, were my first and most basic world. I looked out through my mother's portholes. Her assumptions were the sheets I wrestled, hauled, lashed. I was her stevedore, her sailor, her AWOL midshipman, her ship's doctor, her mutinous crew, her captain — who ever knew for certain? I thought of her as my mother, but rarely of myself as her daughter. When I wrote about her for her memorial service, I was surprised to see how obviously my interests followed hers. Mourning is not just a long goodbye; it is a hard labor of turning away and returning, of swimming free and then poling back.

She died between my second and third visit to the hospital on a Tuesday toward the end of March. After checking with her nurse, who, like me, thought she still had days, I had decided to attend half my evening Italian class. I departed at the break, and arrived back twenty minutes too late. The hand I grasped was still warm. But she was dead, and the conversation between us was over. Eighty-nine years old, she'd had multiple sclerosis for twenty years. For the past eight she'd lived near me year-round, and every Wednesday evening after I finished seeing patients, I would walk the four or five blocks from my office to her apartment and we would eat dinner together. I never found an easy way to be with her. She longed intensely for a confiding intimacy that I wouldn't offer and that she couldn't seem to bear when I did. I have not known a more confounding relationship. Yet we both kept trying, and a good portion of our love located itself within the effort.

We had our moments. I liked best when she passed along news about old friends. "I called Louise." "What did you learn?" A flat exchange. But not between us, for whom it heralded — like a sundapple on the shady dirt road, or a cluster of daisies against white birch — our return to the family home. The beloved summer property, so familiar that the pleasure is in revisiting together, surveying, setting things right; steadying ourselves with the known, and then contemplating the variation a season brings. Louise was my mother's good friend in Oregon half a century ago. Her son, Peter, an age-mate now prematurely dead, was my first playmate. We named our son Peter partly after him. Louise's husband, Chester, was my father's close friend. My mother was attracted to Chester, and on more than one occasion — car out of gas, dead mouse in the bathtub — he rescued her. He had been a paratrooper fighting in Italy during the Second World War, and possessed a resourcefulness in crisis my father lacked. My mother liked being rescued.

Seeing it on the page, I realize this string of associations reveals an aspect of my Crusoe: I early grasped that the surest way to be with my mother was as her rescuer — not dramatically, but in small everyday ways. Childhood was a night watch. My assignment (assumed or ordered, who knows which?) was to stand between her and her self-hatred. Sometimes I gave my all. Other times I slipped away furtively; I could be derelict, fractious. After she died, the figure returning to the shipwreck was a seaman suddenly unemployed; the part of my own psyche whose long labor has just ended. "My duty all ended," Gerard Manley Hopkins wrote after another death.

What is gone and what remains? The first night, all is lost. But the next morning, the ship lies wrecked within reach, a brilliant stroke by Defoe. The reader shares Crusoe's relief. He is no longer alone — not because the boat is peopled, but because its appearance domesticates the alien space, offers comfort by placing within it a bit of home. Perhaps oddly, perhaps not, its reappearance resembles the return of an absent mother to her child. She disappears. He fears for his survival, dependent upon her. She reappears, and the hostile world is tempered. Better yet, she carries provisions to sustain him. The ship's hold, as Crusoe explores it, transforms into a general store absent its proprietor, and he gathers up goods like a lad on a spree. What better way to please a reader, gratify basic fantasy, than with bounty found, not earned — once again, analogous to a dimension of the maternal: the full breast, the free lunch. Certainly, there is something female and mammalian about the ship as Defoe describes it when Crusoe first swims back, a large beast lying on its side, waiting to be suckled. In this case, of that manly sailor's beverage, rum:

> I swam around her twice, and the second time I spy'd a small piece of a rope, which I wondered I did not see at first, hang down by the fore-

chains so low, as that with great difficulty I got hold of it, and by the help of that rope, got up into the forecastle of the ship. Here I found that the ship was bulged, and had a great deal of water in her hold, but that she lay so on the side of a bank of hard sand, or rather earth, that her stern lay lifted up upon the bank, and her head low against the water; by this means all her quarter was free, and all that was in that part was dry; for you may be sure my first work was to search and to see what was spoiled and what was free; and first I found that all the ship's provisions were dry and untouched by the water, and being well disposed to eat, I went to the bread room and filled my pockets with bisket, and ate it as I went about other things, for I had no time to lose; I also found some rum in the great cabin of which I took a large dram, and which I had indeed need enough of to spirit me for what was before me.

At once losing my mother and inheriting from her. I have kayaked places where the wind, current, and tide, the angle of underwater ledge, come together in such inscrutable, turbulent confusion it makes your head spin. There's no sure place to set your paddle, nothing to do but stroke hard and hope you don't tip into hammering ocean. The night after she died, I grabbed a bunch of cash from her wallet and took my family to dinner at a nearby bistro. She didn't need it anymore. I remember the high, so unlikely in the moment, almost giddy, of grasping coin from her purse, the pilferer's simian bark. Within hours, the elation crumpled into grief. The extreme opposite within her death, the unparalleled tenderness — *my mother* — the simultaneous liberation and found wealth spun my feelings: the ship is wrecked, yet I did not drown. Her cargo is mine.

I had not understood that after a person dies, her surround, her physical space, retains life — the pale blue cotton nightgown clean in the dryer, the custard in the refrigerator, the open issue of *The New Yorker,* the bills laid out on the table waiting to be paid. Her used tissue dropped, out of reach, behind the chair. She had resisted visiting her doctor for months, but finally, too weak to protest, had been sent by ambulance to the hospital by one of the women who cared for her. I was briefly out of town. She was determined to die, and I don't know which of us she was sparing by waiting to depart until I turned away. My back to her, she hastened toward death, as if we had been playing some scrambled game of

Mother May I? or Red Light Green Light. I think she knew I would
try to save her. So she chose not to tell me what she foresaw — unlike herself, really, tight-lipped, determined: courageous in a way
that caught me by surprise, that put paid to all clarity about where
between us strength lay.

It fell to me to empty her apartment and distribute her goods. I
shared Crusoe's urgency. The work couldn't wait. The weather
could shift at any moment, and then the precariously resting wreck
would again slide into the sea. But unlike Crusoe, I found it hard
to judge utility, to know just what to keep. Something undesirable
now might become crucial later. I didn't want to create a museum, even in storage boxes. Yet I didn't want to leave myself
unprovisioned in a future season. The sorting, the boxing, the
hauling took three months. I would drive to her apartment (it was
when I pulled into her parking lot that Crusoe usually appeared).
I'd let myself into her home, so familiar and now silent, and gird
myself to look, touch, toss, sell, or give away; brace myself for the
grief — the waves slamming the pebbled beach, then sucking back
in a roar, the clamorous slush of stones. Except for one small, perfect plate, I did not keep the pieces she still owned of her grandmother's floral-patterned china. I did keep a pair of gray knee
socks.

Occasionally, the apartment offered animal comfort, as if it were
breathing with her breath, as if it still held her body heat, or more
than that, the remains of her enthusiasm, her *tendresse*. As when
you walk on a quiet rural road in summer after a rain, and the humid heat wafts up all around you then drifts away. She had worked
hard to sift and order while she still had strength. What she left was
so condensed as to hold emotional weight disproportionate to its
apparent mass. In four small rooms, her life, remnants of my father's, my brother's, my own; time past, piled, pressed dry, gathered into photo albums, into stacks of old pages recording earn-
ings, debts paid, celebrations, bitter exchanges; mementos whose
history became the sediment of hers; photographs everywhere of
my children, of Italian forebears unmet, of friends now dead. I had
to disassemble a universe.

I had no idea how wrenching the labor would be. A space does
not die right away when a person dies, and I was unprepared for
that discovery. She was gone, yet her being still lingered within her

rooms. At one point it brought to mind a story someone had told me years ago after we'd been swimming in a quarry near our summer home — about trapping and grilling the eels that lived in the water there, and the way their bodies squirmed on the grill for long minutes after their heads had been cut off. I was at once Crusoe, comforted by her hoard, a daughter overwhelmed, and some much more violent creature, ripping apart a life; plundering, feeling little of Crusoe's entitlement. A man saving his own life escapes self-doubt; my mission was more ambiguous. Her correspondence with my father, sold to a library, may update a bathroom in our home. I like the Japanese porcelain figure from her father better in my living room than in hers. A nightmare I dreamt early on captured the psychic torque. I am in my mother's bedroom at night sitting on her bed while she is lying in it. It is very dark. Something I cannot see is threatening her life. Desperate, I dive over her to protect her. I become aware that I am both the one murdering her and the one wrestling with some shadowy intruder, trying to save her.

> It blew very hard all that night, and in
> the morning when I looked out, behold,
> no more ship was to be seen.

Crusoe disappeared in July — after I had emptied the apartment and called in the painters. In August my husband and I returned to our summer home on an island in Maine, and I began to settle. One afternoon we spotted a merlin hawk hidden in the aspen, waiting for warblers. On another, we kayaked home from an outing with the wind hard behind us and three ospreys above us, circling, diving for mackerel. Slowly, my feelings — my sorrow, my violence, my greed — came to seem less overblown, less grotesque, more like houses back on the shore, or a dock from which one has untied and departed.

I found myself thinking one day about the way people in the wild sometimes press a spider's web over an abrasion when no bandage is at hand. The sticky mass of threads stanches the bleeding until the body can take over. Crusoe webbed my wound, held my circumstance for me until I could gradually grasp it myself.

JOHN UPDIKE

The Writer in Winter

FROM *AARP Magazine*

YOUNG OR OLD, a writer sends a book into the world, not himself. There is no Senior Tour for authors, with the tees shortened by twenty yards and carts allowed. No mercy is extended by the reviewers; but then it is not extended to the rookie writer, either. He or she may feel, as the gray-haired scribes of the day continue to take up space and consume the oxygen in the increasingly small room of the print world, that the elderly have the edge, with their established names and already secured honors. How we did adore and envy them, the idols of our college years — Hemingway and Faulkner, Frost and Eliot, Mary McCarthy and Flannery O'Connor and Eudora Welty! We imagined them aswim in a heavenly refulgence, as joyful and immutable in their exalted condition as angels forever singing.

Now that I am their age — indeed, older than a number of them got to be — I can appreciate the advantages, for a writer, of youth and obscurity. You are not yet typecast. You can take a distant, cold view of the entire literary scene. You are full of your material — your family, your friends, your region of the country, your generation — when it is fresh and seems urgently worth communicating to readers. No amount of learned skills can substitute for the feeling of having a lot to say, of *bringing news*. Memories, impressions, and emotions from your first twenty years on earth are most writers' main material; little that comes afterward is quite so rich and resonant. By the age of forty, you have probably mined the purest veins of this precious lode; after that, continued creativity is a matter of sifting the leavings. You become playful and theoretical; you invent sequels, and attempt historical novels. The novels and stories thus generated may be more polished, more ingenious, even more humane than their predecessors; but none does quite the essential earth-moving work that Hawthorne, a writer who dwelt in the shadowland "where the Actual and Imaginary may meet," specified when he praised the novels of Anthony Trollope as being "as real as if some giant had hewn a great lump out of the earth and put it under a glass case."

This second quotation — one writer admiring a virtue he couldn't claim — meant a lot to me when I first met it, and I have cited it before. A few images, a few memorable acquaintances, a few cherished phrases, circle around the aging writer's head like gnats as he strolls through the summertime woods at gloaming. He sits down before the word processor's humming, expectant screen, facing the strong possibility that he has already expressed what he is struggling to express again.

My word processor — a term that describes me as well — is the last of a series of instruments of self-expression that began with crayons and colored pencils held in my childish fist. My hands, somewhat grown, migrated to the keyboard of my mother's typewriter, a portable Remington, and then, schooled in touch-typing, to my own machine, a beige Smith-Corona expressly bought by loving parents for me to take to college. I graduated to an office model, on the premises of *The New Yorker* magazine, that rose up, with an exciting heave, from the surface of a metal desk. Back in New England as a freelancer, I invested in an electric typewriter that snatched the letters from my fingertips with a sharp, premature *clack;* it held, as well as a black ribbon, a white one with which I could correct my many errors. Before long, this clever mechanism gave way to an even more highly evolved device, an early Wang word processor that did the typing itself, with a marvelous speed and infallibility. My next machine, an IBM, made the Wang seem slow and clunky and has been in turn superseded by a Dell that deals in dozens of type fonts and has a built-in spell checker. Through all this relentlessly advancing technology the same brain gropes through its diminishing neurons for images and narratives that will lift lumps out of the earth and put them under the glass case of published print.

With ominous frequency, I can't think of the right word. I know

there *is* a word; I can visualize the exact shape it occupies in the jigsaw puzzle of the English language. But the word itself, with its precise edges and unique tint of meaning, hangs on the misty rim of
consciousness. Eventually, with shamefaced recourse to my well-
thumbed thesaurus or to a germane encyclopedia article, I may
pin the word down, only to discover that it unfortunately rhymes
with the adjoining word of the sentence. Meanwhile, I have lost the
rhythm and syntax of the thought I was shaping up, and the paragraph has skidded off (like this one) in an unforeseen direction.

When, against my better judgment, I glance back at my prose
from twenty or thirty years ago, the quality I admire and fear to
have lost is its carefree bounce, its snap, its exuberant air of slight
excess. The author, in his boyish innocence, is calling, like the sorcerer's apprentice, upon unseen powers — the prodigious potential of this flexible language's vast vocabulary. Prose should have a
flow, the forward momentum of a certain energized weight; it
should feel like a voice tumbling into your ear.

An aging writer wonders if he has lost the ability to visualize a
completed work, in its complex spatial relations. He should have
in hand a provocative beginning and an ending that will feel inevitable. Instead, he may arrive at his ending nonplused, the arc of his
intended tale lying behind him in fragments. The threads have
failed to knit. The leap of faith with which every narrative begins
has landed him not on a far safe shore but in the middle of
the drink. The failure to make final sense is more noticeable in
a writer like Agatha Christie, whose last mysteries don't quite
solve all their puzzles, than in a broad-purposed visionary like Iris
Murdoch, for whom puzzlement is part of the human condition.
But in even the most sprawling narrative, things must add up.

The ability to fill in a design is almost athletic, requiring endur-
ance and agility and drawing upon some of the same mental muscles that develop early in mathematicians and musicians. While
writing, being partly a function of experience, has few truly preco-
cious practitioners, early success and burnout are a dismally familiar American pattern. The mental muscles slacken, that first fresh-
ness fades. In my own experience, diligent as I have been, the early
works remain the ones I am best known by, and the ones to which
my later works are unfavorably compared. Among the rivals beset-
ting an aging writer is his younger, nimbler self, when he was the
cocky new thing.

From the middle of my teens I submitted drawings, poems, and stories to *The New Yorker;* all came back with the same elegantly terse printed rejection slip. My first break came late in my college career when a short story that I had based on my grandmother's slow dying of Parkinson's disease was returned with a note scrawled in pencil at the bottom of the rejection slip. It read, if my failing memory serves: "Look — we don't use stories of senility, but try us again."

Now, "stories of senility" are about the only ones I have to tell. My only new experience is of aging, and not even the aged much want to read about it. We want to read, judging from the fiction that is printed, about life in full tide, in love, or at war — bulletins from the active battlefields, the wretched childhoods, the poignant courtships, the fraught adulteries, the big deals, the scandals, the crises of sexually and professionally active adults. My first published novel was about old people; my hero was a ninety-year-old man. Having lived as a child with aging grandparents, I imagined old age with more vigor, color, and curiosity than I could bring to a description of it now.

I don't mean to complain. Old age treats freelance writers pretty gently. There is no compulsory retirement at the office, and no athletic injuries signal that the game is over for good. Even with modern conditioning, a ballplayer can't stretch his career much past forty, and at the same age an actress must yield the romantic lead to a younger woman. A writer's fan base, unlike that of a rock star, is post-adolescent and relatively tolerant of time's scars; it distressed me to read of some teenager who, subjected to the Rolling Stones's halftime entertainment at a recent Super Bowl, wondered why that skinny old man (Mick Jagger) kept taking his shirt off and jumping around. The literary critics who coped with Hemingway's later, bare-chested novel *Across the River and into the Trees* asked much the same thing.

By and large, time moves with merciful slowness in the old-fashioned world of writing. The eighty-eight-year-old Doris Lessing won the Nobel Prize in literature. Elmore Leonard and P. D. James continue, into their eighties, to produce best-selling thrillers. Although books circulate ever more swiftly through the bookstores and back to the publisher again, the rhythms of readers are leisurely. They spread recommendations by word of mouth and "get around" to titles and authors years after making a mental note of them. A movie has a few weeks to find its audience, and television shows flit by in an hour, but books physically endure, in public and private libraries, for generations. Buried reputations, like Melville's, resurface in academia; avant-garde worthies such as Cormac McCarthy attain, late in life, bestseller lists and *The Oprah Winfrey Show.*

A pervasive unpredictability lends hope to even the most superannuated competitor in the literary field. There is more than one measurement of success. A slender poetry volume selling fewer than a thousand copies and receiving a handful of admiring reviews can give its author a pride and sense of achievement denied more mercenary producers of the written word. As for bad reviews and poor sales, they can be dismissed on the irrefutable hypothesis that reviewers and book buyers are too obtuse to appreciate true excellence. Over time, many books quickly bloom and then vanish; a precious few unfold, petal by petal, and become classics.

An aging writer has the not insignificant satisfaction of a shelf of books behind him that, as they wait for their ideal readers to discover them, will outlast him for a while. The pleasures, for him, of bookmaking — the first flush of inspiration, the patient months of research and plotting, the laser-printed final draft, the back-and-forthing with Big Apple publishers, the sample pages, the jacket sketches, the proofs, and at last the boxes from the printer's, with their sweet heft and smell of binding glue — remain, and retain creation's giddy bliss. Among those diminishing neurons there lurks the irrational hope that the last book might be the best.

RYAN VAN METER

First

FROM *The Gettysburg Review*

BEN AND I ARE sitting side by side in the very back of his
mother's station wagon. We face glowing white headlights of cars
following us, our sneakers pressed against the back hatch door.
This is our joy — his and mine — to sit turned away from our
moms and dads in this place that feels like a secret, as though they
are not even in the car with us. They have just taken us out to dinner, and now we are driving home. Years from this evening, I won't
actually be sure that this boy sitting beside me is named Ben. But
that doesn't matter tonight. What I know for certain right now is
that I love him, and I need to tell him this fact before we return to
our separate houses, next door to each other. We are both five.

Ben is the first brown-eyed boy I will fall for but will not be the
last. His hair is also brown and always needs scraping off his forehead, which he does about every five minutes. All his jeans have
dark squares stuck over the knees where he has worn through the
denim. His shoelaces are perpetually undone, and he has a magic
way of tying them with a quick, weird loop that I study and try myself, but can never match. His fingernails are ragged because he
rips them off with his teeth and spits out the pieces when our
moms aren't watching. Somebody always has to fix his shirt collars.

Our parents face the other direction, talking about something,
and it is raining. My eyes trace the lines of water as they draw down
the glass. Coiled beside my legs are the thick black and red cords
of a pair of jumper cables. Ben's T-ball bat is also back here, rolling
around and clunking as the long car wends its way through town.
Ben's dad is driving, and my dad sits next to him, with our mothers

in the back seat; I have recently observed that when mothers and fathers are in the car together, the dad always drives. My dad has also insisted on checking the score of the Cardinals game, so the radio is tuned to a staticky AM station, and the announcer's rich voice buzzes out of the speakers up front.

The week before this particular night, I asked my mother, "Why do people get married?" I don't recall the impulse behind my curiosity, but I will forever remember every word of her answer — she stated it simply after only a moment or two of thinking — because it seemed that important: "Two people get married when they love each other."

I had that hunch. I am a kindergartener, but the summer just before this rainy night, I learned most of what I know about love from watching soap operas with my mother. She is a gym teacher, and during her months off she catches up on the shows she has watched since college. Every summer weekday, I couldn't wait until they came on at two o'clock. My father didn't think I should be watching them — boys should be outside, playing — but he was rarely home early enough to know the difference, and according to my mother, I was too young to really understand what was going on anyway.

What I enjoyed most about soap operas was how exciting and beautiful life was. Every lady was pretty and had wonderful hair, and all the men had dark eyes and big teeth and faces as strong as bricks, and every week there was a wedding or a manhunt or a birth. The people had grand fights where they threw vases at walls and slammed doors and chased each other in cars. There were villains locking up the wonderfully haired heroines and suspending them in gold cages above enormous acid vats. And, of course, it was love that inspired every one of these stories and made life on the screen as thrilling as it was. That was what my mother would say from the sofa when I turned from my spot on the carpet in front of her and faced her, asking, "Why is he spying on that lady?"

"Because he loves her."

In the car, Ben and I hold hands. There is something sticky on his fingers, probably the strawberry syrup from the ice cream sundaes we ate for dessert. We have never held hands before; I have simply reached for his in the dark and held him while he holds me. I want to see our hands on the rough floor, but they are visible only every block or so when the car passes beneath a streetlight, and then for only a flash. Ben is my closest friend because he lives next door, we are the same age, and we both have little brothers who are babies. I wish he were in the same kindergarten class as me, but he goes to a different school — one where he has to wear a uniform all day and for which there is no school bus.

"I love you," I say. We are idling, waiting for a red light to be green; a shining car has stopped right behind us, so Ben's face is pale and brilliant.

"I love you too," he says.

The car becomes quiet as the voice of the baseball game shrinks smaller and smaller.

"Will you marry me?" I ask him. His hand is still in mine; on the soap opera, you are supposed to have a ring, but I don't have one.

He begins to nod, and suddenly my mother feels very close. I look over my shoulder, my eyes peeking over the back of the last row of seats that we are leaning against. She has turned around, facing me. Permed hair, laugh lines not laughing.

"What did you just say?" she asks.

"I asked Ben to marry me."

The car starts moving forward again, and none of the parents are talking loudly enough for us to hear them back here. I brace myself against the raised carpeted hump of the wheel well as Ben's father turns left onto the street before the turn onto our street. Sitting beside my mom is Ben's mother, who keeps staring forward, but I notice that one of her ears keeps swiveling back here, a little more each time. I am still facing my mother, who is still facing me, and for one last second, we look at each other without anything wrong between us.

"You shouldn't have said that," she says. "Boys don't marry other boys. Only boys and girls get married to each other."

She can't see our hands, but Ben pulls his away. I close my fingers into a loose fist and rub my palm to feel, and keep feeling, how strange his skin has made mine.

"Okay?" she asks.

"Yes," I say, but by accident my throat whispers the words.

She asks again. "Okay? Did you hear me?"

"Yes!" This time nearly shouting, and I wish we were already home so I could jump out and run to my bedroom. To be back

here in the dark, private tail of the car suddenly feels wrong, so
Ben and I each scoot off to our separate sides. "Yes," I say again, almost normally, turning away to face the rainy window. I feel her
turn too as the radio baseball voice comes back up out of the quiet.
The car starts to dip as we head down the hill of our street; our
house is at the bottom. No one speaks for the rest of the ride. We
all just sit and wait and watch our own views of the road — the parents see what is ahead of us, while the only thing I can look at is
what we have just left behind.

JERALD WALKER

The Mechanics of Being

FROM *The Missouri Review*

A DECADE AFTER dropping out of high school, I'd managed to arrive, like some survivor of a tragedy at sea, on the shores of a community college. My parents were thrilled when I phoned to say I was pursuing my childhood dream of being an architect. They were just as happy when I decided to be a sociologist instead. And after that a political scientist. Finally, a writer. "I'm going to write a novel based on my life," I said to my father one day. I was in an MFA program by then, starting my second year. I'd recently found some statistics that said there'd been a sixty percent chance I'd end up in jail; I had stories to prove just how close I'd come. But after writing the first draft, my tale of black teenage delinquency seemed too clichéd to me, told too often before. I decided to write about my father instead. He, like my mother, was blind.

My father lost his sight when he was twelve. Climbing the stairs to his Chicago brownstone, he somehow fell backward, hitting his head hard against the pavement and filling his cranium with blood. It would have been better had some of this blood seeped out, alerting him to seek medical attention, but when the area of impact did no more than swell a little and throb, he tended to himself by applying two cubes of ice and eating six peanut-butter cookies. He did not tell anyone about the injury. He also did not mention the two weeks of headaches that followed, the month of dizzy spells, or that the world was growing increasingly, terrifyingly dim.

His mother had died of cancer four years earlier. His alcoholic father was rarely around. So at home my father only had to conceal his condition from his grandmother, Mama Alice, who herself could barely see past her cataracts, and his three older brothers and sister, who had historically paid him little attention. His grades at school suffered, but his teachers believed him when he said his discovery of girls was the cause. He spent less and less time with his friends, gave up baseball altogether, and took to walking with the aid of a tree branch. In this way his weakening vision remained undetected for three months until, one morning at breakfast, things fell apart.

Mama Alice greeted him as he sat at the table. She was by the stove, he knew, from the location of her voice. As he listened to her approach, he averted his face. She put a plate in front of him and another to his right, where she always sat. She pulled a chair beneath her. He reached for his fork, accidentally knocking it off the table. When several seconds had passed and he'd made no move, Mama Alice reminded him that forks couldn't fly. He took a deep breath and reached down to his left, knowing that to find the utensil would be a stroke of good fortune, since he couldn't even see the floor. After a few seconds of sweeping his fingers against the cool hardwood, he sat back up. There was fear in Mama Alice's voice when she asked him what was wrong. There was fear in his when he confessed he couldn't see.

He confessed everything then, eager, like a serial killer at last confronted with evidence of his crime, to have the details of his awful secret revealed. And when pressed about why he hadn't said anything sooner, he mentioned his master plan: he would make his sight get better by ignoring, as much as possible, the fact that it was getting worse.

For gutting out his fading vision in silence, Mama Alice called him brave. His father called him a fool. His teachers called him a liar. His astonished friends and siblings called him Merlin. The doctors called him lucky. The damage was reversible, they said, because the clots that had formed on, and now pressed against, his occipital lobes could be removed. But they were wrong; those calcified pools of blood were in precarious locations and could not be excised without risking immediate paralysis or worse. The surgeons inserted a metal plate (my father never knew why) and later told Mama Alice that the clots would continue to grow, not only destroying the little sight he had left but also killing him. They gave him one more year to live, but they were wrong again.

They were wrong, too, in not predicting the seizures. He'd have them the rest of his life, internal earthquakes that toppled his body and pitched it violently across the floor. I remember these scenes vividly: as a young child, I would cower with my siblings at a safe distance while my mother, her body clamped on top of my father's, tried to put medicine in his mouth without losing a finger or before he chewed off his tongue. My father was a big man in those days, bloated on fried food and Schlitz — one wrong move of his massive body would have caused my mother great harm — but she rode him expertly, desperately, a crocodile hunter on the back of her prey.

I expected one of those attacks to be fatal. But their damage would be done over five decades rather than all at once, slowly and insidiously eroding his brain, like water over stone. So we knew it wasn't Alzheimer's when he began forgetting the people and things that mattered and remembering the trivia of his youth. He knew it, too. That's why, at the age of fifty-five, he retired from teaching, moved with my mother to an apartment in the suburbs, and waited, like we all waited, for the rest of his mind to wash away. By the time I started teaching, when he was in his mid-sixties, he had forgotten us all.

According to the American Foundation for the Blind, every seven minutes someone in this country will become blind or visually impaired. There are 1.3 million blind people in the United States. Less than half of the blind complete high school, and only 30 percent of working-age blind adults are employed. For African Americans, who make up nearly 20 percent of this population, despite being only 12 percent of the population at large, the statistics are even bleaker.

There are no reliable statistics for the number of unemployed blind prior to the 1960s, but some estimates put it as high as 95 percent. Most parents of blind children then had low expectations, hoping only that they would find some more useful role to play in society than selling pencils on street corners or playing a harmonica in some subway station, accompanied by a bored though faithful basset hound. Usually the blind were simply kept at home.

Mama Alice expected to keep my father at home for just a year, but even that was one year too many. She was elderly, diabetic, ar-

thritic, and still mourning for her daughter and other accumulated losses. Now she had to care for a blind boy who spent his days
crying or, when his spirits lifted, smashing things in his room. His
school had expelled him, his friends had fled, and his sister and
brothers had not been moved by his handicap to develop an interest in his affairs. And so, on the second anniversary of his predicted death, Mama Alice packed up his things, kissed him goodbye, implored him to summon more bravery, and sent him to jail.

My father never told any of his children about this. I read about
it in his chart at the Sight Saving School, in Jacksonville, Illinois,
where he'd been transferred after fifteen months in juvenile detention, and where, in 1994, the same year he and my mother
moved to the suburbs, I went to visit.

Thirteen years later, the trip for me is a blur, punctuated now
and then with random vivid images. I cannot see the face of the
principal who greeted my wife and me, and I cannot visualize the
office we were escorted to, but my father's chart is seared in my
mind, a black three-ring binder with "Thomas Keller Walker"
handwritten in the top right corner. Before I read it, the principal
gave us a tour of the facilities. It was a twelve-acre complex that included basketball courts, a baseball diamond, a swimming pool . . .
and classrooms. We were taken to the library, which was a museum
of sorts, where the history of blindness was laid out in pictures and
graphs behind glass cases. We ate lunch in the cafeteria where my
father had eaten lunch. We went to the dorm room where he'd
slept. Outside, we walked on the track where, cane in hand, my father had learned to run again.

After the tour, the principal took us back to her office and left us
alone with his chart. It contained his height, weight, vital signs, and
a summary of his academic performance before he lost his sight,
which I cannot recall, though my guess is that it was exceptional. I
also cannot remember the progress reports during his two years
there. What I do remember was a description of him as "trauma-
tized." That seemed about right to me. He'd lost his mother, his
sight . . . and his freedom. The only person who'd consistently
showed him love had put him in prison. He was sixteen. I thought
about my own life at sixteen, my delinquency and lack of purpose,
and I suddenly felt as disappointed in myself as I know he must
have been.

When we arrived back at our home in Iowa City, I typed up my notes from the trip. I decided not to call my father to ask about being put in juvenile detention; he'd had a reason for keeping it a secret, and I figured I should probably honor it.

In 1997 my parents moved again. My father was having difficulty with his balance and could not manage the stairs to their second-floor apartment. They bought a house in Dolton, a suburb in south Chicago; its primary appeal, besides being a single-level ranch, was its screened-in porch. For two summers they pretty much lived in there, crowding it with a swing set, a glider, a card table on which sat an electric water fountain, and four reclining chairs. My father was in one of those chairs enjoying a refreshing breeze and the faint sound of gurgling water when he had a grand mal seizure, the worst in years. For two weeks he was in intensive care on a respirator. When he was finally able to breathe on his own, he was moved to a regular room, and a month later, when he could finally speak, he asked everyone, including my mother, his wife of forty-two years, who they were. While he languished in this state of oblivion, struggling to recall his life, I finished the first draft of my book, having him die peacefully in his sleep. Wishful thinking. Another massive seizure put him back in the ICU.

A month later he was transferred to an assisted living facility. Speech therapists helped him talk again, and occupational therapists showed him how to move with a walker. But no one could fix his brain. His thoughts were in a thousand fragments, floating in his skull, I imagined, like the flakes of a shaken snow globe. His filter gone, my father, this intensely private man from whom I'd had difficulty extracting just the basic facts of his life, was now a mental flasher. My mother called me on occasion to report what he'd revealed.

"Mama Alice arrested me," he announced to her one day.

"I drink too much," he said on another.

"That Lynne can sure fry some chicken," he mentioned as well. After my mother relayed this last comment, there was a long pause before she asked me, "You *do* know about Lynne, don't you?"

Lynne was the woman he'd left her for. That was in 1963, thirteen years after my parents had met at the Chicago Lighthouse for the Blind, an organization that, among other services, provides employment for the visually impaired. My father was there assembling clocks while home on summer break from the Sight Saving

School, and my mother, blind from a childhood accident, had been hired to do the same. They were seventeen when they met, eighteen when they married, and at twenty-five the parents of four children. My mother was pregnant with two more when my father moved out. That was all I knew, told to me one day by an older brother when I was in my mid-teens.

My parents had never discussed any of this with my siblings or me. My mother spoke openly about it now, though, and then she segued into talking about the man she'd dated during the two-year separation and about the son they'd had together. Her story I knew more about because when my twin and I were ten or so, her son, our half-brother, would come to our house to play with us. Occasionally he'd be accompanied by his father, a lanky blind man who chain-smoked and had a baritone voice that made me think of God. These attempts at civility lasted two summers before suddenly coming to an end. I never again saw my mother's son. And I never met my father's. I did not even know that he and Lynne had one, in fact, until three years ago, when one of my brothers mailed me a newspaper clipping from the *Chicago Sun-Times* describing his murder. His girlfriend had stabbed him thirty-one times. In the margin next to his picture, my brother had inscribed, "He looks just like *you!*" At first glance, I thought it was.

I made no mention of my stepbrothers in the novel, nor of my parents' separation, even though my mother, after speaking about this tumultuous period in their lives and of the resilient love that saw her and my father through it, suggested that I should. But at the time these details seemed peripheral to my point, too far astray from the topic at hand, not so much character development and depth, in my view, as dirty laundry. After chronicling how he'd lost his sight, I described how my father had navigated the sighted world: his learning to walk with a cane, his mastery of public transportation, how he'd earned his college degrees with the help of students and technological aids, his purchase of a Seeing Eye dog. Chapter after chapter focused on the mechanics of blindness when I should have focused on the mechanics of being. I should have explored my father's life beyond his handicap, just as, when I set out to write my own story, I should have explored my life beyond the trials common to inner-city black males. The novels I had written said no more about the range of my father's experiences or mine, no more about the meanings we had shaped from the chaos of our lives, than the newspaper clipping had said about his murdered son's.

I realized this while at my father's funeral. He died in September 2005, fifty-six years after the surgeons predicted he would, succumbing not to the blood clots after all, but rather to pneumonia. My wife and I left our two toddlers with their grandmother and flew from Boston to Chicago to attend the service. We sat in the second pew, just behind my mother, whose shoulder I would reach forward to pat as we listened to the organist play my father's favorite hymns. A cousin of mine read Scripture, a family friend recited a number of poems, and then the pastor gave the eulogy, a thorough account of my father's accomplishments, punctuated by the refrain: *and he did this while blind.* As I listened to him try to convince us that sightlessness was the core and sum of my father's existence, I understood that my novel had failed.

At some point during the eulogy, when I could no longer stand to listen, an incident I had long forgotten came to mind. I was probably thirteen years old, and my father, as he had so often done before, asked me to take some of his clothes to the dry cleaner's. Ordinarily this wasn't a big deal, but I had plans to join some friends at the park, so I whined and complained about being called into service. A mild argument ensued, which I lost, and a short while later I slumped out of the house with a paper bag full of his things. At the cleaner's, I watched the clerk remove each article of clothing, my lack of interest turning to horror as her hand, now frozen in midair, dangled before us a pair of my father's boxers. The clerk, very pretty and not much older than me, smiled and said, "We don't clean *these.*" I couldn't believe that my father had made such an unpardonable mistake, a blunder of the highest order, and the more I thought of it, the more upset I became. Halfway home, swollen with anger and eager to release it, I started to run. When I arrived, out of breath, my hands clenched by my sides, my father wasn't in the living room where I'd left him but was sitting on the porch. The second I barked, "*Daddy!*" he exploded in laughter, his large stomach quivering beneath his T-shirt, his ruddy face pitched toward the sky. I could not, despite my best effort, help but join him. I rose after the pastor finished his eulogy and told this story to the congregation. If I ever attempt to write another novel about my father, this is where it will begin.

Contributors' Notes

SUE ALLISON graduated from McGill University, and after two years as a freelance writer based in London, writing for publications that included the London *Observer* and the London *Sunday Times,* she moved to New York, where she was a reporter for *Life,* serving at various times as a writer, editor, and Washington correspondent. When *Life* ended its publication as a monthly magazine, she earned an MFA from the Vermont College of Fine Arts. She has published a book on the Bloomsbury group; had a story included in the Selected Shorts Series at Symphony Space in New York, the performance of which was broadcast on NPR; received an honorable mention in the World's Best Short Short Story Contest of the *Southeast Review* and a third place in the short short story contest of *So to Speak;* and has been twice nominated for a Pushcart Prize.

CHRIS ARTHUR is the author of four highly acclaimed essay collections: *Irish Nocturnes* (1999), *Irish Willow* (2002), *Irish Haiku* (2005), and *Irish Elegies* (2009). *Words of the Grey Wind* (2009) offers a selection of new and previously published essays. Born in Belfast, he worked as a warden on a nature reserve before attending the University of Edinburgh, where he took a First Class Honours degree followed by a Ph.D. His work has appeared in many U.S. periodicals, including the *American Scholar,* the *North American Review, Northwest Review, Orion,* the *Southern Review,* the *Southern Humanities Review,* and the *Threepenny Review.* He was the Gifford Fellow at the University of St. Andrews and has been the recipient of several literary prizes and awards. He teaches at the University of Wales, Lampeter. For further information about his work, see www.chrisarthur.org.

Storyteller, novelist, essayist, screenwriter, dramatist, and critic, JOHN BERGER is one of the most internationally influential writers of the last fifty years. His many books include *Ways of Seeing*, the fiction trilogy *Into Their Labours, Here Is Where We Meet*, the Booker Prize–winning novel *G*, and most recently, *From A to X: A Story in Letters*.

WENDELL BERRY'S nonfiction books include *What Are People For?; Standing on Earth; Sex, Economy, Freedom, and Community; Another Turn of the Crank; Life Is a Miracle; Citizenship Papers;* and most recently, *The Way of Ignorance*. *That Distant Land: The Collected Stories of Wendell Berry* appeared in 2004, and two of his recent novels are *Hannah Coulter* and *Andy Catlett: Early Travels*. The recipient of many awards, including Guggenheim and Rockefeller fellowships, Berry lives and farms with his family in Henry County, Kentucky.

BRIAN DOYLE is the editor of *Portland* magazine, at the University of Portland, in Oregon. He is the author of five collections of essays, two nonfiction books (*The Grail*, about a year in an Oregon vineyard, and *The Wet Engine*, about how hearts work and don't), and two collections of "proems," most recently *Thirsty for the Joy: Australian and American Voices.*

DAVID JAMES DUNCAN is a lifelong resident of riverbanks and wilderness edges and the author of the novels *The River Why* and *The Brothers K.* His many essays and four-hundred-plus public talks celebrate free-flowing rivers, imaginative and religious freedom, the tragicomedy of the writing life, the irreplaceable biological and spiritual importance of wild salmon, and the charms of a nonmonastic contemplative life haunted by wild birds. David lives with his family in Montana, where he's at work on a novel that tries to resolve his six well-worn translations of the *Bhagavad Gita* with his five well-worn pairs of cowboy boots.

PATRICIA HAMPL is the author of many award-winning books, *including Blue Arabesque: A Search for the Sublime, A Romantic Education, I Could Tell You Stories: Sojourns in the Land of Memory,* and *Virgin Time: In Search of the Contemplative Life.* She has also published two volumes of poetry. Her most recent book is *The Florist's Daughter,* which was selected by the *New York Times* as one of the one hundred notable books of 2007. She teaches at the University of Minnesota in Minneapolis and is on the permanent faculty of the Prague Summer Program. "The Dark Art of Description," in a slightly different version, was the keynote address at the Bedell NonfictioNow conference at the University of Iowa in November 2007.

GARRET KEIZER is the author of *Help, The Enigma of Anger, God of Beer, A Dresser of Sycamore Trees,* and *No Place but Here.* His work has appeared in *The Best American Science and Nature Writing 2002, The Best American Poetry 2005,* and *The Best American Essays 2007.* A contributing editor for *Harper's Magazine,* he is writing a book about the politics of noise. He and his wife live in northeastern Vermont.

VERLYN KLINKENBORG was born in Colorado in 1952 and raised in Iowa and California. He graduated from Pomona College and received a Ph.D. in English literature from Princeton University. He is the author of *Making Hay* (1986), *The Last Fine Time* (1991), *The Rural Life* (2003), and *Timothy: Or, Notes of an Abject Reptile* (2006). He is a visiting professor at Bard College and the visiting writer in residence at Pomona College. He is also the recipient of a 2007 Guggenheim fellowship and has been a member of the editorial board of the *New York Times* since 1997. Mr. Klinkenborg lives in rural New York State.

AMY LEACH received a Rona Jaffe Award in 2008. She has an MFA in creative nonfiction from the University of Iowa, and her essays have appeared in *A Public Space,* the *Iowa Review,* and the *Massachusetts Review.* She lives in Evanston, Illinois.

MICHAEL LEWIS is a contributing editor for *Vanity Fair* and the author of a number of books, including *Moneyball* and *Liar's Poker.* He lives in Berkeley, California, with his wife, Tabitha, and their three children.

BARRY LOPEZ is the author of two collections of essays, *Crossing Open Ground* and *About This Life,* and eleven other works of fiction and nonfiction, most recently the story collection *Resistance.* He is a recipient of the National Book Award.

JAMES MARCUS is the author of *Amazonia: Five Years at the Epicenter of the Dot-Com Juggernaut* (2004). He has translated six books from the Italian, the most recent being *Collusion: International Espionage and the War on Terror* (2007) and Saul Steinberg's *Letters to Aldo Buzzi.* His work has appeared in the *Atlantic, Raritan, Harvard Review, Salon,* the *Los Angeles Times Book Review,* and many other publications. He lives in New York and is currently working on both a novel and a history of anonymity.

JILL McCORKLE is the author of five novels — *The Cheer Leader, July 7th, Tending to Virginia, Ferris Beach,* and *Carolina Moon* — and three short story collections: *Crash Diet, Final Vinyl Days,* and *Creatures of Habit.* Her new collection, *Going Away Shoes,* will be published in fall 2009. Her work has appeared in the *Atlantic, Ploughshares, The Best American Short Stories,* and *New Stories from the South,* among other publications. The recipient of the New England Book Award, the John Dos Passos Prize, and the North Carolina Award for Literature, she has taught creative writing at the University of North Carolina at Chapel Hill, Tufts, Harvard, Brandeis, and Bennington College. She is currently on the faculty of North Carolina State University.

KATHRYN MILES is an associate professor and the director of the environmental writing program at Unity College. She has written extensively on issues of place and memory, environmental change, and human ecology. Most recently, she is the author of *Adventures with Ari: A Puppy, a Leash, and Our Year Outdoors*. For more information, visit her website: www.kathryn-miles.com.

GREGORY ORR is the author of ten collections of poetry, most recently two book-length lyric sequences, *How Beautiful the Beloved* (2009) and *Concerning the Book That Is the Body of the Beloved* (2005). Among his other volumes of poetry are *The Caged Owl: New and Selected Poems, Orpheus and Eurydice, City of Salt* (a finalist for the *Los Angeles Times* Poetry Prize), *We Must Make a Kingdom of It, The Red House, Gathering the Bones Together,* and *Burning the Empty Nests.* The recipient of a Guggenheim fellowship, a Rockefeller fellowship, and two poetry fellowships from the National Endowment for the Arts, he was presented the Award in Literature by the American Academy of Arts and Letters in 2003. *Publishers Weekly* chose his memoir, *The Blessing* (2002), as one of the fifty best nonfiction books of 2002, and Adrienne Rich characterized *Poetry as Survival* (2002) as "a wise and passionate book." Earlier prose collections include *Richer Entanglements: Essays and Notes on Poetry and Poems* and *Stanley Kunitz: An Introduction to the Poetry.* A professor of English at the University of Virginia since 1975, he was the founder and first director of its MFA program in writing. He served from 1978 to 2003 as poetry editor of the *Virginia Quarterly Review.* He lives with his wife, the painter Trisha Orr, and his two daughters in Charlottesville, Virginia.

CYNTHIA OZICK is the author of ten works of fiction, including the novels *The Puttermesser Papers* and *Heir to the Glimmering World,* which was a *New York Times* Notable Book, a Book Sense Pick, a finalist for the International Man Booker Prize, and was chosen by NBC's *Today* Book Club. Her essay collections are *Art & Ardor, Metaphor & Memory, Fame & Folly,* a finalist for the 1996 Pulitzer Prize, *Quarrel & Quandary,* the winner of the 2001 National Book Critics Circle Award, and *The Din in the Head.* She served as guest editor of *The Best American Essays 1998.* Ozick received the Presidential Medal for the Humanities in 2007 and both the PEN/Nabokov Award and the PEN/Malamud Award in 2008. Her most recent book, *Dictation: A Quartet,* is a collection of novellas. An expanded version of "Ghost Writers" was published in *Standpoint* (September 2008) and can be found at www.standpointmag.co.uk.

RICHARD RODRIGUEZ is the author of *Hunger of Memory, Days of Obligation,* and *Brown.* He writes principally personal essays. In an essay on racial impurity he describes himself, living in San Francisco, as "a queer Catholic Indian Spaniard at home in a temperate Chinese city in a fading blond state in a post-Protestant nation." He is writing a book about monotheism and the desert.

JANNA MALAMUD SMITH is a writer and psychotherapist. She has lectured widely and has published in many newspapers, magazines, and journals. She is the author of three books. The first two, *Private Matters: In Defense of the Personal Life* (1997) and *A Potent Spell: Mother Love and the Power of Fear* (2003), were chosen as Notable Books by the *New York Times Book Review.* Her latest, *My Father Is a Book: A Memoir of Bernard Malamud* (2006), was selected as a *Washington Post* Best Book of the Year and a *New York Times* Editors' Choice. She has worked part time since 1979 in the Cambridge Health Alliance, in Cambridge, Massachusetts, and has a private practice. She is currently writing a book about the emotional perils that inhibit art-making, and researching a book about fishing in the Gulf of Maine.

JOHN UPDIKE was born in 1932 in Shillington, Pennsylvania. After graduation from Harvard in 1954 and a year spent at an English art school, he worked for two years for *The New Yorker*'s "Talk of the Town" department. Since 1957 he lived in Massachusetts as a freelance writer. His most recent books include a novel, *Terrorist,* and *Due Considerations: Essays and Criticism. The Widows of Eastwick,* his twenty-third novel, was published in 2008. He died on January 27, 2009. A volume of poetry, *Endpoint,* and two collections of fiction, *My Father's Tears* and *The Maples Stories,* were published in 2009. In a long and distinguished career, Updike was elected to the National Institute of Arts and Letters and received numerous awards, including the National Book Award, the National Medal of Art, the National Medal for the Humanities, the National Book Critics Circle Award, the Rosenthal Award, the Howells Medal, and was twice a recipient of a Pulitzer Prize for fiction.

RYAN VAN METER's writing has appeared in *Gulf Coast,* the *Colorado Review,* the *Indiana Review,* the *Gettsyburg Review,* and the *Iowa Review,* among others. His essays have also been included in the *Touchstone Anthology of Contemporary Creative Nonfiction: Work from 1970 to the Present,* edited by Lex Williford and Michael Martone, and *You Must Be This Tall to Ride: Contemporary Writers Take You Inside the Story,* edited by B. J. Hollars. A recent graduate of the nonfiction writing program at the University of Iowa, he is currently finishing a collection that includes "First," titled *If You Knew Then What I Know Now.*

JERALD WALKER is an associate professor of English at Bridgewater State College. "The Mechanics of Being" will be included in his memoir *Street Shadows*, which will be published in January 2010. Other essays have appeared in publications such as *The Best American Essays 2007*, *The Best African American Essays 2009*, *Mother Jones*, the *Oxford American*, the *North American Review*, the *New Delta Review*, the *Chronicle of Higher Education*, the *Barcelona Review*, and the *Iowa Review*.

Notable Essays of 2008

SELECTED BY ROBERT ATWAN

ROBERT FINCH
  When You Wish Upon a Star,
  Ecotone, 4/1 and 2.
TOM FLEISCHMANN
  Fist, *Pleiades,* 28/2.
JONATHAN SAFRAN FOER
  My Explosion, *Washington Post
  Magazine,* July 13.
RUTH FRANKLIN
  Dreams of Reason, *Granta,* 101.
JONATHAN FRANZEN
  The Way of the Puffin, *New Yorker,*
  April 21.
HILARY FRASER
  The Morals of Genealogy, *Raritan,*
  Spring.
MILES FULLER
  First Words, *Bellingham Review,*
  Spring.

ERNEST J. GAINES
  Louisiana Bound, *Oxford American,*
  62.
JOHN GAMEL
  The Funnel, *Epoch,* 57/3.
DAVE GARDETTA
  The Burning Wind, *Los Angeles,*
  November.
PHILIP GARRISON
  Pain, Pride, and the Permit That
  Never Expires, *New Madrid,*
  Winter.
WILLIAM H. GASS
  The Literary Miracle, *Iowa Review,*
  Spring.
GAYNELL GAVIN
  What We Have, *Prairie Schooner,* Fall.
DAVID GELERNTER
  Feminism and the English
  Language, *Weekly Standard,*
  March 3.
DAVID GESSNER
  Those Who Write, Teach, *New York
  Times Magazine,* September 21.
BENEDICT GIAMO
  Played Out, *Sport Literate,* 6/1.

JOSH GIDDING
  On Not Being Proust: An Essay in
  Literary Failure, *Agni,* 67.
JULIA GLASS
  Real Life, *Washington Post Magazine,*
  July 13.
HERBERT GOLD
  A Night Scavenger, *Michigan
  Quarterly Review,* Winter.
ALBERT GOLDBARTH
  Some Ugly Truths and a Whisper,
  River Styx, 76/77.
ANNE GOLDMAN
  In Praise of Saul Bellow, *Michigan
  Quarterly Review,* Winter.
EUGENE GOODHEART
  The Thin Man, *Sewanee Review,*
  Spring.
ADAM GOPNIK
  The Real Work, *New Yorker,* March
  17.
LORI GOTTLIEB
  Marry Him, *Atlantic Monthly,* March.
MARK GREIF
  On Food, *N+1,* Fall.
MARGARET MORGANROTH
GULLETTE
  No Longer Suppressing Grief:
  Political Trauma in Twentieth-
  Century America, *Life Writing,*
  5/2.
LORRENCE GUTTERMAN
  Mistake, *River Teeth,* Spring.

ALLE C. HALL
  Girl Feelings, LiteraryMama.com,
  October.
MEREDITH HALL
  The Simplest Questions, *Kenyon
  Review,* Summer.
MARK HALLIDAY
  Prospectus, *Pleiades,* 28/1.
JENNA HAMMERICH
  Undark, *Quarterly West,* Summer.
KAY HAREL
  "It's Dogged as Does It": A
  Biography of the Everpresent

Canine in Charles Darwin's Days, *Southwest Review*, 93/3.

DANIEL HARRIS
Celebrity Bodies, *Southwest Review*, 93/1.

ELIZABETH LOGAN HARRIS
Black and White TV, *Colorado Review*, Fall/Winter.

LISA OHLEN HARRIS
Evil Eye, *Jabberwock Review*, Spring.

ROBIN HEMLEY
Field Notes for the Graveyard Enthusiast, *New Letters*, 75/1.

CHRISTOPHER HITCHENS
Believe Me, It's Torture, *Vanity Fair*, August.

NOELLE HOWEY
Never Give Up? *Real Simple*, September.

VALERIE HURLEY
The Whisky on Her Breath, *The Sun*, September.

SIRI HUSTVEDT
My Father, Myself, *Granta*, 104.

CHRIS IMPEY
Exohumanities, *Western Humanities Review*, Fall.

LAWRENCE JACKSON
The Beginning of Slavery, *Antioch Review*, Spring.

ANJALI JAIN
Crossing the Atlantic, *Health Affairs*, March/April.

TRELLIE JAMES JEFFERS
From the Old Slave Shack, *PMS*, 8.

HA JIN
Arrival, *Washington Post Magazine*, July 13.

CHARLES JOHNSON
Northwest Passage, *Smithsonian*, September.

MICHAEL L. JOHNSON
Math, *Under the Sun*, 20.

JEREMY B. JONES
In Search of Dreadlocks (and Captain Zero), *Relief*, Fall.

DIANA JOSEPH
The Devil I Know Is the Man Upstairs, *Willow Springs*, 61.

REED KARAIM
Getting Away, Yet Going Home, *Preservation*, March/April.

MERILEE D. KARR
Plant Life, *Bellevue Literary Review*, Spring.

ROBERT KIMBER
Big Jim, *Missouri Review*, Spring.

JOHN KINSELLA
Lightning: Stranger Than Fiction, *Notre Dame Review*, Summer/Fall.

DAVID KIRBY
The Ninety-nine Names of the Prophet, *TriQuarterly*, 132.

JUDITH KITCHEN
The Speed of Light, *Georgia Review*, Fall.

GEORGINA KLEEGE
Blind Imagination: Pictures into Words, *Southwest Review*, 93/2.

AMY KOLEN
Moenkopi Dance, *Minnetonka Review*, Winter.

ANNE KORNBLATT
The Writer of the Body, *Cream City Review*, Spring.

NICK KOWALCZYK
As I Lay Dying, *Ninth Letter*, Spring/Summer.

LEONARD KRIEGEL
Learning the Code, *Sewanee Review*, Spring.

AARON KUNIN
Awkward Without W, *Seneca Review*, Fall.

KIM DANA KUPPERMAN
Paved with Good Intentions, *Hotel Amerika*, Spring.

NATASHA TRETHEWEY
 The Gulf: A Meditation of the
  Mississippi Coast after Katrina,
  Virginia Quarterly Review,
  September.
J. M. TYREE
 Other Brooklyns, *Mid-American
  Review,* 28/2.

LEE UPTON
 Purity: It's Such a Filthy Word,
  TriQuarterly, 132.

ROBERT VON HALLBERG
 Sob-Ballads, *TriQuarterly,* 132.

GARRY WALLACE
 A Topper for the Pickup, *Owen
  Wister Review,* 2008.
WENDY S. WALTERS
 Lonely in America: Contemplating
  the Remains of Slavery, *Harper's
  Magazine,* March.

STEVEN WEINBERG
 Without God, *New York Review of
  Books,* September 25.
ANNE WELCH
 Lady Undressing, *Image,* 58.
KATHRYN WILDER
 The Last Cows, *Fourth Genre,* Spring.
LOIS WILLIAMS
 The House of Provisions, *Granta,*
  103.
JASON WILSON
 On the Nose, TheSmartSet.com,
  December 17.
S. L. WISENBERG
 Cancer Bitch, *The Pinch,* Fall.

LEE ZACHARIAS
 Geography for Writers, *North
  Carolina Literary Review,* 17.
PAUL ZIMMER
 Practicing for Doomsday, *Gettysburg
  Review,* Autumn.

Notable Special Issues of 2008

Antioch Review, Medical Memoirs: Pain
 and Pills, ed. Robert S. Fogarty,
 Spring.
Ascent, Excellence, ed. W. Scott Olsen,
 Spring.
Bidoun, Objects, ed. Lisa Farjam,
 Spring/Summer.
Black Warrior Review, Contributor Love
 Issue, ed. Alissa Nutting, Spring/
 Summer.
Crab Orchard Review, The In-Between
 Age: Writers on Adolescence, ed.
 Allison Joseph, Summer/Fall.
Creative Nonfiction, Anatomy of
 Baseball, ed. Lee Gutkind, 34.
Daedalus, On Nature, ed. James Miller
 and Leo Marx, Spring.
Ecotone, The Evolution Issue, ed. David
 Gessner, 4/1 and 2.

Granta, The New Nature Writing, ed.
 Jason Cowley, 102.
Granta, Fathers, ed. Alex Clark, 104.
Indiana Review, Funk Feature, ed.
 Abdel Shakur, Summer.
Isotope, Our Bodies, ed. Christopher
 Cokinos, Spring/Summer.
Manoa, Literature and the Ethical
 Imagination, ed. Frank Stewart and
 Barry Lopez, 20/1.
Massachusetts Review, An Especially
 Queer Issue, ed. John Emil Vincent,
 Spring/Summer.
McSweeney's, Reviving the Fable, ed.
 Jess Benjamin and staff, 28.
Michigan Quarterly Review, China, ed.
 Laurence Goldstein, Spring.
Mississippi Review, Literary Magazines,
 ed. Travis Kurowski and Gary
 Percesepe, 36/3.

New Literary History, Literary History in the Global Age, ed. Ralph Cohen, Summer.

PMS, Current Black Women's Writing, guest ed. Honoree Fanonne Jeffers, 8.

Representations, On Form, ed. Jean Day, Fall.

Salt Hill, Prose Poetry, ed. Daniel Torday and Tara Warman, Winter.

Sport Literate, Our Football Best, ed. William Meiners, 6/1.

Threepenny Review, A Symposium on Fear, ed. Wendy Lesser, Fall.

Tin House, The Political Future, ed. Rob Spillman, Fall.

TriQuarterly, The Other, guest ed. Henry S. Bienen, 131.

Virginia Quarterly Review, No Way Home: Outsiders and Outcasts, ed. Ted Genoways, Summer.

Correction: The following essay was inadvertently omitted from Notable Essays of 2007: JOHN GAMEL, Pendulous Beauty, *Boulevard*, 65/66.